A CORNISH STRANGER

There's an old Cornish saying: "Save a stranger from the sea, he'll turn your enemy . . ."

When her reclusive grandmother Jaunty becomes too frail to live alone, Gabriella Blythe moves into the remote waterside cabin on Frenchman's Creek which has been her grandmother's home for decades. Once a celebrated artist, Jaunty's days are coming to a close but she is still haunted by events in her past, particularly the sinking of a ship during the war.

Everything is fine until a handsome stranger arrives in a storm, seeking help. Fin has been left a family legacy: a delicate watercolour of a cabin which leads him to this beautiful stretch of Cornish water. As Fin begins to pick at the clues of the painting, he is drawn into the lives of Gabe and Jaunty, unravelling a remarkable story of identity and betrayal . . .

A CORNISH STRANGER

LIZ FENWICK

ISIS
LARGE
PRINT

First published in Great Britain 2014
by
The Orion Publishing Group Ltd.

First Isis Edition
published 2015
by arrangement with
The Orion Publishing Group Ltd.

A catalogue record for this book is available
from the British Library.

ISBN 978-1-78541-026-0 (hb)
ISBN 978-1-78541-027-7 (pb)

Published by
F. A. Thorpe (Publishing)
Anstey, Leicestershire

Set by Words & Graphics Ltd.
Anstey, Leicestershire
Printed and bound in Great Britain by
T. J. International Ltd., Padstow, Cornwall

This book is printed on acid-free paper

For Dom

Save a stranger from the sea
And he'll turn your enemy

Loving and caring for a stranger
gives us a chance to entertain angels.

Heb. 13:1–2

Part One
Jaunty

Prologue

As a sailing boat tacked in the mouth of Frenchman's Creek, it lost wind and the incoming tide carried the lugger onwards, bathing it in the afternoon sunlight. Jaunty squinted but it made no difference. Colour would not return to the scene. The world had become monochromatic grey, if there was such a thing. There must be, for everything was just a different blend of light and shadow. Her brain and her eyes received the same stimulus as before but something was now lost in the translation.

The sail appeared dark so she knew it wasn't white. Maybe it was crimson. She closed her eyes, capturing the image like a faded black-and-white photograph. The lines of the boat were so familiar — but it couldn't be *Jezebel*. Pain stabbed her heart, forcing open what was locked away, almost forgotten. That was too long ago and Jaunty wasn't even sure her memories were true. It would have been a blessing if her mind had gone when she had fallen and hit her head instead of the ability to see colour.

Her chest tightened. She coughed and it eased. She looked out to the terrace where bees frantically moved from one lavender flower to another, reminding her that there was so little time. Sitting down at her desk, she picked up a pen and began to write. Her hand shook. Gone were the rounded shapes of her letters. They were replaced by jagged lines and sharp spikes where they shouldn't be.

The time has come to tell the truth. For years the lie has been everything and the truth existed only in my thoughts. But now that the end is close, I need to explain before it is too late and the truth, such as it is, dies with me.

CHAPTER
ONE

School uniforms and rucksacks filed past the graveyard gates across the street three storeys below. Even now, fourteen years since Gabe had last worn a uniform, she remembered the scratch of the woollen fabric of her kilt against her legs and the dig of the straps of her bag into her shoulders. She held the phone to her ear and it rang again. It would take her grandmother, Jaunty Blythe, at least six rings to reach the table where the Bakelite handset sat. Jaunty would not be far away, but she had become so frail of late that getting out of her chair by the big picture window was an effort.

On the fifth ring, Gabe turned towards the packing boxes scattered around her. The removers would arrive tomorrow — with a crane to get her piano out of the window. How many years ago had they done the reverse? Four years? Time flies when you're not looking.

"Manaccan 325."

"Hello, Jaunty." Gabe smiled. No one answered the phone that way any more. It really wasn't relevant or precise. But it did put off cold callers if they had allowed the phone to ring long enough for Jaunty to answer it. Their confusion, Gabe was sure, gave her

5

grandmother a small bit of pleasure. And when it was the glass people calling about replacement windows or conservatories that Jaunty didn't want and couldn't afford, she would lapse into fluent French, German or Italian. She had never explained to Gabe how she had become fluent in so many languages. Her reply had always been, "I had an ear for it, dear."

"Gabriella, how lovely to hear from you."

Gabe noted a breathless tremor in her grandmother's voice.

"How are you?" Gabe asked, knowing that she would not receive a true answer.

"Well enough, thank you."

Gabe pictured her grandmother pulling her thin body up as straight as she could. Even at the age of ninety-two she maintained a remarkable posture and grace which Gabe envied. When Gabe had been on stage she'd tried to project Jaunty's poise, to hold it to her like an invisible cloak that would protect her. She grimaced. She hadn't performed on a stage in four years — life had taken a different route and now Gabe used that aloofness like a garment every day. It served her well.

"I've just had a call from Mrs Bates." Gabe took a deep breath. "She told me you refused to have your prescription refilled." Gabe sat on a large cardboard box. Everything in the top floor flat was packed and ready. Not that there was much: a piano, a keyboard and, of course, a few of Jaunty's paintings. These were Gabe's most important belongings. Gabe had packed the boxes with her books and fragments of her old life and it had been strange sifting through old programmes, scores, press cuttings, reviews and cast photos. There had even been a dried yellow rose from the bouquet that Jaunty had sent her after her first opera at the conservatory — in year one Gabe had risen above the chorus of brilliant voices to have a solo role. Now echoes of her former self were shoved in a box labelled BITS. It wasn't much, but then it had only been the beginning.

"I don't need the wretched stuff any more." Jaunty coughed. "It gives me indigestion and there is little enough left in life that I can enjoy and food is one of them."

"Did the doctor approve this?" Gabe knew the answer before Jaunty replied.

"No."

"Jaunty, you have diabetes. I don't need to tell you what that means."

"No, you don't."

Gabe closed her eyes, hoping this was just Jaunty having a moment of stubbornness. Despite her age and her diabetes, she had been in good shape until quite recently. "OK, I won't tell you. I'll be there tomorrow evening and we'll talk about it then."

"I don't know why you're doing this. I'm fine on my own. This is foolish! No, it's downright stupid." Jaunty took a raspy breath. "The young should be in London and living, not becoming hermits in remote cabins."

Gabe sighed. "You lived there when you were young."

"Things were different. I was a war widow with a child, not a single woman."

"So you've said, and you can say it again tomorrow and each day thereafter."

"Am I repeating myself?"

"Only when you have a point to make." Gabe knew Jaunty wouldn't let go of this and she also understood that Jaunty didn't want to accept that financially they could no longer afford to run two homes. Her grandmother was no longer painting and had only a small pension, and Gabe's income fluctuated — composing music for commercials wasn't steady — so selling the flat in London made sense. She didn't need to be there to do her job and it would give them a good financial buffer.

"I'll see you tomorrow night — and keep taking your pills. Mrs Bates will be round shortly with your supply." Before Jaunty could argue, Gabe put the phone down. She couldn't escape the feeling that her grandmother was giving up. It was one of the reasons Gabe knew this move to Cornwall was the right thing to do. Jaunty needed help, but she was too set in her ways to let anyone from the village assist with more than running errands and a bit of cleaning.

Out of the window Jaunty could see the creek, the opposite shore, and the river beyond. These views kept her sane and had been her constant companion for almost seventy years. There had been so much to hide. This place, the water and the trees, had helped to conceal her secrets. The river hadn't changed and the view had only differed with the addition of several farm buildings and a few new houses built across the river. The creek and the riverbed had silted up as the rains had washed the fields, yet to her eye the soul of the river, the water itself, remained the same. She laughed. Of course that was completely wrong. The water refreshed with each tide and every heavy downpour. The unaltering but all-changing nature of the river *was* her life. It held her memories, and its beauty had provided inspiration and solace.

Rotating the pen, she studied her fingers. Once they had been one of her best features, but now rheumatism and liver spots covered the thin skin and her joints looked overlarge on the long digits. She moved the pen above the paper. Where should she begin? There was so much to tell and even now she wasn't sure if she wanted to. What was the benefit? There was none, she thought; it would just provide the relief that would come from confessing. Except, maybe, Gabriella needed to know. It might help her.

I was born Jeanette Maria Christina in Rome. I was baptised by Pope Benedict XV, which made my mother's family very happy and angered my father's parents. Their only consolation was that I was not the son and heir they so desperately wanted, and my early life was spent almost exclusively in Europe.

Jaunty looked up, picturing the large apartment in Milan with its grand windows and its smell of ground almonds, until what was actually in front of her erased the past. An egret walked along the opposite bank, its stark whiteness dramatic against the mud. Jaunty couldn't feel the colour any more. It was as if the world were flat. She was empty and the mud was mud, not crimson, Prussian blue, Hooker's green and burnt umber with a hint of indigo. The egret was white or, more correctly, held simply the absence of colour, nothing more. She blinked, hoping that the subtleties would come back but the bird was still white and the mud simply dark. She wrote on.

For most of my early childhood, I had governesses and travelled with my parents as they followed my mother's career. They were sunlit years of freedom, music and colour, particularly purple. It was my mother's favourite and she wore every shade from the grey-washed lavender to the deepest imperial hue.

Happiness fills me when I look back. I was spoiled and adored. Europe was my playground and schoolroom. Languages surrounded me and I slipped effortlessly from one to another, unaware of doing so. My parents' love for each other embraced me and nothing punctured the bubble of our life except the annual trips to England to my father's family.

My paternal grandparents lived in Cornwall, in Polruan House which was set on the upper reaches of the Lynher River. When I was very young it seemed like an enchanted place, with lawns that swept down to the water and hills covered in dense woodland. My memories of those early visits were coloured with happiness and laughter. But then as I grew up and my grandfather died, the atmosphere changed. My mother stopped coming with us and I sensed that my grandmother was not delighted with me in any way. As my parents had not had another child, I was simply a reminder of my father's failure to produce an heir. So each year we would come to Cornwall and cold silence filled the beautiful rooms along with the watery sunlight.

As the years passed I took to the river with my father. He taught me to sail in an old dinghy and on the water or in the boathouse we were free from his mother's silences and pursed lips. She never smiled. So my father and I excelled at spending our days in a boat, no matter what the weather. At the end of each visit I would return to my mother who would shake her head at my brown, freckled face. She would complain to my father that he had ruined my chances of finding a husband with such tanned skin and my father and I would laugh . . .

The phone rang. Jaunty sighed and stopped writing. Who was interrupting her now? She needed to write this down before it disappeared, but the phone was ringing on and on and on. She capped the pen and used both hands on the arms of the chair to push her body upright. Each joint clicked into place and she grimaced with every step she took towards the phone.

11

★ ★ ★

The small panes of the windows above her desk framed the view on three sides. To the south Frenchman's Creek filled with the tide. Directly in front of Jaunty the river wound west towards the setting sun; to the north the banks of Calamansac were slowly being covered with water. She opened the desk drawer and pulled out the notebook. Sunlight fell on the pages, brightening them, and Jaunty looked out of the window. The sky was almost cloudless and she knew it would be cerulean touched with a hint of rose madder but all she saw was a graded grey sky.

Colour. It has gone. I can't see it. Life is becoming dark and that which lit my life has gone. My memory is failing and the reason I am still here is you, Gabriella.

There was so much to say, so much in her head, confusing her mind and her fingers. Jaunty scanned what she had written the day before and continued on.

I thought those days would never end. I grew tall and slim — I had my mother's dark hair and my father's blue eyes — and I was more Italian than English. Yet when I hadn't been sailing my complexion was fair "like a china doll" my Italian grandmother, my nonna, would say. She would run her thumb across my cheek then kiss the tip of my nose, and if I close my eyes I can still feel the tickling caress across my cheek and her scent, rose and cinnamon, becomes fresh, as if she is here. She had a passion for both: her house and garden were filled with roses and in her cooking she loved using cinnamon.

Steam twisted away from Jaunty's tea. She couldn't think of Nonna without hunger. Even if she walked to the kitchen for a biscuit it wouldn't remove the emptiness in her. She sighed.

At sixteen, I was sent to England to go to school and become respectable enough for my English grandmother. I was against this plan from the start because I didn't like her and she didn't like me. Cheltenham Ladies' College was not going to rectify that situation. It was like being put into a straitjacket, except that it was there that my love of art was first properly harnessed and trained. Well, you see, painting was acceptable for the granddaughter of Lady Penrose — but only as a hobby.

My drawing tutor had spotted the promise in me. She encouraged me and I spent every spare moment in the art studios experimenting with every medium available. The freedom of oil, clay and metal after years of pencils, watercolours and crayons opened my eyes and my future. Everything was new and exciting.

Jaunty ran her fingers over what she had written. Did this really matter? For years she had convinced herself that the truth wasn't important, that the lie hurt no one. And in all these years no one had uncovered the secret. She sighed. For a time she had almost forgotten it herself because the fiction was more believable. So did anyone need to know? She could let the truth die with her and who would care? Weren't some things better left unsaid and unknown? But no, no. Lately the compulsion to be honest had grown overwhelming; she knew she needed to tell Gabriella and the world the truth.

The racket of stones on the track announced Gabriella's arrival. Jaunty would have done almost anything to prevent her granddaughter from moving here, but Gabriella was as stubborn as she was herself.

"But my death will speed her back to the living. When I am gone she won't stay here." Jaunty spoke aloud and glanced about the room. "There is nothing for her here but memories." Her glance fell on a picture of her son, Philip. They had lost him so long ago now.

Jaunty stood. As she willed her body to do as it was told, she could almost count each vertebra as it sought alignment. Most days she coped with the pain, but on some, when the dampness from the river seeped into the cabin, the freezing of her joints would make her cry out. Thankfully, until now, no one had been here to listen. And recently the memories made her cry out too. How could she stop them from coming into her thoughts? She must for Gabriella's sake.

The Helford gig went upriver towards Gweek, the sound of the cox's instructions drifting in through the window. Once essential for commerce, racing the pilots out to boats, the gigs now carried on for sport.

14

Most days Jaunty saw the various crews pass the creek, practising, and all she could do was watch. Jaunty sighed and put the notebook in the desk drawer. Locking it, she put the key into her smock pocket. She didn't want Gabriella to see it until she was gone and that would come quickly enough.

Gabe rolled her head back and forth as she put the window down, enjoying the fresh air. She was almost there. Passing a tractor she waved at the farmer and continued down the lane. The last stretch always took too long, yearning as she did to be home at Bosworgy, the house above the water. It was far from the world, safe. It had always been that way. As she passed the turning to Orchard Lane and Penarvon Cove, she took the track and slowed to glance out towards Falmouth Bay. Over the years the trees had grown, almost obscuring the view but not quite. She grinned, feeling the tension drift away in the clear air.

The track was potholed and her overstuffed car complained as she hit each one despite her efforts to avoid them. Putting the car into second gear, she descended, passing three walkers enjoying the sunny afternoon. A few hundred yards more and she arrived at the gate. She stopped the car and climbed out. Righting the sign that warned trespassers to beware, she wondered again what they needed to watch out for. Here there was simply a reclusive artist living on her own; there were no mean dogs or even a big bloke, just an old woman. Thankfully, over the years the only trespassers had been occasional lost ramblers to disturb Jaunty's life of art and solitude.

Gabe smiled again as she opened the gate, grateful that no one had preyed on her grandmother. Jaunty had never seemed to be afraid of living such an isolated life, something that astonished Gabe. She drove through the gate then closed it behind her before travelling down the drive to park by the shed.

Opening the door, Gabe took a deep breath. The air was damp, fragrant with the smell of eucalyptus and pine. Home. The bamboo that lined one side of the path rustled as if a strong breeze had whipped through it, but the leaves on the eucalyptus towering above were still; so, an animal, hunting, must be the cause. Gabe opened the boot and disturbed a jackdaw that complained bitterly as he flew off. She leaned against her little car and looked up at the blue sky. A few clouds rushed past the pines that protected the cabin from the harsh north wind and it felt very warm for September . . . Indian summer.

Pulling out grocery bags, Gabe walked down to the cabin, noting the weeds sprouting where the gravel had become thin. Sometime very soon she would need to get out the strimmer and push the wilderness back a bit. She knew there was much to do. On her last visit six weeks ago she had noted the steep decline in her grandmother's health — not that Jaunty would acknowledge it. She would have a battle on her hands to make Jaunty see that she needed Gabe. A woman of ninety-two could not live in an isolated cabin on her own and they couldn't afford to have live-in help, not that Jaunty would even entertain such an idea. Adjusting the bags in her hands, she stopped to listen to the cry of a gull. The river was visible through the pines and the cedar-clad cabin almost blended into the hillside. This first glimpse of Jaunty's hideaway always created a lump in Gabe's throat. This was home, and it was so right she was doing this that she wasn't sure why she'd left it so long.

Late afternoon sunlight baked the cedar cladding and Gabe could see her grandmother sitting at her desk, staring out of the window at the river. A small sailing boat tacked in front of Groyne Point. It looked so peaceful. Gabe's glance fell to the immediate surroundings. The small garden was booming with agapanthus, lavender and weeds — in the weeks since her last visit the weeds had almost overtaken the proper plants. She had serious work to do, but if the weather remained this fine it would be a joy. Turning towards the cabin again she saw the kitchen door was open, welcoming her home.

Gabriella walked in weighed down with bags. Jaunty paused in the doorway to the kitchen, noting the dark circles under her granddaughter's eyes. "I told you not to come."

"What sort of greeting is that?" Gabriella placed the bags down, came towards Jaunty and embraced her, then pulled back and studied her.

Too much scrutiny was a bad thing. Jaunty knew how to hide, but attack was the best method. "The only one you deserve."

"You're stuck with me." Gabriella began to put away the groceries.

"That's enough to feed a family of five." Jaunty shook her head.

"You said you weren't enjoying your diet so I thought I'd cook for you and see if we can overcome the indigestion."

"Doubt it."

"I think the indigestion is because you live on biscuits, not proper food." Gabriella stopped and turned to her. "You looked tired. Go and sit in the sun while I unpack, then I'll bring you a cup of tea." Gabriella smiled, yet her eyes appeared sad. Jaunty knew those eyes. They had haunted her for years.

Jaunty went to the front of the cabin and out on to the terrace. Weeds were sprouting from between the stones. She bent to the ground but didn't have enough strength to pull the wretched things out. They had been there too long. How had she not seen them until now?

She sank into a chair. So much had slipped, not just the weeds embedded in the terrace. The roses had been left to their own devices for so long they looked more like brambles than garden delights. Had she seen them, Nonna, her Italian grandmother, would have been appalled. Tilting her face upwards, Jaunty closed her eyes for a moment. Although nearing the end of September, there was still strength left to the sun and it warmed her face. Jaunty was tired as Gabriella had said, and every day each breath took more energy; more importantly, nothing captured her interest or her appetite. She didn't have much strength left and she needed strength to do what she had to do. Maybe Gabriella's arrival, with all the fussing and food that came with it, was a good thing. It would build her up to finish.

"Why are you here?" Jaunty blinked.

Her grandmother's eyes were not as bright as Gabe remembered. The radiant blue had clouded and faded. Jaunty turned to look at the creek and Gabe recalled all the times she had found her grandmother staring at the river, not the view but the water itself. For hours on end Jaunty would gaze at the creek or the river, not painting or sketching, just looking, as if she were searching for something. The sea had nearly taken Jaunty's life towards the end of the war, but in the end it had saved her by putting food on the table.

"I want to be here." Gabe knew there was no point in reminding Jaunty how tight money was. Jaunty knew and that's why she'd been living on cheap biscuits.

"No, you are here because I am dying." The weary eyes focused on Gabe.

Gabe paced the terrace, wondering how she was supposed to respond to this. In a way it was true. But there was more to it than that.

Jaunty laughed. "I am no longer fit for purpose. Nothing works properly any more and sometimes it doesn't work at all." Jaunty flexed as she straightened her top. Her grandmother still dressed, as Gabe had always seen her, in her navy sailing smock and trousers, plimsolls on her feet, white for summer and black for winter. Halfway to standing Jaunty stopped and dragged in a breath and Gabe could see the spasm of pain that crossed her grandmother's face, but she didn't move. She knew Jaunty didn't want her help: it would only make things worse, make them stand out. Independence was the thing that Jaunty valued above all else.

Jaunty was all the family that Gabe had had since she was thirteen. They'd gone from a family of three — Jaunty, Gabe and Philip, her father — down to two in an instant when her father had died on an explosion on an oilrig in the North Sea, and soon it would just be Gabe. There was nothing she could do to alter that. However, she could make what time they had left special. She hoped that her being here could ease some of Jaunty's discomfort, even just a little. Jaunty turned as she entered the cabin and smiled. "It's good to see you."

Gabe forced herself to remain in the garden as her grandmother made slow progress back inside. It was one thing wanting to help and another to make her grandmother feel worse about how far she had declined, so rather than race to Jaunty's side, Gabe began pulling up the weeds that had sprouted between the paving slabs. She could tell the weather had been good because many came out easily, scattering dry soil on to the terrace, but a few were more persistent; their roots had ventured deep, their stems breaking at the surface, sure to grow again.

Jaunty's eyelids fluttered and eventually the sparse lashes rested on the thin skin. Her breathing became more regular, moving the faded eiderdown in shallow undulations. Gabe backed out of the room, leaving the door ajar. How many times had she crawled under that eiderdown, scared of something in the night? Too many times to count. Jaunty was so slight now she was barely visible on the bed. The mattress below her was ancient and moulded to fit Jaunty's younger form because Jaunty had ceased turning the mattress years ago, around the time Gabe's father had died.

Standing just outside Jaunty's bedroom, Gabe looked closely at the sitting room. Although the covers on the chairs and sofa were faded, the room was cosy. Gabe had always loved the almost square, utilitarian shapes of the chairs and the rectangular sofa. They must have been expensive to last so well all these years. A pine-scented breeze came through the open French windows and the sky was brilliant crimson on the horizon, fading to pale blue as she looked directly up when she stepped outside. The air had cooled and pink shades still washed the few clouds lingering above the hillside.

"Red sky at night, sailors' delight. Red sky in the morning, sailors take warning." As Gabe uttered the words she frowned. She really didn't know if they held any truth. Despite spending so much of her life here in Bosworgy she had never sailed; rowed yes, but sailed, no. Her father had never sailed either, as far as Gabe knew. She wondered if this was because of Jaunty. Her grandmother's relationship with the sea was complex. She would swim and she would row as far as Helford but never further and she would stare at the sea endlessly. Jaunty had never spoken of her experience to Gabe but Gabe's father, Philip, had told her of Jaunty's bravery many times. He had been so proud of what his mother had done during the war and of her success as an artist. Sadly, he had never been too detailed about Jaunty's war years or maybe she had just been too young to be interested. Maybe Jaunty would talk about it if Gabe asked now.

Gabe picked up the weeds she had pulled out earlier and, climbing the steps to the old shed, she put them down on the bonfire pile then walked to the car and collected her suitcases. She had to find out the exact state of Jaunty's health. Her grandmother was evasive but Gabe was sure that Mrs Bates would be able to bring her up to speed. That woman managed to know everything and always had. It was Mrs Bates who had known when she and Jenna Williams had been scrumping pears from a house in the village.

In her room, Gabe smiled at the things still on the bookshelves above the windows. There was the prize she'd won for singing at school. Her father had been so pleased. He'd loved her voice and had encouraged her singing for as long as she could remember. She was sure he wouldn't be happy at the turn her life had taken, but she hoped he would have understood if he were still here. On the chest of drawers sat a picture of her at a piano with her father turning the pages. She remembered it all so clearly. She had just finished singing his favourite Scottish ballad, "Ailein Duinn", and little had she known then that the sea would take her father from her. She had only known that the sea was important in their lives, mostly because of the cabin's location perched above the water.

As she unpacked she began humming the tune, before singing the words. She hadn't done any vocal exercises today so her voice wavered at first.

How sorrowful I am
Early in the morning rising
Ò hì, I would go with thee
Hì ri bhò hò ru bhi
Hì ri bhò hò rinn o ho
Brown-haired Alan, *ò hì*, I would go with thee

If it is thy pillow the sand
If it is thy bed the seaweed
Ò hì, I would go with thee
Hì ri bhò hò ru bhi
Hì ri bhò hò rinn o ho
Brown-haired Alan, *ò hì*, I would go with thee

If it is the fish thy candles bright
If it the seals thy watchmen
Ò hì, I would go with thee
Hì ri bhò hò ru bhi
Hì ri bhò hò rinn o ho
Brown-haired Alan, *ò hì*, I would go with thee

I would drink, though all would abhor it
Of thy heart's blood after thy drowning
Ò hì, I would go with thee
Hì ri bhò hò ru bhi
Hì ri bhò hò rinn o ho
Brown-haired Alan, *ò hì*, I would go with thee

As she sang the last note she looked out of her window and the water of Frenchman's Creek was glass-like in the fading light. Now that she was here permanently, she would learn to sail. It couldn't be that hard and with the river on her doorstep it would be a shame not to. Tomorrow she would go to the sailing club and find out about lessons.

In the kitchen she grabbed a scrap of paper. As always, this was recycled paper from a sketch or painting that Jaunty had rejected. There had always been evenly torn fragments by the phone. Nothing was ever wasted. Gabe wondered how many works hadn't reached Jaunty's exacting standards over the years and had become the shopping list or even one of Gabe's own pathetic attempts at art. She looked up to the far kitchen wall to see her own framed painting of a summer picnic and laughed at her rendition of Jaunty, her father and herself with a cake bigger than they were in the centre. Her priorities were clear. Cake was everything.

She wrote down "sailing lessons" then looked in the cupboard to see if the ingredients were there for her to bake a cake for Jaunty tomorrow. She was sure she could do some form of cake that would be diabetic friendly, low in sugar, high in slow-release carbohydrates. It was a challenge she could rise to. Gabe grinned at her unintended pun as she mentally listed the key ingredients, then sighed as she wondered what her grandmother had been eating because the cupboard was bare except for a few soup tins, some terrible biscuits and a loaf of stale bread growing a life of its own. This was not good at all. If she had had any doubts about moving down here they disappeared.

Going through the sitting room towards Jaunty's bedroom on the far end of the cabin, Gabe stopped to admire Jaunty's paintings hanging on either side of the wood burner. One was a study in blues, ranging from aqua to deepest cobalt, and the other was soft white tinged with lavender and pale green. Gabe thought of bright afternoons when the sun made diamonds sparkle off the surface of the river. Somehow Jaunty captured a mood or moment so precisely, yet when Gabe actually studied the work it looked almost like nothing more than random brush strokes. That was Jaunty's genius.

Something dropped to the floor in Jaunty's room and Gabe stuck her head through the door. Carefully she slipped in, picked up a pen and placed it on the bedside table. Gabe loved this room. It was almost as big as the sitting room, only a little bit narrower and it was puritan in its furnishings: a bed, a chest of drawers, a desk and a Windsor sack-back chair. The walls were lined with windows and behind the bed was another of Jaunty's paintings, one that reminded Gabe of the sunsets reflected in the river, all fiery, passionate reds and magenta.

The works hanging in the cabin were impressionistic and abstract, whereas the ones that had vaulted Jaunty to fame in the first place were more realistic and very slightly primitive. Someday it would be wonderful to see a retrospective of Jaunty's work. In the past, when Gabe had raised the subject with Jaunty, her grandmother had said nothing, but waved her hand in the air and gone back to whatever she'd been working on. It had been clear that Jaunty didn't want the attention that a retrospective would bring, which Gabe thought was a shame. Jaunty had earned it but she only desired a quiet life.

Gabe crept out of the bedroom and walked out on to the terrace. A light breeze stirred the treetops, then the leaves stilled as if someone had switched a machine off for the evening. Entering the house again, she glanced through Jaunty's bedroom door. The eiderdown moved regularly so Gabe headed to the car, still laden with things from the flat. Her mouth watered at the thought of a glass of wine. She paused and leaned against the doorjamb. Did she really have the energy to do any more today? Why not just collapse on the sofa? No, she had better do it, and then she needed to compose some music for a baked bean commercial. She shrugged. This was her life now — but at least she would be living it at Bosworgy. She smiled as she set off.

CHAPTER
TWO

Sunlight broke through the flimsy white curtains. Jaunty had chosen the fabric years ago because of the simple daisy pattern, not because of the practicality. It didn't keep out the light or the draughts, but it was covered with embroidered daisies and there had been so many daisies in the field that summer . . . Jaunty had been eighteen in the summer of 1939 and he was beautiful. Closing her eyes, even after all these years, she could still feel his skin under her fingers. Now she touched her shrivelled hands, abused by the turpentine and the paint. One of those hands had drawn slow circles across his smooth back.

Daisies had been her favourite flower ever since. He had woven them through her hair, the flower so simple in its beauty. No shouting, just narrow petals and a glorious drop of golden yellow. If she painted the daisy's eye she would use cadmium yellow and a touch of umber.

Before the memory faded, Jaunty rose and unlocked the desk drawer and retrieved the notebook. Studying the pen in her fingers before she began to write, ink dropped on to the page and spread into it, creating an amoeba shape. The nib touched the page then lifted as singing floated in on the morning breeze. An aria from Puccini, "O Mia Babbino Caro". The purity of Gabriella's voice stirred memories: Vienna, Paris, Rome, and Berlin. No, no, Gabriella shouldn't be here. With her talent the world should be at her feet as it had been with Maria Lucia, Jaunty's mother.

Gabriella should be in London, not trying to play nursemaid. Had Jaunty left this all too late? She tapped the pen on the page again and watched another drop of ink bleed into the grain of the paper. Gabriella must let her go, but it was clear she didn't know how to, so Jaunty must teach her.

I have become good at farewells. I'm almost ready to say goodbye for the last time. I don't want to go on until I don't know who I am — and I'm the only one who does know.

Jaunty looked up from the page and laughed. Why hadn't she gone loopy? That would have been simple, or at least she thought it would have been. It would have been easier for her than her world turning to grey. Jaunty rubbed her temples.

However, the last thing I want to do is to hurt you, Gabriella. But what I have to say will and that troubles me. I have barely enough oomph to rise from my bed and see the morning light on my beloved river. It is the river that saved me and it forced me to choose life. It is where I first found love and where I still seek it, foolishly.

The raspy noise of my breathing drowns out the birds and my thoughts. It is too loud and too laboured. Each breath takes too much effort, but what should I expect at my age? My body is too old, despite what my brain sometimes thinks.

Yet hearing you sing makes me feel I am eighteen again, listening to my mother. It is such a foolish thing to do, to revisit the past. It is finished, but it calls to me like the river does.

Gabe sat on a tree trunk near the creek, clutching her mug, listening to a symphony of morning sounds just as she had spent most of the night listening to Jaunty's uneven breathing. Gabe had held her own while waiting to hear her grandmother's, which meant she'd had virtually no sleep and the first thing she had done when she'd woken, exhausted, had been her exercises to try and release the constriction across her chest.

At least here in Bosworgy she wasn't plagued by the nightmares that haunted her in London. The therapist had said that they might never go and that was when Gabe had given up therapy. She couldn't see the point if it wasn't going to help her sleep at night. In fact, the nights after a session had been the worst. Dragging the whole thing up, over and over, making her live through it again. Each time it was more dreadful than before and she hadn't thought that was possible. Lying awake at night, not being able to fall asleep, reliving each moment, wondering whether, if she had done something differently, would it not have happened? So fruitless, because it had and it couldn't be changed now.

Here she would be able to leave it behind, begin again. Life was simpler at Bosworgy; well, at least Jaunty's way of life was. Everything was pared down. No television, only the radio to bring the outside world into the cabin. Gabe sighed and let her shoulders relax.

The air was thick with fog that hung a few feet above the creek and yet the water below was so clear she could see the rocks on the bottom and a small crab scuttling away. Swimming was her sanity; it had always brought clarity of thought. Discarding her towelling robe she went carefully to the steps. She was home again, and that's all that mattered.

Checking the thick rope was still sound and securely tied, she made her way down a few of the steep steps carved out of the rocks and dipped her foot in the water, wishing it were warmer. And while the wind blew gently from the south, it didn't carry any heat at this early hour and so the air was cool too.

The tide was on its way out but still high. Everything revolved around the tides living this close to the sea, she thought. She made circles with her foot in the water but there was no way to make this less painful so she took a shallow dive into the creek. The coldness of the water sucked the air from her lungs and she broke through the surface, gasping, then struck out in a fast crawl across the creek to the other side. The temperature really wasn't too bad. In fact, she knew from experience that the river was at its warmest at this time of the year, but her body hadn't believed that when she dived in.

She swam back and forth until her tension disappeared, then flipped on to her back and floated while the current pulled her out into the river. She could hear the distant thud of a fishing boat engine and the cry of a gull above. Fog still hung heavily over the surface of the water, trapping the silence. She was fully out into the main part of the river and when she turned her head she could just make out Jaunty's studio tucked in the trees. From this angle, the pines that protected it looked as if they were taking a bow.

Gabe smiled then turned over again. With the tide on its way out, she would have a good workout to swim back to the steps, but she was looking forward to it. From an early age she had swum in the river, even if a wetsuit was needed at certain times of year. Her father had never worn one and called her a sissy, but she didn't care. No matter what he said it was bloody cold in mid-January. Jaunty always stated it wasn't that the temperature of the water changed so much during the course of the year, it was the air and the wind howling at you when you stepped out that made the experience painful. Gabe shivered at the memories of Christmas morning swims — always fun but often freezing.

Kicking double time, Gabe managed to make the turn into the creek where the pull of the current was less intense. She was out of shape. How could two weeks of not swimming have made the tide so hard to beat? She didn't know and on a peaceful morning she didn't care. She changed to breaststroke and enjoyed the serene atmosphere. A cormorant dived towards the water but pulled up before it pierced it.

Stillness enclosed the creek and she made her way past the steps and the quay in the silence. Branches hunched to touch the surface of the water, and in the low cloud Gabe imagined she could see ghosts lingering by the banks. The thud of the fishing boat's motor grew louder.

Something touched her foot and she squirmed, but knew it would most likely be one of the many grey mullet that lived in these waters. Halfway, she stopped and turned around, seeing that the mouth of the creek was now obscured by the fog rolling in, and everything was muffled. Magic. If only she could block out the rest of the world so easily. She shook her head and began a brisk crawl back to the steps.

Out of the water and wrapped in her robe, Gabe stared at the river, watching the fog begin to dissolve as the sun grew stronger. It was going to be a glorious day. Hopefully the piano would arrive early and she could then go for a long, solitary walk. Her heart lifted as she climbed up to the cabin. The sky was blue, the sun was warm and the north shore was bathed in golden light. It was good to be home.

Moving the sofa to the side of the room, Gabe pushed her hair out of her eyes. It just wasn't going to work. No matter how she tried she wasn't going to fit a grand piano into the sitting room unless she lost the dining table, which was too big for the small but functional kitchen. Everything about the cabin spoke about

Jaunty's practical way of life. The kitchen contained only what it needed, nothing more than a sink, a stove, a fridge and a large dresser. No space was wasted or overfilled. It was as though Jaunty's surroundings needed to be plain to let her imagination soar.

Although Gabe knew the cabin already existed when Jaunty had moved here after the war, it could have been designed for her grandmother. The kitchen and utility room were outside Gabe's bedroom on the south side, while the sitting room was next to Jaunty's bedroom on the north, and the cabin looked west with just a few small windows on the east side, which backed into the hill. Virtually everything about the place focused on the river, with almost every glance from the windows providing yet another view.

Gabe leaned on the dining table and looked out at the bright day. It was so hot it could be midsummer. She opened a few windows and dodged a sleepy wasp. Turning, she sighed. The piano wouldn't fit in here. There was, of course, Jaunty's studio, perched on the edge of the cliff among the pines overlooking the river. It was almost as big as the cabin, but it hadn't been used much recently and would most likely be damp. The question was how damp, because pianos and damp didn't make good companions.

This morning, sitting near the mudflats on the old quay, she had heard the music of the creek as the tide began to pull the water from the banks. It had soothed her as it tapped, gurgled and popped its way out to sea. The fog had trapped the sound, which clung to the shore like horns, muffled. She had lost track of the time, listening to the array of tones, and a composition had begun forming in her head, a sonata of the tides.

Gabe shifted the small sofa slightly. Jaunty was dying and Gabe was OK with that. She swung around. No, she really wasn't, but she had to be. Jaunty, at ninety-two, wasn't going to live for many more years, probably only months, and Gabe would try and make them the best that they could be.

In the kitchen the water for Jaunty's egg had reached a fierce boil. For Jaunty the egg must be placed into the water only when it reached this point, then cooked for three minutes exactly. Gabe set the silly yellow duck timer she had given her grandmother the Christmas Gabe had been ten. Life was better then; she'd still believed in Father Christmas and her father had been alive. Innocence had not been lost.

Gabe sighed. Some days she felt she'd been born under a bad moon. Her mother had died from an infection three days after she'd given birth to Gabe; when she was thirteen her father had died; and four years ago, when her career was just about to make a giant step forward . . . well, she had walked away.

The timer rang. She scooped the egg from the water and placed it in an eggcup, quickly covering it with a hat. She and Jaunty had made the hat together twenty years ago and she grinned, looking at the wonky shape. She had never been very good at crafty-type things but that hadn't stopped her trying. Gabe placed the single egg, the china teapot, and toast on a tray, everything just as Jaunty liked it. Gabe couldn't change her grandmother, but maybe if she built up Jaunty's strength she would enjoy what time she had left.

"Good morning." Jaunty walked from her bedroom into the sitting room, rubbing her hip joints, hoping they would loosen and ease her movements. Breakfast was on the table and Jaunty smiled, but Gabriella was wrinkling her nose, a clear sign that something was troubling her. She had done that repeatedly when her father had died and she was trying to be brave. When tears would threaten she would screw up her nose to hold them back and though Jaunty would say they were better out than in, the child had always tried to control her emotions. That self-control had not been a major problem at thirteen, but now it was.

Just looking into Gabriella's eyes sent Jaunty back in time but she needed to focus her mind on the present, she told herself. Yet everything about Gabriella tugged Jaunty backwards. She took so much from her great grandparents — her vibrant red hair was the same shade Jaunty's father's had been, and the purity of her singing came from Maria. All that was missing from Gabriella's voice was the depth that Maria's had had, the depth acquired from time and practice.

Lowering herself into a ladder-back chair at the table, Jaunty could see up close how much Gabriella had let herself go. She took no time with herself. The glorious flame-coloured locks were scraped back in a careless chignon and the porcelain skin was dry for the lack of a bit of moisturiser. It was as if Gabriella were hiding. But how could a woman so naturally beautiful, so striking, hide? She had hair the colour of a sunset, yellow-orange eyes and a voice that could bring down God from heaven. Why was she concealing it all? There had always been an air of fragility about her — of course, losing her mother just after she had been born had not helped, but this — this carelessness of self had a deliberation about it that made Jaunty uneasy.

"You slept in." Gabriella joined her at the table with a mug clasped in her hands. Chewed fingernails topped the long elegant fingers and Jaunty ran her own over the scars in the oak table top. In a previous life the table had been a door that someone had discarded but Jaunty had salvaged it, stripped it of its chipped paint, then waxed it until it glowed. It had served as the dining table, but more frequently as a work surface, and in the early years, before the studio was built, she had painted and sketched here.

"I stayed in bed watching the morning light bounce off the north shore," Jaunty lied, but her room, in the mornings, with the sound of the gulls and the waves, was like being on a boat, something that soothed and stimulated at the same time. The water beckoned her, called to her in the way it could to one who had experienced its power. It had let her go all those years ago, but her time was coming to an end and it was demanding payment for the years of reprieve. Would her death pay her other debts? No.

"Jaunty?" Gabriella touched her arm.

"Yes." Jaunty frowned.

"I asked if you wanted any fruit this morning?"

"Prunes, dear." Gabriella was lovely and always had been, ever eager to please. But something had happened to her, something that wasn't good. Jaunty sensed it, but Gabriella never spoke of it — whatever it was. Everything was always "fine", which said nothing at all. And though Gabriella worked like a demon on her music, it was not her singing but her music. When Jaunty listened it was beautiful and sad, but it wasn't enough to sustain a passionate woman — and Gabriella was passionate, Jaunty knew it.

She was, what, thirty? Jaunty wasn't sure. She could be younger or older. Jaunty should know Gabriella's age. Her daughter-in-law had gone into labour a month early and it was so cold so it must have been winter. Philip, dear Philip . . . He had still been at sea on a rig somewhere and her daughter-in-law had died by the time he'd reached her. Heartbreaking.

Jaunty puzzled how some events like Alex threading flowers through her hair in the summer of 1939 were so clear, but the date her only grandchild had been born had disappeared. Her mind was too full. A life too long does that and the brain picks and chooses what it wants to hold on to. She had no control. She still had her wits, but not all her memories, and certainly not all that she sought to keep. No, her devious mind had selected the memories to hold tight to and who was she to tell it it was wrong.

Gabriella placed a bowl of prunes in front of her. "Is there anything in particular that you want to do today?"

Jaunty raised an eyebrow. "Run a marathon?" Gabriella knew there was little that Jaunty could do any more because taking anything but a few steps was too painful. However, Gabriella was putting a bright face on it as she had always done, and her smile lit the room.

"The day is fine so I will sit on the terrace and watch the birds," Jaunty said. How they tormented her with their freedom. But this was not new. They had done this since the day she was plucked out of the sea by a fisherman and brought to Falmouth, to live thereafter in a cage of her own making.

"Are you sure?" Gabriella wrinkled her nose again.

"Please stop that! You will give yourself unnecessary lines." Jaunty sucked some air into her lungs. She knew she shouldn't snap, but her fuse had never been long. Her mother's cautionary words about appearance and freckles echoed in Jaunty's mind. Gabe mustn't be so careless with hers.

As Gabriella cleared the plates, Jaunty noted her granddaughter appeared almost hollow, a skeleton of the woman she used to be. Gabriella thought she was doing the right thing by coming here; she was good like her father and grandfather had been. But deep inside something had altered her. She lived alone and Jaunty knew she was lonely, which was one reason why she was here.

But an old woman was not the company she needed. Jaunty's fingers moved around the rim of the teacup, enjoying the delicate feel of something that, although beautiful, was robust enough to hold its scalding contents. Could Gabriella become strong again or would she let whatever had happened defeat her?

Jaunty sighed inwardly. She herself had become resilient, but she had lost so much that wholeness was never possible, not when you were not who you said you were.

"Wrinkles are good. Look at yours." Gabriella smiled and those beautiful eyes glinted with laughter.

"I am an exceedingly old woman and I have earned mine. Gabriella, you are a woman in your prime — your face is as important as your voice or your hands."

Gabriella lifted her chin then turned away. This argument had been raised too many times. She hadn't listened then and Jaunty knew she was a fool if she thought her granddaughter would now. She was a woman — a broken woman — not a child. Gabriella had matured into someone as stubborn as Jaunty had been. It would do her good to remember that, but her mind refused to accept it. Jaunty wanted Gabriella fixed and as whole as she could be.

The dew soaked the bottom of Gabe's jeans as she walked through the overgrown grass to reach the studio. The morning chorus was still in full voice despite the late hour and although the studio was only two hundred feet from the cabin, it felt to Gabe as if it was in a different county or even country. It was a place of magic. Blank canvases, sheets of paper, pieces of wood and even old cereal boxes were transformed into paintings of blue, green, grey, black, purple. Jaunty portrayed the water in every colour on the chart, each shade reflecting a mood, a moment, an emotion.

Jaunty, too, altered the second she walked through the studio door. Her grandmother was like a patchwork quilt made of pieces of fabric discarded by others as unworthy of keeping, but salvaged by Jaunty, and in her they became stunning. Jaunty's nose was positively patrician, her hair was now white and downy but had been thick and black. Those eyes now somewhat clouded had been bright cornflower blue. But it was her voice, especially when she was painting, which didn't fit her gypsy-like grandmother at all. When she was lost in her work her voice was cut-glass with impeccable diction, if she was interrupted and answered a question. But when she spoke in public, when she was aware of people near, her voice softened, her vowels became rounder. Only when she was transported by her art did she sound like an old-fashioned BBC newsreader.

There seemed to be something about Jaunty's hands flying across the canvas or paper that removed a filter, or maybe added one. Her hands never stilled when she was working, even if she held no brush, no palette knife, no charcoal. It was as though her movements were her brainwaves, creating the magic that would transform the canvas.

Gabe closed her eyes and saw the flash of movement that always preceded each stroke of the brush. It was as if Jaunty was taking a practice swing in golf. Gabe smiled at the image in her head. Jaunty and golf didn't go together. Philip, her father, had loved the game; indeed, a golf course was where he'd met Gabe's mother and she wondered when he had learned to play.

There were so many things she didn't know. Maybe she should ask Jaunty now, before it was too late. In the past she had hesitated because it had felt like poking an open wound that had never healed. But time was running out. If she didn't ask now, she would never know.

The door to the studio didn't open when Gabe released the latch. She wondered if it might be locked, but a shove with her shoulder released it. Inside, dust covered all the surfaces and the scent of turps still lingered in the air. Canvases were stacked against the far wall. When had Jaunty last been in here? Gabe looked around, noting the neatness, and it didn't feel right. Yes, there was still paint splattered on the floor and even some on the ceiling, but it was old. The room looked like a museum exhibit, down to the half-finished painting on the easel.

The painting was obviously Jaunty's work, but while the subject was right, the colours were wrong. Gabe touched the heavy brushwork on the canvas. It was hard, which meant it was at least six months old, and grey muddied the deep purple. Gabe fought the sadness welling up inside as she studied it. Jaunty's paintings always stimulated deep emotions in her, but this one spoke of despair, of loss. Shivering, Gabe turned away.

The studio was dry with only a hint of moisture around the skylights in the ceiling. Dampness was always an issue beside the river, and even in high summer the night storage heaters were supposed to kick in, but sometimes didn't. This year they had obviously been doing their work well.

Gabe sat on the single divan bed in the far corner and looked out through the ceiling-to-floor windows that faced north on to the river. She had spent so many hours curled up here while Jaunty painted, totally absorbed in the work, oblivious to Gabe's presence. Gabe stroked the needlepoint cushion that lay on the bed. She had made it at school and had given it to Jaunty the first Christmas they had been alone. Gabe swallowed. Christmas was a few months off. Would Jaunty make it?

These thoughts weren't helpful. Gabe rose. The studio was fine and she could set up her keyboard and piano in here so as not to disturb Jaunty. She glanced at her watch. The delivery van was due any time now. Once her things were here she could begin to re-establish normal life with its rigid practice routines. But as she stepped out of the studio and pulled the door closed behind her, she wondered why she bothered any more.

The crocosmia Gabe placed in a black plastic vase brightened the slate gravestone. This place featured in so many of her thoughts. When she was little, she and her father would visit regularly and talk to her mother, but for too many years she had been coming here on her own. Gabe looked at the sunlight falling through the trees. It was so quiet here. She squatted down and ran her fingers over the letters. Jaunty had never visited the grave with her; she lived by putting the past firmly away. Gabe frowned. Maybe she should try and adopt that way of living too. The past was written and couldn't be altered, so she must let it go, yet it had changed her. She sighed. What would she have been like if her mother had lived? If her father had been on leave when the rig went up? She shook her head. Leave it. Wasted thoughts.

"Hello, both." She glanced around to make sure she was alone. No one, just a robin jumping about then fluttering on to the headstone. She touched the stone again. "I'm worried about Jaunty."

The bird tilted its head as if it was listening, even understanding. It flew from the stone and landed by the flowers, even closer to her. "Is there anything beyond death?" She laughed. "I must think there is because here I am talking to a robin and a gravestone." Jaunty wouldn't talk about God — or death, for that matter. She had said there couldn't be a God, but she never said why. Gabe knew there had to be a reason Jaunty felt this way. Whether there was a God or not, Gabe was grateful to all the musicians who had composed glorious works evoking the power, the glory, and the love of God. Without the composers' genius the world would be less beautiful. Their music, their words, made her life worth living. Gabe watched the robin fly off.

One last glance at the grave and she closed the gate behind her, intent on booking lessons at the sailing club after she stopped in the village shop. She pulled the shopping list out of her pocket as she walked down the lane to the store. A multicoloured butterfly landed in the hedge and Gabe stopped and tried to remember the name for it. It flew away and she set off again, wishing her memory were better for things like this.

"Gabriella, how wonderful to see you!" Mrs Bates was puffing her way up the hill. "In fact, it couldn't be better timing."

Gabe frowned, but before she could ask why the older woman had taken her by the arm and was leading her down the hill. "This couldn't be more fortunate." She turned to Gabe just before they crossed the square. They seemed to heading for the village hall. "It's so wonderful that you're back. Jaunty will perk up no end now that you're here."

"Thank you, but why are we going to the hall?"

"You still play the piano?"

Gabe nodded.

"Well, Max's car broke down near Goonhilly and he has just rung to say he won't be back in time to hold the rehearsal."

"I'm not sure I'm following you. Max who?" Gabe tilted her head, studying Mrs Bates and hoping for some clue as to what was happening.

"Max Opie. There's a rehearsal for the fund-raising concert for cancer research that's going on next week. We're all so excited about it and it's for such a good cause. Of course, you'll have heard about poor little Jeremy Smith and how he was rushed to London for treatment?"

Gabe stopped just inside the outer door to the hall. The last time she'd been in here was for the summer jumble sale a few years ago. Inside she saw a group of teenagers and some younger children. One of them was playing scales on an old upright piano. A tall boy covered in spots was on his phone and another one was staring at the ceiling. One blonde girl was shuffling through music and glancing through the French windows towards the square while a small girl stuck close by her. In all there were twenty that Gabe counted.

"No, I hadn't heard, Mrs Bates, and I'm not sure how I can help."

"But of course you can help. They need someone to play while they sing. I remember your singing so well, my dear. It's a shame that the programme is all sorted otherwise it would have been wonderful to have you join them."

Gabe sent up a silent prayer for the small miracle of a preprinted programme. The last thing she wanted to do was to try and tell Mrs Bates that she wouldn't sing.

"Hannah, can you show Gabriella what needs playing and she'll be able to help."

The blonde girl turned from the window.

"Gabriella's very clever and composes music for a living." Mrs Bates gave Gabe's arm a little squeeze and disappeared.

Hannah came forward with a big smile. "Hi, sorry about Mrs Bates, but we really would be grateful if you could accompany us while we practise."

Gabe looked at all their faces and their eyes were intent on her. Phones were shoved in pockets and headphones removed. They were keener than she would have initially guessed. She looked at her watch. The sailing club would have to wait for another day. "OK," she said, "show me what you were working on." Gabe followed Hannah to the piano and they all gathered round. Gabe sifted through the sheets; Faure's Requiem, beautiful. She wondered who would be singing the solo, "Pie Jesu".

She looked up. "I don't know who is doing what so I will have to rely on you all." They nodded and were soon assembled on to the stage. The youngest child stayed by her side.

"Before we begin, can you tell me where the concert will be held?" Gabe ran her fingers over the keys while she studied the faces on the stage.

"Manaccan church," the young girl said.

"Will you have any other instruments accompanying you besides the organ?"

The girl shook her head back and forth energetically, sending her plaits flying. "No."

Gabe smiled at her. "Thanks. Will you tell me your name?"

"Emily."

"OK, Emily, you know what's happening but why aren't you up on the stage?"

"I don't sing but I can read music and I know when to turn the pages."

"You don't sing?" Gabe looked into the serious brown eyes.

"Well, I can sing but it's awful."

Gabe shrugged. "I doubt that's true but we had better get started — at the beginning."

The girl nodded and straightened the score.

Gabe flexed her fingers. She remembered singing this in school herself. "Do you need any direction or should I just accompany?"

Emily turned to her. "They can do it."

"I'm sure you're right."

The group arranged themselves and the sounds of sheet music being shuffled filled the hall. She waited a moment then played the opening bars, but almost stopped when they began, they sounded so lovely. Whoever had been working with them was doing an excellent job.

"How was that, miss?" Emily asked after the second run-through.

"Excellent. Is there anything you want to go over again?" Gabe asked them, amazed at how quickly the time had gone.

"Um, no," said Hannah, who had turned out to be the soloist singing "Pie Jesu". Gabe smiled at her. She had sung well but Gabe felt she could do with some more practice. Most of the kids took Hannah's words as a cue to leave and were grabbing the bags. One by one they headed out the door, waving thanks. Emily straightened all the music and left "Pie Jesu" on the top before scooting out of the door.

Hannah walked slowly to the piano. "I just wanted to say thanks again for stepping in."

"I enjoyed it and you all sang so well. Who knew there was so much talent locally?"

Hannah looked up from under her fringe, which had fallen across her eyes.

"Shall we go through this?" Gabe ran her finger across the "Pie Jesu" sheet.

Everything that had been relaxed about Hannah disappeared.

"No, it's fine. I'll manage without running through it again."

"It's always been one of my favourite pieces." Gabe smiled at Hannah. She could see her nerves. "We could just do a quick run through. Wouldn't take a moment."

Hannah bit her lower lip.

"Why don't you try an ascending arpeggio to loosen up a bit?" Gabe hit the F above middle C and gave Hannah an encouraging glance. But Hannah stood straight as an arrow by the piano, not opening her mouth. Gabe swallowed as Hannah's fear infected her. But she wasn't performing. No. This wasn't the same. Images of standing by a piano, voiceless, circled in Gabe's mind. No. This wasn't performing, this was teaching. Gabe coughed, then hit the note again, and when Hannah didn't begin, Gabe sang. Her voice faltered, but by the time she followed with a descending scale, her tone rounded and began to open.

"Wow!" Hannah's eyes were wide.

"Well, yes. Now let's see you try it." Gabe hit the note and Hannah wriggled her arms before she began. Gabe waved her hand for Hannah to continue while she played the accompanying chords and Hannah's shoulders opened. Gabe stilled her hands but Hannah continued to go one tone higher.

"Now it's my turn to say wow."

Hannah grinned.

"Good, now shall we run through 'Pie Jesu'?"

"Sure."

Gabe glanced at Hannah, who began. When the short piece finished, Hannah kicked her toes against the piano. "I fu — messed up."

Gabe's mouth twitched. "Only here." She played the section and Hannah nodded. "Try it again and this time relax more when you sing Pie, pie Jesu."

"Relax?"

"Yes, like this." Gabe played the notes then sang part of the closing segment. "Did you notice what I did?"

"Yes." Hannah frowned. "You finished the previous note a little early, then you took in all the air you needed."

"Now it's your turn to try it — and remember, cheat the breath."

Hannah smiled and this time she sang it fluently.

"That's much better, and I bet it was easier to sing when you weren't worrying about having enough breath."

Hannah nodded.

"OK, let's run through the whole piece again." Gabe played and Hannah sang the motet without fault.

"Wonderful."

"Thank you so much." Hannah looked down and then to Gabe. "Would you sing it for me so I can hear how it really should sound?"

"You already sing it how it should sound." Gabe glanced out of the window. Afternoon sunlight caught the dust motes, bringing back memories. Like Hannah, she had been a student once, wanting to learn, and she had been helped by so many people. How unfair of her not to help this talented girl. She could do this. Gabe's glance darted to the door. "OK."

Gabe closed her eyes for a moment then straightened her back. She played the opening note on the piano and began to sing, forcing everything, including where she was, out of her head and thinking only of music. As the last note ended she heard a slow clapping coming from behind her. Her throat closed.

"Hello." A man's voice said.

"Max." Hannah beamed.

"Sorry, I couldn't make it earlier but it was worth it to hear you sing." He walked up to the piano and extended his hand. "Mrs Bates tells me that you are Gabriella Blythe. It was a real pleasure to hear you."

"She's amazing, isn't she?" Hannah said.

"Yes." Max nodded. "We don't often hear sopranos of your calibre here." He paused. "Actually, not just here."

"Um, well . . ." Gabe stood up from the piano and tidied the music. "I'm off."

"Thank you so much for taking the rehearsal — I really appreciate it." The overhead light made his auburn hair seem brighter and it picked out the jewel colours in his brocade waistcoat. His dress sense was . . . unique. Gabe smiled as she looked down at his jeans and Converse high tops.

"They all sang well. You should be fine for the concert next week." Gabe picked up her bag.

"Will you be coming?" Hannah hovered by the door watching the two of them.

"I don't know." Gabe turned to Hannah. The air of fear around her had disappeared. She now leaned against the piano, projecting confidence.

"Does that mean you live around here?" Max asked.

Gabe nodded. "I've just moved in with my grandmother."

"Wonderful news."

Gabe walked towards the door.

"Hannah, shall we buy Miss Blythe a drink at the pub to say thanks?" Max stood a few steps behind.

"Brilliant idea." Hannah grinned and, linking her arm through Gabe's, led her out of the door and down the hill towards the pub.

A lone yacht with a French ensign motored out of the river, the tide helping it on its way. Jaunty recalled those precious summer days mucking about in a boat before everything changed. The task of fighting — no, working with the wind and tide filled her. The feel of the sea spray and the pounding of the blood in her veins were distant but pleasant memories and she missed the thrill. Now a snail could overtake her as she hobbled back inside the cabin. Gabriella had gone out so Jaunty had space to write. She needed space.

Removing the notebook from under the mattress, Jaunty picked up the pen.

My thoughts are rambling, but I don't think it matters in what order I tell the story, just that it is told. Today, France.

Jaunty sat back. She could see the flat she shared with Jean but it was hard to remember how they had met. She rubbed her temples. It had to be there in her mind. These things didn't go away, they were just pushed to the back.

Paris 1938.

Jaunty took her pen from the page. She closed her eyes, running through things she did remember about 1938. Her mind strayed to Alex but she opened her eyes again, erasing him with the view of the river in front of her. Of course! It had been Pierre who had introduced them. It had been the first day of her training.

I walk into the big studio and immediately feel at home with the smell of paint and dust. A woman, nude, sits in the centre of the room on a stool. Light falls on her from the window in the ceiling, creating marvellous shadows. My fingers twitch. I want to paint immediately but Pierre comes to greet me and kisses me three times. He smells of tobacco and wine although it is only ten in the morning. When he releases me I see this elegant woman dressed like a man sitting quietly in the corner. I wonder who she is and if she is painting the nude. I am jealous for so many reasons, but mostly it is her confidence. I love her hair. It is cut in a short bob and is sleek, black and glossy. I touch my own and feel out of date, although I know it suits me.

Pierre takes my hand. "Come and meet Jean. I know you will love her. She is English, like you."

Jean looks up from her work and smiles. Her face is alight with mischief and instantly I am happy. I know we will be friends.

Jaunty touched the pen to the paper again, everything now clear in her mind. She only needed to write what Gabriella needed to know.

I moved to Paris in September. I was there to study art with Pierre François. A month after I arrived I moved in with my fellow student, Jean. We were already good friends, seeing each other every day, but living in a small flat bonded us closer than I could ever have imagined. We were so different but shared the same passion — art.

Jaunty smiled, remembering. She rubbed her knuckles to ease the stiffness. She needed some coffee so she walked to the kitchen and boiled the kettle. Opening the coffee canister, the scent filled her nostrils. It was almost better than the drink itself.

"You will learn to like coffee." I sip mine.

"Never. Give me decent strong tea with milk and sugar." Jean frowns at the tea in her cup. "Not this stuff."

"It's good tea."

"Never! When we are back in England I will treat you to a decent cup. It's your foreign roots that have ruined your taste buds."

I laugh and flick my newly cut hair. It is not as short as Jean's — I didn't let her take that much off. But I feel freer and lighter and slightly mad.

Jaunty touched her hair. No longer black but white, it was now very short and much coarser than those days. So much had changed.

The pub was busy and Gabe wasn't sure about this, but she hadn't been able to think of a way of refusing without being rude. Still, she would make it quick because she needed to get back to Jaunty.

"What can I get you?" Max asked.

"A glass of white wine would be lovely, thanks." Gabe looked around the pub and recognised a few faces from her past. One of them left the bar and headed straight for her with arms open.

"Hey, Gabe! I hear you're home for good." She hadn't seen Mike Gear in years. Her recent visits had been too short and totally focused on time with Jaunty.

"That's right." Gabe smiled as he stepped back.

"Change in job?" He raised an eyebrow.

"Same job, which I can do anywhere — and Jaunty needed me."

"Good thinking." Max came up and handed her the wine.

"I see you've met our resident musical genius." Mike raised his glass towards Max.

Gabe nodded.

"You two should have a lot in common. People still talk about your rendition of 'Once in Royal David's City'."

"Mike, that was years ago," she protested, laughing

"Yeah, but it blew us all away. We didn't know you could sing. You never opened your mouth half of the time, then, bam! All I can say is the Christmas crib service has never been the same again."

Gabe looked into her wine glass. It wasn't until sixth form that she'd been willing to sing in public. She hadn't wanted to stand out in any way, which was hard enough with red hair and unusual eyes. As an orphan away at school, and with a grandmother who was more than something of an individual, she was already different enough from everyone

"Max, you have to hear her sing." Mike was warming to his subject and Gabe needed to do something to move him away from it.

"Mike, are you still fishing?" Gabe asked.

He smiled. "Yes, thanks to Jaunty. She gave me the seed money to buy my own boat. If it weren't for her I'd still be working for someone." He took a sip of his beer. "Didn't she tell you?"

Gabe shook her head and then smiled. "I'm so glad she did."

"Me too. You have to come around, and bring Jaunty if she's up to it. She hasn't met the kids yet."

"Love too." Gabe couldn't see Jaunty leaving the cabin at the moment. Her mobility had reduced so much this year.

Hannah, who'd been talking to friends, walked back to them. "Thanks again for your help today. It was really cool singing with you."

"No problem." Gabe rubbed her palms against her jeans. She shouldn't have sung. But it wouldn't happen again.

CHAPTER
THREE

Jaunty looked up from the page. Sunlight no longer hit the desk. It wasn't too hard to think back in time and to write it down. She only wished her thoughts would follow chronologically, but she had no control over them. She sighed and considered the river. It changed, yet it didn't. Each minute the water level altered, making the landscape appear transformed but it remained a sunken valley flooded by the sea and marked by the tides. The river was with her, but Alex was not. Was he ever? Had she imagined it all? What was real and what was a lie?

Glancing across the room Jaunty saw the lunch plate that Gabriella had made up for her before she'd left. Dearest Gabriella — she always thought ahead. In fact, sometimes she was far too practical for someone so artistic. She was an odd mix of her parents.

Why couldn't Jaunty remember Gabriella's age? Jaunty hated that some things were slipping away, but other things remained as if branded on her skin. Yes, she wanted to hold on to Alex, but there was so much she wanted to forget about that time and those things had never left her.

I met Alex through his sister, Rebecca. I was at Cheltenham with her and once, when my parents were in New York, I spent a holiday with her family. I remember little of the week except for Alex. He was in his final year at Oxford and was home only for the weekend. We were beneath his notice, or so I thought until my shy glances met his knowing look. With hindsight, I realise that, in truth, he was actually far more innocent than I. My breath still catches when I think of the first time he held me. It was months later at a ball. We waltzed but I can't recall which one, or even the music, and yet I can taste the frustration of being close, but not nearly close enough. His eyes hinted at desire and I knew then that my future lay with him.

It was another year before I saw him again. It was on the King's Road in London and I was very distracted. The talk of war was everywhere and so were uniforms, and I wasn't looking where I was going when I bumped into a man in one. Alex.

Jaunty stretched. Gabriella doesn't need to know this, she thought. She leaned back into the chair, feeling the wooden uprights press into the thin skin of her back. *Alex.* Everything changed that day.

"Well, hello." Alex steadies me with both hands.
"Alex!" I blink, noting how the uniform hugs his broad shoulders and that his hands have remained on my arms.

"How wonderful to see you." He steps back and I feel myself flush as he takes in my crazy apparel. "I'm on my way to meet Rebecca for tea. You must come."

I open my mouth to say no, but he grabs my hand and I know I would follow him anywhere. Grandmother Penrose will be furious when I don't appear for tea but I don't care. Alex is holding my hand.

The phone rang. Jaunty put the pen down and stretched. Who would be calling? Probably Gabriella, to check on her. It was on the fifth ring by the time Jaunty reached it, and the line was dead. It was so infuriating. The newspaper sat on the kitchen table. Gabriella must have walked to the shop this morning. Jaunty read the headlines. The news was not good, but then it never was. The names changed but the content didn't. At least now there wasn't a war in Europe. That had dominated too much of her life and altered its course — and she was following it until the bitter end.

She walked back to the sitting room, which was filled with a soft golden light. The lugger she'd seen a day ago was becalmed in the creek and Jaunty could see the sailor's dark curls and expanse of shoulders. Her breath caught. She could almost be eighteen again, the way her body yearned. It was funny how the mind played tricks. Alex was fair and he had been dead since June 1943. But there was something about the boat and the sailor . . .

★ ★ ★

"Jaunty, I'm back." Gabe put the shopping on the table and looked around. Her grandmother wasn't in her usual spot on the terrace or in the sitting room. Gabe dashed to the bedroom, hoping to find her napping, but the bed was empty. Jaunty's mobility was limited, so where could she be? Running out of the cabin to the studio, Gabe nearly fell in her haste. She had been gone hours by the time she'd picked up the things she needed from Helston. The studio was empty. Where could her grandmother have gone? She rushed along the path and found the gate was open. "Jaunty?" she called. No answer.

Gabe moved forward, peering through the trees towards the creek. Some walkers stood aside. "Have you seen an old woman about?" she asked, but they shook their heads and Gabe raced on, leaping over exposed tree roots and avoiding the worst of the brambles covered with nearly ripe fruit. Where on earth could her grandmother be? She couldn't go far but she wasn't in any of the likely spots. Taking a deep breath and trying to think logically, Gabe walked down the small path to the creek's edge and stepped on to the mud. The tide was on its way back into the creek but the foreshore was still exposed. The mud was treacherous in places, but she knew she was safe close to the trees. Her grandmother wouldn't be here, she told herself, and yet so often in the past she had found Jaunty down by the water's edge.

As she made her way past the old wreck that had been there for ever, she was even more certain that

Jaunty couldn't have made it down the path to the water, beautiful though it was there and so peaceful. Seaweed dried on the rocks and hung from the low branches, and in the distance she could see the quay. With the tide out it was obvious where it needed to be repaired but it appeared mostly sound.

"What on earth are you doing knee-deep in mud, Gabriella?" Jaunty read the mixed emotions displayed across Gabriella's face. She worried about so much. Jaunty could see the questions that Gabriella wanted to ask but didn't. She was so like her father and her grandfather in the way that she wouldn't pry. So unlike Jaunty herself, who would have dug and persisted until she found out what she wanted to know. Gabriella was too careful. She risked nothing, but she hadn't always been that way. When did it change? Even Philip, her cautious father, had never been that bad. Yes, he had married late, but at least he had found true love, however fleetingly.

"How on earth did you get down here?" Gabriella pulled herself out of the mud and climbed the rusty ladder on to the quay.

"On my bottom." Jaunty shifted. It hadn't been dignified but it had worked, and the peace of listening to the water in the creek had been glorious.

"Jaunty!"

"Don't Jaunty me. I can do as I like." Jaunty knew she sounded like a toddler. This whole regression was awful. She uncrossed her arms and looked at her granddaughter, then turned from her intense stare. In the distance Jaunty could see Groyne Point and Merthen Wood, a beautiful and mystical ancient wood that had to be filled with fairies. It was, she believed, the only place left in the county where they could be safe. Once, many years ago, she'd ventured on to the shore at low tide and tried to find a way through the cluster of trees, but she hadn't been able to penetrate more than a foot of the dense scrub and the tree cover was so thick the temperature dropped immediately. Goosebumps had covered her skin and she'd felt a thousand eyes watching her. She wondered if they watched her still from this distance. Could fairies see that far?

"Jaunty, where are you?" her granddaughter asked.

She smiled. "Away with the fairies, dear."

Gabriella shook her head, smiling in turn. She couldn't hide her love, and Jaunty didn't believe she deserved it. If — when — Gabriella knew the truth, would she feel the same?

"When you came down did you consider how you would get back up?"

"No." Jaunty shook her head. "I don't suppose you found some muscled handsome young man on your travels today?"

"No such luck."

Jaunty shook her head. She doubted Gabriella would know what to do with one if she did. It was such a waste of beauty and youth. Her granddaughter stood with her jeans splattered in mud. Did Jaunty have a washing machine? She couldn't remember, but she must. She frowned. Her memory was disappearing. Was this how it happened? Information departing in random haphazardness?

"I suppose it's a good thing you're so slight these days," Gabriella said, looking Jaunty up and down.

"Before you pick me up like a piece of luggage, let me tell you that I don't want to go yet." Jaunty crossed her arms again.

"Just when would you like to go?"

"Shall we have a picnic supper here like we used to?"

Gabriella smiled and her eyes twinkled. Jaunty was reminded again of the girl's beauty.

"OK."

Jaunty was content. Now that Gabriella was onside, her granddaughter would do all in her power to make it a magical evening. Jaunty looked to the sky. It promised to be a beautiful sunset — and the fairies would approve.

Digging through the shed, Gabe found the barbecue and some charcoal. She wasn't sure why she was doing this, because it would require a fair bit of work, but it was a beautiful evening and a simple meal of sausages and salad should be manageable if the charcoal wasn't too damp. Seventeen years ago she had done this with her father. He was on leave and he'd spent a magical six weeks in summer with her here. It had been the last time she'd seen him, and it was a fun and happy memory, a memory to repeat with Jaunty.

With a bag full of equipment and a bottle of rosé wine, she made her way carefully down to the quay, telling herself that she must remember a torch on the next trip. Jaunty should be light enough to carry as she was so small now, but Gabe had the feeling that they wouldn't be leaving until the sun had long set and the tide was fully in. The path was tricky enough in daylight but in darkness it could be hazardous.

"There you are."

Gabe felt Jaunty's scrutiny.

"Good, you brought wine. Did you remember the corkscrew?"

Gabe placed her burdens down and looked at her grandmother. "Don't need it. It has a screw top."

"Will the wine be drinkable?" Jaunty squinted doubtfully at the bottle.

Gabe shook her head. "Yes, many good winemakers now prefer screw tops to corks."

Jaunty folded her arms across her chest and Gabe laughed. She supposed that at ninety-two you had a right to be stuck in your ways and Jaunty had always been particular about her wines, although she had never explained how she knew so much about them.

Before setting up the barbecue, Gabe opened the wine and handed Jaunty a glass. Her grandmother's glance was fixed on the river as if she was expecting someone. This, of course, was ridiculous because Jaunty had always kept to herself. She communicated with the world only as necessary: the shop, the postmistress, the doctor, the bank, the gallery and Mrs Bates, who knew everyone and everything. And Jaunty never left Cornwall. She hadn't done so even for Gabe's graduation. Gabe had been the only one without any family there to celebrate their achievement.

Gabe poked the charcoal. After the fourth attempt it took and she climbed back up to the cabin to gather the rest of the supplies and the essential torch. Already the sky was turning pink. It never ceased to amaze Gabe how quickly the night closed in at this time of year. A few wispy clouds divided the horizon, making it look like sheet music without the notes.

Today was the second day that Gabe hadn't composed in a long time. She stretched her fingers. Tomorrow she would set up the keyboard in the studio. At the moment it was still wrapped in cardboard and propped in the sitting room. She needed to call a piano tuner as well. God knows what had happened to the instrument on its journey. She sighed and grabbed a cushion off a chair for Jaunty. The quay couldn't be too comfortable for Jaunty's small bottom, although of course she hadn't complained; she never did.

The boat, with what Jaunty assumed were scarlet sails, came into view again. She pictured where it might have been up-river. The sailor was fighting the incoming tide, trying to make it past Merthen Wood, but he wouldn't get far with so little wind. The boat was so similar to Alex's . . . If she closed her eyes, it was all so clear, her first love and the sea. She could see it, feel it and taste it. For her, salt was the taste of love. She shook her head. Did everyone remember their first love so precisely? She wouldn't know, for she had kept the world so far, so very far, away.

"The sausages shouldn't take too long." Gabriella poked them.

"Chipolatas never do," Jaunty said, watching the dark head in the boat. The sailor didn't seem perturbed by his lack of progress, just content to be on the river, Jaunty supposed. How she envied him his freedom . . .

"Jaunty, I asked if you wanted more wine?"

"Of course." She smiled at her granddaughter. Had she had a first love — or any love for that matter? Jaunty had never asked, which was wrong. Without her mother Gabriella must have needed to confide in someone, but Jaunty had never encouraged it. Confidences could lead to questions, and that was a risk that she couldn't take. Gabriella's father had been very independent and bright, winning a scholarship to Eton. In fact, Jaunty's father had attended but she had never told Philip of the connection, depriving him of what so many of his friends had — that sense of belonging.

Had Jaunty been distant with him? No, it had been different. Philip had been affectionate physically, but hadn't required conversation other than the normal whys. He hadn't been one for words, just building things. Gabriella had been different. She loved Gabriella, but had that been enough?

The sailing boat was closer to the mouth of the creek. It welcomed him and Jaunty's heart reached out, calling to Alex.

"Please eat . . ." Gabriella spoke softly, but it was a plea nonetheless.

Jaunty looked at the sausages and salad in front of her. Despite the inviting smell, she had no hunger for food. "I'll just be heavier to carry later."

"I don't think a sausage and a few green leaves will make much difference to your weight."

"You are a good girl."

Gabriella pursed her mouth. She was about to reply she wasn't a girl, Jaunty could tell, but she was. There was something untouched, no, frozen, that made her girl-like. She was not a woman. Gabriella had never given her heart in love, Jaunty could see that clearly now. But why? Even though everything had gone wrong in Jaunty's life and there had been no fairy-tale ending, let alone a happy one, Jaunty wouldn't change it.

But Gabriella was a lost soul. And it was Jaunty's fault in some way. It's not that she hadn't loved her. She had, but not the way a mother would have or the way her father had. For Philip, Gabriella had been the sun and everything revolved around her, even though her birth had taken his beloved. *That* was love. Jaunty looked at Gabriella and those eyes followed her.

The boat came fully into the creek and Jaunty waved to the sailor.

"Do you know him?" Gabriella squinted.

The dying rays of the sun caught the curl of his hair, making it appear golden. *Alex.* All moisture drained from Jaunty's mouth. *He's come for me.* But, "No, it just seemed the thing to do when he glanced this way."

The man in the boat waved back. A light breeze picked up and the incoming tide took him up the creek. He disappeared from view and Jaunty found her thoughts travelling with him.

The day had been warm when she and Alex had tied up to the quay and scrambled up to the cabin, for then it was truly a cabin. Had she known what would happen? Yes. It was all so clear, even now. She licked her lips, remembering the taste of him, and yet she couldn't recall the taste of the sausage she'd just eaten. Still, at least she remembered she'd eaten it. She shook her head. She needed to focus on the here and now with Gabriella. She owed that to her.

"Lovely dinner."

Gabriella laughed and put another sausage on Jaunty's plate.

Jaunty pushed it with her fork. "It was. Food always tastes better outside and beside the water. There's a freshness to it."

Gabriella shook her head. "If I'd pulled a few fish out of the creek and cooked them then I might agree, but supermarket sausages and bagged salad? I think not."

"You have no romance in you."

"In fact, you are right." Gabriella looked away, blinking.

"Why?" The word slipped out and now she couldn't take it back. Gabriella stared at her.

"I . . ." Gabriella stopped. "Never mind." She stood and poured water over the burning charcoal.

Jaunty put her hand out to stop Gabriella but she was just out of reach. Then she opened her mouth to speak but no words came out. Pain stabbed her chest. She sputtered.

Gabriella swung around. "Jaunty!" She fell to her knees and took Jaunty's pulse. "Cough," she commanded.

Jaunty tried to oblige and some sound emerged. But she wasn't having a heart attack. It was a different pain, an unfixable one.

Jaunty swatted Gabe away. "Don't fuss. There's nothing wrong."

Gabe didn't believe her.

"Clear up these things and let me be." Jaunty waved her hand at the remains of their dinner but Gabe grabbed Jaunty's wrist and felt for her pulse. It was normal and regular. Maybe Jaunty was right and she was fussing unnecessarily. God, she must relax, but it was not something she was good at any more.

Placing Jaunty's plate back in front of her, Gabe cleared everything except that and the barbecue, which could wait until tomorrow morning. Scolding herself for arguing with Jaunty, Gabe climbed back to the cabin, reminding herself that she and Jaunty hadn't lived together for years. It was bound to take some time for them to adjust to each other.

Gabe turned and looked down to the quay before it was out of view. Her grandmother sat holding her wine, staring at the boat with the red sails that was leaving the cradle of the creek. In the cabin Gabe deposited the dishes in the sink and sighed. She needed to treasure each moment with Jaunty, not lose them in worry.

Halfway down to the quay she heard Jaunty laughing, but not her normal laugh. It was lighter, higher pitched. In fact, if Gabe didn't know better, she would call it playful. What on earth had caused it? Jaunty was alone on the quay, after all.

"Your boat is beautiful and in such fine condition for an old lugger."

"Yes, *Jezebel* has been well loved and in my family since the twenties," a deep male voice replied. Gabe went rigid as she reached the last step on to the quay. Her grandmother was chatting to a tall man with loose dark curls and the boat in question was the same one they had watched earlier; now it was tied to the quay. Jaunty handed her uneaten sausage to the stranger.

"Gabriella, there you are." Jaunty smiled and her eyes gleamed. The man turned to Gabe. In the dwindling light, his skin looked pale and his almond-shaped eyes secretive. She stood tall and breathed out slowly to release the tension that had gripped her when she heard the unknown voice.

"This is Fin." Jaunty paused.

"Fin Alexander." He smiled at Gabe.

"He's the owner of that fine boat, *Jezebel*." Jaunty's voice caught on the name of the boat.

He held out his hand and Gabe realised hers were in fists. She forced them to unfold then wiped the sweat from them on to her jeans before she took his hand. His grip was firm and he had a warm smile, but there was something about him that niggled at the back of Gabe's mind. She looked from her grandmother's smiling face to his. What was it about him that had made Jaunty so bright? Gabe stepped back. Why was he here?

"I thought I could ask this young man . . ." Jaunty paused and sipped her wine ". . . if he would help me up to the cabin rather than you struggling with me." Jaunty beamed and Gabe blinked. Her grandmother seemed so perky all of a sudden. Reluctantly, Gabe assessed the stranger. His shoulders were broad and his cheekbones were almost classical. She guessed he was older than her by at least five years.

"I can manage quite well. No need to ask a stranger," Gabe said, wondering what spell he had cast over Jaunty.

"It's been a long, long time since I've been swept up by a handsome man," Jaunty said, laughing.

Gabe reminded herself to limit Jaunty's wine intake in the future. Somehow, the thought of Jaunty in the arms of a stranger was all wrong.

He took the piece of kitchen roll that Jaunty offered him. "More than happy to help."

"Then, thanks." Gabe forced her mouth into a smile and, as her lips stretched, the skin cracked. She wasn't sure why she felt uncomfortable about this, but she did. If it had been Mike Gear or someone else from the village she would have been relieved not to have to carry her grandmother; maybe it was simply because she didn't know this man that she was uneasy.

Jaunty extended her hand to Fin and he grasped the frail one.

"Thank you," Jaunty said as he scooped her into his arms.

A quick glance showed Gabe that his muscles had barely registered her grandmother's weight. She must feel like a feather to him. Gabe bent and collected the cushion from the quay, not quite sure what to do with herself. Jaunty was clearly drunk. Her accent had

71

slipped into cut-glass mode and she was a woman that Gabe didn't know.

With her arms wrapped around his neck, an expression she had never seen before crossed her grandmother's face, followed by a fleeting smile. Gabe wasn't sure her grandmother was here or lost in her own memories . . .

Gabe grabbed her grandmother's empty plate and glass then followed them up to the cabin, trying not to admire the stranger's firm bottom. He made light work out of what would have been a struggle for her, and when they reached the terrace he placed Jaunty carefully on her feet. He looked into the cabin and his glance lingered on Jaunty's paintings. They were valuable and the thought crossed Gabe's mind that he might be a thief.

Jaunty smiled up at him. "Thank you, Fin. Would you like a coffee?"

Gabe stared, astonished. Jaunty never entertained anyone. The woman protected her privacy above all and it had been a struggle to bring friends home. Only a few had been allowed to come, and never their parents. After a time, Gabe had given up trying. Looking at her suddenly animated grandmother, Gabe blamed the wine.

"Thank you, but no. I need to secure the boat for the night." He smiled. "And many thanks for allowing me to use the quay."

Gabe just stared at Jaunty. There was nothing else she could do.

He turned to Gabe. "Thank you for the sausage."

"Um . . ." How was she supposed to respond to that? "Thanks for helping my grandmother." She looked at him then turned away from his questioning glance. He nodded to Jaunty then disappeared down the path, Gabe watching his dark figure until it was out of sight. The wind blew in from the east, rustling the trees, a sure sign the weather was about to change, and when Gabe went into the cabin again, Jaunty had disappeared. Gabe found her in her room.

"What was all that about?"

"What, dear?" Jaunty stifled a yawn. "So tired. Must be all the fresh air."

And the wine, Gabe added silently. "How are you feeling now? I'd like to call the doctor."

"I'm absolutely fine," Jaunty said firmly. "Do *not* call the doctor. I am fine, just old." She began to undress, but when Gabe didn't move she said even more firmly, "Goodnight, Gabriella." She pointed to the door. "Close it behind you."

Gabe followed the order but then stood staring at the door.

CHAPTER
FOUR

Gabe paced the sitting room, glancing at the phone. Jaunty had been adamant that the doctor should not be called, but Gabe wasn't so sure. The peace of the evening had been shattered by the arrival of the man, and he had certainly been a help — Gabe would have struggled to get Jaunty up to the cabin — so she couldn't pinpoint why, but unease filled her. The stranger's dark eyes came to mind.

She went into the kitchen to do the dishes and saw there was some wine left in the bottle. Pouring it into a glass, she walked to the big window in the sitting room. Rain had arrived without warning, lashing the windows, and the winds assaulted the Monterey pines on the point. The eerie half-light that preceded lightning softened the details of the landscape and added to the tension in the air. Gabe sipped the wine, then took a few deep breaths, trying to loosen her shoulders. It didn't work. She jumped when lightning heralded the thunder that swiftly followed. She remembered the storms of her childhood, how even at sixteen she had crawled into Jaunty's bed seeking reassurance. After a few tut-tuts, Jaunty would wrap her arms around her and pull her close. And it had been a night like this when they had received the phone call that had brought them news of her father's death. She hadn't cried. She couldn't — it hurt too much.

Gabe shook her head. That was a long time ago. She knocked back the wine in one gulp then coughed. Not a good idea. Placing the glass on the table, she decided she'd do the dishes in the morning. Rain pelted against the windows and rattled the frames. In the wind she heard a note and thought of Hannah. The girl had talent, but it was early days. At sixteen Gabe had been full of promise too. At least today she had sung. Her throat hadn't closed, killing her voice. She should be thankful, but instead she was restless. So much had been lost.

Thunder boomed. The storm was growing. The trees, with their leaves still on, were at risk of being uprooted. The next flash of lightning revealed one almost bent in half with the force of the gust. Gabe counted fifteen seconds. The storm was still some way away, probably over Falmouth, wreaking havoc with the boats seeking shelter in the bosom of the harbour. But maybe it was further away than that. She counted the next interval. No, it wasn't moving. It was content to release its fury in one spot for the moment, and it was building the tension inside her. She waited for the next crescendo before she checked on Jaunty. Her grandmother was peacefully asleep; she was fine. In her room, Gabe changed into an old T-shirt. As she pulled the covers over her head, the chorus of a hymn from school, "Hail Queen of Heaven", came to her:

Refuge in grief, Star of the sea,
Pray for the mourner, Oh pray for me.

A tear slipped down her cheek and a draught pushed through a gap in the window. Gabe shivered, then fell into a half sleep, dreaming of standing on stage unable to produce a single note, until a loud crack sounded and she came fully alert. A tree or a large branch must have given way in the ferocity of the storm and she slipped out of bed to check Jaunty. Goosebumps covered her skin as she walked through the sitting room. She flicked the light switch but the lights didn't come on. Maybe a tree had taken the power lines down. The rain drummed on the roof while the overgrown buddleia scratched on the window.

She closed her eyes and slowed her breathing so that she could listen for Jaunty's gentle snores, but she heard nothing. Finding the torch on the kitchen counter, Gabe walked through the cabin, checking it and her grandmother. Maybe the shed or even the studio had been hit. Gabe grimaced, thinking about her piano, but there was nothing she could do about it tonight. The storm was moving closer and she stood by the sitting-room windows waiting for the next flash of lightning. Through the raindrops covering the glass she could just about make out the dark silhouettes of the pines on the point. Then the hairs on the back of her neck rose as she peered into the darkness and lightning flashed, revealing the creek below. There was someone in the water!

She ran to the kitchen and thrust her feet into wellies before racing out of the door, making sure it was tightly closed behind her. The steps on the path were slick and as she ran she slipped and landed on her backside, but she pulled herself up and continued. The quay appeared empty when she arrived, but then she saw the mast had snapped off the boat. The weak beam of the torch revealed debris but she didn't see the stranger. Gabe shouted over the wind while the boat bashed against the quay. Lightning flashed again and she saw what looked like a body in the water. The storm was picking up pace like an orchestra. She kicked off her wellies, marked where she had seen the body, and slipped into the icy water.

Her whole being contracted with the cold but she forced herself into action. Every second counted, but without her torch and the advantage of the raised outlook, she was swimming forward by instinct. The tide was flowing out again, pulling everything, including Gabe, with it. She was a strong swimmer, but the water felt different, overpowering. What if she didn't find him? She was treading water, trying to locate him, but the swell made everything difficult. The whole time she felt the current taking her out to sea. Then she heard a sound, a human sound. Lightning flashed and she spotted the body again and struck out towards it, thinking of the hymn again, changing the words as she swam. *Pray for the mariner, Oh pray for me.*

Jaunty's eyes fluttered open. The wind rattled the windows and her curtains billowed in the draught. She climbed out of bed, cursing her stiff joints, and tied the curtains back. Lightning illuminated the landscape and created an etched print. She pressed the switch and the lamp flickered before it came fully on. Walking to her desk she picked up a piece of charcoal and swiftly sketched out the looming shapes of the trees; a study in light and dark.

Tonight the river had brought a young man, so like Alex she could almost believe it was him, and *Jezebel*. Her senses hadn't been wrong. Had the stranger and lugger appeared now to help her to remember what had happened? Or was it more likely to remind her what she had lost?

Jaunty dropped the charcoal, rubbing her fingers together to remove the sooty remains. The wind howled and she thought she heard Gabriella singing an old hymn, but Jaunty knew it must be her desire to hear her sing that was making the wind's whining through the trees sound like music. Collecting her pen and notebook she settled back into bed, looking up at the ceiling as a thump hit the roof. The light blinked but remained on. She looked at her watch, then the bedside table. It was one thirty but the alarm clock showed one. The power must have gone off at some point. She hoped Fin had secured his boat well. He should be protected from the worst of the storm in the creek. It was a haven and had always been.

This cabin has been my refuge although when I bought it, it didn't feel that way. This room was cold and so damp. A local builder helped me to make it watertight and since his true passion was boats, much of the walls and ceiling are wood cladded. Even now when I look at the way he fitted the cupboards I think of a yacht.

When Philip and I arrived here it was barely habitable but it was safe, safe for me but not for a small child. I had to build walls and terraces so an active toddler didn't fall off on to the rocks below. I was grateful for the safety of the trees that protected us from winter storms and I became quite proficient at providing for us, fishing and foraging. You, Gabriella, won't remember, but for years our only water came from a well and I didn't have electricity installed until the sixties.

What I had here was so different from my childhood.

Looking back I wonder how I managed at all — but I did. Just getting water from the well was a long project when Philip was little. The well . . . Now it's closed off, not needed, but several times a day I used to make my way to it. Have you ever found it? I suspect not, as it is so overgrown, but people still visit it I think. I used to find things tied to the holly tree beside it. Some said it was a holy well. I never believed it but they said there had been a hermit who, like me, had sought refuge in this place away from the world. Many people had come here seeking miracles and forgiveness from him and from the water of the well in the wood.

Jaunty's eyes kept closing and with a sigh she put the pen and paper away. Maybe sleep would come again.

Shutting off the light, she closed her eyes and listened. The wind called to her and stirred the emptiness within. Everything was changing with it. Maybe there was hope after all.

All her muscles ached and despite the exertion Gabe was freezing. She fought the current to swim across to the body. What she was doing was madness. How could she save someone when she was struggling with almost everything she had to beat the current? The next flash came and she found him just feet in front of her, but the water pulled him just out of her reach. White horses converged where the creek met the river. The north-east wind was whipping them up higher and she lost sight of him again, lost sight of the shore. The body drifted further away and she forced her arms out to reach him. There was no movement. He was either dead or out cold but she didn't have time to check or she'd be dead before too long. What the hell was she doing? she asked herself. She wasn't going to be able to save him and she would probably end up killing herself. But she had to try, she had to.

The one thing she could tell as she lifted him by the chin was that he was the man from the boat. If she had thought him big when he carried Jaunty, he felt enormous as she fought against the current to try and reach the bank. He was a dead weight, pulling them both down. She didn't want to think about dead. He must still be alive. She must survive. The wind grew stronger, swirling above them, whipping water at them. Slowing down, she took in a mouthful of water. No!

Mother of Christ, Star of the sea, Pray for the mariner, pray for me. The words ran through her head with each stroke. She changed arms and pulled harder but opened her mouth at the wrong time and took in water again. Her muscles complained and her kicking wasn't as forceful as it needed to be. The pull of the river was winning. Her muscles seized and she began to go under. He stayed afloat, held up by his life vest. Forcing her legs into action she stayed above the water. She could see the bank of rock covered with holly branches. There was no way she could get them to safety there.

She went under again and almost lost her hold on him. She had no strength left. Maybe she should just give in, let the sea take her. She had been living half a life for years. She knew that. Jaunty was dying and Gabe had no one. She could just stop swimming. The man might yet survive but she could stop trying. Gabe ceased kicking. This was the answer.

The man moved in her grasp. She came up, gasping for air. He was alive. He fought with her and she felt she might have to leave him to the river because he was going to drown them both. The words of the hymn wouldn't leave her head. *Mother of Christ, Star of the sea, Pray for the mariner, pray for me.*

The storm continued to grow and he stilled in her grasp. Wind and rain whipped savagely about them, flashes of lightning showed Gabe how perilous their situation was. The darkness was better. She could imagine they were closer to shore, to safety. She struck out towards the nearest branch, kicking with full force.

81

Eventually she was able to grab it. The holly pierced her hand, but she held on despite the pain as the water did its best to pull them back out.

Lowering her feet, she made contact with the bottom. Once her feet were secure, she released the branch and reached out for another, pulling them around until they were back in the creek where the force of the current lessened.

The man spluttered. Gabe was trying to get her breath back and to find the strength to get them out of the water. Her hand was bleeding but the water was so cold she couldn't feel anything and didn't care. She hadn't thought this through. They were safe from the tide and protected from the wind but not saved. Far from it — the quay was still some distance from them and the bank was too steep to climb even if she had the strength. Now that she had stopped moving, shivering began to take over her body. Her brain echoed with Jaunty's words that the river was at its warmest at this time of year, but right now it felt like the Arctic.

The stranger kept going in and out of consciousness. He was alive, but neither of them might be for much longer if she didn't find a way out. Think, think, *think*. But her mind was blank except for the hymn. She didn't want to pray. If they didn't get out of the water, they would freeze to death or drown. Despite her lack of strength, Gabe knew she must get them out. She couldn't walk along, as the footing was treacherous, so she grabbed another branch. Again the holly leaves pierced her hand. She sank her teeth into her bottom lip, trying to distract herself from the pain with another pain. As she reached for the next branch she lost her hold on him. He turned and pulled away.

"What the hell?" she shouted and took in a mouthful of water. His arms flailed about and he bashed her on the head in his scramble. She went under. This was the nightmare she'd been dreading. Gabe fought her way to the surface, only to be pushed down again. He was going to drown her! She swam underwater, away from him. She couldn't save him but maybe, just maybe, she could save herself.

She came up spluttering and looked around but didn't see him. She was still close to the shore and she grabbed another branch, finding him caught in the holly. He was stuck, but at least he was caught above the waterline.

Lightning revealed the scene and she saw they were not far from safety. She had to make one more attempt to get them to the quay, but she needed him aware of what was happening. He had to be awake. There was no way she would have the strength to pull him on to the quay. She would be lucky if she could get herself on to it.

Gabe slapped his face repeatedly and finally he spluttered.

"Come on, you bloody man! Open your eyes. I can't do this without you and if I leave you out here you will die and I will have nearly killed myself for nothing."

She began shaking and shock took over. She had been in the sea for what felt like hours, but had been only a matter of minutes she was sure. If she could wake him they could both make it.

"Come on!" He was breathing but not responding. She glanced around, hoping for some inspiration but nothing came. She looked up and let the rain blend with her tears.

"Someone help me!" she shouted.

The stranger, Fin, opened his eyes, staring almost through her. Gabe gasped. She didn't know what he was seeing but she felt exposed. "Can you move?"

He nodded.

"Right, we need to get out of the water and on to the quay. Follow me."

She lay on the quay gasping for breath, trembling. They were both alive, which was a miracle because he'd damn near killed her. His shoulder pressed against her arm and his breathing was more like gasps, which shook her whole body. She had only enough energy to breathe and for her teeth to chatter. The trembling became violent shivering.

He moved and before she knew it he was on his feet, pulling her up out of the shallow water that was washed over the quay. Her legs shook so much that standing was almost impossible. He wrapped an arm around her and half dragged, half carried her to the cabin without a word. The thunder and lightning had stopped but the rain continued to beat down on them. By the time he thrust them through the door Gabe couldn't speak even if she wanted to. It might be shock but it was certainly the cold that had turned her incapable. He looked around. "Bathroom?" Gabe managed to point with a hand that was far from steady. He took the wobbly hand and led her through her bedroom. Everything in Gabe froze and she refused to move any further. He released her hand and went into the bathroom where he turned the shower on full. Steam followed him back into the bedroom. Gabe stood in a puddle of water. Her T-shirt, now transparent, clung to her. She tried to think, to move, to act in some way.

Fin approached and took her hand. Instinct took over and she fought, lashing out.

"I'm not going to hurt you but you need to get warm, and so do I." He held both of her hands down and manoeuvred her into the bathroom and into the shower. Once he was sure she could stand he stepped out of the room and closed the door.

Gabe leaned against the tiles on the wall. Her skin stung with pin-like pricks of pain, but slowly the shaking began to subside. What had just happened?

He knocked. "Are you OK?"

"Yes." But she wasn't so sure. Gabe pulled off the T-shirt then stepped out of the hot water. Securely wrapped in the towel she entered her room. He wasn't there. *Jaunty*.

Gabe rushed through the kitchen and walked straight in to him, staring at Jaunty's paintings. His hands steadied her, then she noticed he was naked except for a small towel around his hips and there was blood on his cheek. It triggered a memory and she went rigid.

"I'm frozen too. May I use your shower?"

Gabe blinked. "Yes — yes, of course."

He stepped around her. And sensations she had hidden away for years fought to come to the surface along with sheer panic.

CHAPTER
FIVE

Gabe screamed but a hand came over her mouth. Aftershave. Cloying. Vodka. Music. Her voice. He'd asked her to sing for him and her voice rose with the music. This was her chance. All her passion went into it. Puccini's wonderful "Vissi d'arte". Her voice filled the room and while she was lost in the moment, he approached. She should have known, she should have known! She'd been warned. She had won. The world was hers. And then fingers circled her throat. His other hand pushed up her dress and ripped away her knickers. Gabe struggled and he slapped her face. His hand grabbed her breast, squeezing it until she screamed again. Why was he doing this to her?

"You want this." He laughed as he threw her to the ground. "They all do. This will make you sing. It will colour your words and give them the passion you lack."

"No!" He had her arms pinned above her head as he pulled himself out of his trousers and wedged her legs open with his knee. She twisted and turned but he brought his knee down on her thigh.

"You've been begging me for it all night."

"No!"

"You came here with me. Every move you made told me." He released her hands so that he could enter her. "You want it." She beat him, clawed at him, but he didn't stop. Finally she drew blood as her nails cut into his face.

"You bitch!"

She screamed until she had no voice and no one came. All the time Puccini's music played in a loop.

"You whore! That's all you are, teasing everyone. You'll never sing again, Gabriella — you don't deserve to."

He finished and stood, pulling up his trousers. He touched his cheek and looked at the blood on his fingers. Gabe tried to scream again, but no sound came out of her mouth. He licked the blood from his fingers then walked out, leaving her on the floor sobbing silently.

Gabe woke in a sweat, her throat constricting, her skin crawling. She headed to the shower but then stopped. She couldn't wash him away. She had tried, oh she had tried. She looked down at her body. The signs of the violation were long gone, but somewhere, on a police file, every bruise, every scratch, even his semen, was recorded. It was all there. It hadn't gone away.

The storm was over. The air was cooler and the tension, which had been almost suspended in the air, had been released as if the world had sighed. Jaunty climbed from bed. It was six. Silence filled the cabin, broken only by the screech of crows and curlews rising from the creek. Pulling on an old cashmere cardigan, she sat at her desk, wondering where she'd left off and knowing it didn't matter.

Jean.

I owe my life to Jean and I thought at the time it would be the other way around. Her French, although she had been in Paris for two years before I met her, was appalling — she just managed to feed herself. Her vocabulary when it came to art was different. This she knew. Even now, I think this was instinctive as was everything to do with art for her. I am still jealous of her talent.

I throw my brush down and walk to the window. Jean chuckles behind me and hands me a cigarette.

"It's in you."

"No. My work is pedestrian."

Pierre joins us. "What is wrong?"

"Self-loathing." Jean grabs the cigarette from my hand and takes a drag. Her red lipstick stains it. She hands it back.

"Self-loathing is essential to learning and so is wine. So now is the time to drink." He takes my hand, then Jean's, and leads us out on to the roof. My stomach growls.

"Always hungry," He turns to me. "But for food."

Jaunty's stomach gurgled. As in the past, she was in the present. She was hungry but she didn't want to take a break. She must stop simply remembering and write it down. Her hand shook as she put pen to paper.

She was jealous of my upbringing. There wasn't a major museum in Europe that I hadn't spent time in and, of course, money was never an issue. Despite the jealousy, our bond was tight. But I lacked her hunger then. I have learned her hunger since.

Jaunty put the pen down and walked through to the sitting room. Tea. She looked at the painting on the wall. At least the work was true. It was so different. She stopped in mid-step. There were large puddles all over the sitting-room floor and on the sofa there was a man. Fin. In sleep he looked even more like Alex than he had last night because the relaxed facial muscles made him appear younger. It was if her longing had brought Alex here.

The cheekbones. Jaunty's fingers stretched out, but then she pulled them back. Someone was having a laugh with her. If there was a God, then he must be enjoying this.

His hair curled in the same way as Alex's had.

Jaunty walked closer. A very different hunger stirred in her. She laughed. Who would believe that at ninety-two desire still existed, if fleetingly? She closed her eyes. Her hands moved, feeling Alex's body again. It was so real but it wasn't.

"Morning." Fin rubbed his chin.

Jaunty stepped backwards. "Good morning. Tea?"

He sat up. He was naked to the waist and so beautiful, the *latissimus dorsi* appearing carved as he moved his arm. Jaunty turned away and walked to the kitchen. Filling the kettle she reminded herself he was not Alex, but all she could think of was how long it had been since she had made love. The kettle clicked. She shouldn't complain. She'd had two brilliant lovers and some women were never that lucky.

Carrying a tray she walked back in to see his body outlined by the window. He was naked, a beautiful specimen, clutching a pillow. Broad shoulders down to lean hips; shapes, angles, shadows — but no colour.

He turned, adjusting the pillow. "I'm sorry, my clothes are still drenched."

Jaunty smiled. "I'm not offended." She looked him up and down. "But you must be cold. Shall I have a look for something for you to wear?"

He walked back to the sofa and picked up the blanket. "This will do."

"Indeed."

He glanced at the puddles. "I'm sorry about the mess."

"What happened?" Jaunty poured the tea and handed him a cup.

"The storm was bigger than forecast. I was asleep, then I heard a noise." He took a sip of the tea and looked at Jaunty. "Thank you."

Jaunty settled in her chair and he remained standing with the blanket wrapped about his hips. He shook his head. "I put on my life jacket and went on deck. The creek looked like the sea and it was pushing the boat against the quay. I knew I needed to secure the boat, but before I could do anything a gust rocked it and I must have hit my head." He paused. "The next thing I knew I was fighting for air." He sat down on the sofa, cradling the cup in his hands. "I wouldn't be alive if it wasn't for your granddaughter. How she found me I don't know. I'm very lucky to be alive." He shook his head.

Jaunty's breath stopped. Gabriella. Forcing air into her lungs Jaunty looked at the man her granddaughter had saved. She could have lost her granddaughter to the sea as well and that would have been too cruel. She looked at him again, pushing thoughts of death away. "What brings you here in the first place?"

"I was at a bit of a loose end in my life." He shrugged.

"A loose end?"

He gave her a lopsided smile. "It's a simple way to describe a nasty divorce." He looked down at his hands while he turned the cup around.

"I see."

He looked up. "I think you might."

"So you are sailing around trying to find yourself?"

"Maybe not myself, but something." He laughed. "I gave, no, I *lost* everything in the divorce."

Jaunty raised an eyebrow. He had been saved for a reason just as she had. She wondered what it was.

"It seemed easier at the time." He laughed. "Now, with hindsight, it's tricky. After last night the boat is gone and I have nothing to return to."

"Are you ready to return?"

"No." He looked at her closely. "Not at all."

"Well, maybe I can help, at least in the short term." Jaunty rose slowly, an idea forming in her mind.

"Really?" He stood, adjusting the blanket about his hips.

"I can give you a place to stay." She smiled. "Follow me."

Debris was strewn all over the path to the studio. Last night had been wild and had brought this young man more closely to them. She stopped and turned to him. "You should be able to stay in here."

His eyes darkened. Jaunty knew pain when she saw it. He looked away. "Thank you."

A large branch blocked the door of the studio, but it appeared not to have hit the building. She did worry about it. There was so much in here and she rarely came near it any more. Fin moved the branch for her and she opened the door. As always she stopped on the threshold and took a deep breath. It was as if filling her lungs with the right air allowed the muse back into her body. The muse was nonsense, but part of her still held on to the idea. Nothing had turned out as she had expected in her life. Because she had gone against her father's wishes and returned to Paris to finish her studies, her world had changed for ever. She stepped into the studio. Desire swelled in her. The longing was almost physically painful. It was like being next to your lover but not being able to feel him, only see his ghost.

"You're an artist." Finn's intense gaze scanned the room.

"Once." Jaunty turned to the bed in the corner. His feet might stick out of the bottom, but it would have to do. She noted that Gabriella had put her piano in here. Well, they would just have to work around each other.

He turned to her. "So you are J?"

Jaunty nodded. The letter defined her now.

"I love your work." He walked slowly around the room and Jaunty knew that he was not an uninterested viewer but a connoisseur. She watched his eyes as his glance studied each work, saw how they stopped on certain types of brush and palette-knife work. This man knew painting. She looked at his hands. No, he was not an artist.

"Thank you."

He stopped in front of the easel. A study in grey; well, Jaunty assumed it was. For that was all she could see now, and she wasn't even sure if the colours she'd mixed were what she thought they might be. All she knew was that the depth and the intensity of hue was right. It had been in the middle of this work that she had known it was over. She'd put her brush down, hadn't cleaned it, and walked away. This was the first time she'd been into the studio since that day.

"Sorry about the smell, but I'm sure that within a few days of proper airing the intensity of it will abate."

"This is incredibly kind of you."

Jaunty stopped and looked at him. It wasn't kind, it was reckless, and both of them knew it. She did not know this man. He was a stranger who looked like an old lover, that was all.

94

★   ★   ★

Sunlight streamed through the windows and every part of Gabe ached. She stretched, opening her hand, then squealed. Holding it up to the light, she turned it over, looking at the gashes. They weren't pretty but they were superficial and there was no permanent damage. Blood seeped out of the corner of a newly formed scab. Last night she had saved a stranger from the sea and damn near killed herself in the process.

She rubbed her temple with her good hand. The worst part was that the man was probably still in the cabin. Where would he go? Nowhere. Taking great care she got out of bed and dressed. She stood in front of the mirror and brushed her hair until she could tame it into a ponytail. She was paler than normal and her lips still had a tinge of blue about them, which matched the circles under her eyes. Her skin seemed almost translucent.

She turned from the mirror when she heard the kitchen door open. Jaunty was chattering like a schoolgirl. When Gabe reached the kitchen, her grandmother was handing the man his clothes out of the tumble dryer. He currently sported a blanket and his feet were bare, with bits of wet grass stuck to them. What on earth had they been doing outside with him dressed like that? He would have frightened the neighbours if they had had any near enough to see him.

"Morning." He looked at her and smiled.

"Yes, how are you?"

He grinned. "Alive. Thank you."

Jaunty looked between the two. "Yes, I hear you risked life and limb to save him. What were you thinking, trying to attempt a rescue on your own in a storm?"

Gabe studied her grandmother. She hadn't heard that tone from her in years. Jaunty had rarely scolded her because Gabe had never given her much reason too. She met Jaunty's piercing glance and then she knew. The sea. "I lost all sense of perspective," Gabe said. "I was mad to have even tried."

"But you did." He tilted his head to one side. "I'm alive because of your madness."

Gabe shivered. He'd nearly killed them both.

"You both could have drowned." Jaunty stormed off.

Gabe looked at Fin.

"I'm sorry." He appeared as sheepish as she felt. "I've got you into trouble."

It had been totally crazy but they were alive. Still, she could understand Jaunty's concern.

"If you'll excuse me, I'll go and change." He glanced down at his attire and gave her a crooked smile. She thought he looked pretty good in the blanket, if she was honest.

Gabe walked through the sitting room to Jaunty's bedroom. Jaunty was straightening the eiderdown.

"What were you doing outside?" Gabe leaned against the doorframe.

"I took him to the studio." Jaunty looked up. "He'll be staying there for a bit."

"What?"

Jaunty frowned. "He has lost his boat and he tells me his ex-wife took his flat, so he's homeless."

"He doesn't appear to be a down and out. What was wrong with a hotel, a bed and breakfast?"

Jaunty looked out the window.

"Right, so you offered your studio that you rarely let anyone into?"

"I'm not using it." Jaunty walked to her desk. "Now leave me be."

Gabe watched her grandmother staring at the river. This was a side to her Gabe didn't know.

Jaunty's fingers bent around the small piece of charcoal and she sketched Fin. Although swiftly done, she had captured the confidence in the stance yet somehow had conveyed the vulnerability. She'd seen it as he'd stood there, legs apart, staring out at the view, but it was only when she asked what he was going to do now that a few careless words revealed his pain.

Jaunty put the page aside and picked up her fountain pen. She could hear Gabriella talking to Fin. How could she have risked her life like that?

"Jaunty, I'm heading into the village to get milk." Gabriella popped her head through the doorway.

"Fine." Jaunty blocked Gabriella's view of the desk with her body.

"Do you want anything?"

"No." Jaunty waved her away and listened to them leave together. She put the pen down and picked up the charcoal again. This time she drew Alex in profile, focusing on his neck. She rubbed the dark, sooty colour into the paper, almost feeling the tendons. A few quick strokes and his long eyelashes appeared. Oh, if it was only so simple to recreate him and to have him here with her . . . Her hands went limp and the charcoal dropped on to the paper. It was Fin's resemblance to Alex that was making it all so much harder. She swallowed and looked at the dark dust on her fingers, shades of grey. That still worked. It was the colour that was gone. The bright jewel hues and the subtle shifts in tone. Her joy, removed in an instant. She picked up the pen again.

I have always been an artist. I was never, even as a child, without pencil and paper. My many governesses knew that I would sit for hours in a museum sketching, even from the age of five. I sometimes wonder if those early works exist somewhere. Mother had kept them all. What has become of my parents' things? I know when she died, and father too. I researched it when I first came to Truro. Both of them had had obituaries in the Telegraph and The Times. Mother's coverage had been bigger. Both obituaries said her heart had been broken and her voice had lost its power because of the deaths of her daughter and her husband.

Jaunty closed her eyes. She had been the cause of so much pain, so much death.

So my early work may have been thrown out or more likely it could be in the attic in my nonna's house. That is, if it still exists, if it survived the war. There is so much that I don't know and now never will.

Then, of course, there was Polruan House. How I hated and loved that house at the same time. When my father was with me it was bliss, but when I was there without him it was dire. To my grandmother I was a disappointment because I was not the male heir she wanted for the Penroses. She did nothing but frown at me, then tell me how wonderful things would be when my mother bore a son. When the years passed and it was too late, she told me that it was my fault that my mother never had a son because she had given birth to me. I heard the whispered discussions about how sick my mother had been after my birth. I knew I must have been the cause.

Jaunty looked up. Jackdaws were complaining in the pines and the wind blew in from the east. The sky should clear but the river would remain disturbed.

Gabe felt for the keys in her pocket. Her muscles were so sore that the thought of taking the car to the shop appealed, but if she moved her legs the pain might lessen, and the sun was shining, showing no storm that had raged only hours before. In fact, the sky was so blue Gabe wasn't sure she had ever seen it so bright and clear. Were her senses heightened because she had damn near died? She glanced sideways at Fin. Although he was about a foot from her she could almost feel him. There was something about him that bothered her. Was it the way he looked so intently at her, almost seeing the pain locked away inside. Or was it his effect on Jaunty? More frightening, was it the thought of his hard, lean body? Part of her froze and the other . . . well, best not to think about it. But with him beside her that was proving difficult.

She went past the car. The walk would help. He moved silently beside her, like a shadow, as if by saving him he'd become attached to her by invisible strings. She shivered.

"Still cold?" His deep voice rumbled over her goosebumps.

"No, someone must have walked over my grave." Damn! That was not what she meant to say — it was too close to the truth. Despite what Jaunty had said about him being homeless, he oozed power and confidence and that was what was making her uncomfortable. He was a powerful man.

"Ah." He studied her, then turned away, looking out at the yellowed field, which sloped upwards towards the tall pines that marked its boundary at the top of the hill. Gabe had always loved this view. The trees, she thought, were like guardians of the river. How many times had she made this walk? Too many to count. Jaunty hated using the car so, no matter the weather, if they had needed more milk or bread then she had walked to the shop. The car remained parked except for a once-a-week trip to the shops and to Camborne for art supplies. Where possible everything had come by post. Gabe always suspected that the person who knew Jaunty best was the postmistress because her grandmother lived in a world of parcel deliveries and cheques and struggled so much with the new world of technology. In the end, many suppliers spoke to Gabe in order to resolve payment issues, and Gabe had managed her grandmother's bank account for the last few years — the gallery had insisted because Jaunty became muddled by the amounts being transferred into her account.

Gabe sighed. Jaunty was old and the world had moved forward. But because Jaunty had locked herself away in her studio, she hadn't seen it nor had she wanted to take part in it. It was too late now.

"Do you want to take the quick route or the scenic one?" Gabe stopped on the cattle grid at the top of the track, wondering what she herself felt like doing.

"Scenic." He shrugged, and Gabe watched the play of muscles under his shirt. She had seen them up close . . . Shaking her head mentally she strode out ahead of him down the lane towards Penarvon Cove, pushing the images away. Instead she filled her mind with the height of the trees above. It felt as if she was in a magic world where she became tinier the lower down the lane she went and the trees above closed into tunnel. She inhaled, filling her lungs, wanting to sing but releasing the breath in a slow sigh.

"OK?" He turned to her.

"Yes, a bit stiff, that's all. How are you?"

"Same, but glad to be alive."

They reached the beach and signs of the storm were strewn all over the pebbles. Among the seaweed were bits of wood and empty bottles which told an interesting tale in themselves. The wood was mixed, a few branches, some plywood and a turned table leg. The bottle selection consisted of a milk carton and an empty bottle of Château Latour. Gabe wondered if it had been consumed last night on one of the few visiting yachts still moored on the river.

They followed the narrow path above the cove and into Helford, passing the pub. Signs of damage were evident here too. A roof slate from a nearby cottage was lying smashed on the road and Gabe was glad she hadn't been walking back from the pub last night when that had come down. She looked out to the river. This morning there was no wind, but the water still displayed signs of the storm. Even from in front of the shop she could see the swell as a boat made its way out to the bay. She climbed the stairs and Fin followed.

"Morning." Gabe didn't recognise the woman behind the counter.

The woman smiled. "Quite the night, last night. Three boats broke anchor on the river."

"Really?" Gabe looked up from the bread selection.

"Yes. Wild, it was."

"Do they know the owners of the boats?" Fin asked.

"Not all — there was one they couldn't identify."

"That's probably mine."

Gabe watched the woman study Fin over and could see the appreciation in her eyes. He certainly was handsome, Gabe gave him that, but wouldn't give him anything more. It was something about his cheekbones and smile. But she was still in shock that Jaunty had offered him a bed in her studio. She didn't understand why he needed it or, more importantly, why Jaunty had offered.

A woman walked in the shop. "Oh, how lovely to see you, Gabriella."

"Hello, Mrs Bates."

"Thank you for helping the choir, by the way."

Gabe swallowed. "No problem." She noticed Fin studying her.

"I'm thrilled you're back with us. Jaunty will be better now that you are with her." Mrs Bates eyed Fin up and down. "And who is this good-looking stranger?"

He smiled and extended a hand to Mrs Bates. "Hi, I'm Fin."

"Is this your boyfriend?" Mrs Bates positively glowed.

Gabe gagged. "No, I rescued him last night in the storm."

"A stranger from the sea? How poetic. Now, if only I could remember these things . . ." Mrs Bates put her basket down. "What was it they always said? Save a stranger from the sea —"

A man stuck his head through the shop door. "Mrs Bates, can you move your car? They're trying to get a trailer down to the pub."

"I'll be back." She waved and disappeared, leaving her basket on the counter. Gabe took the opportunity to pay, then set off out of the shop at a pace that hurt her aching legs, wondering how Mrs Bates could take two and two and come up with six.

As they reached the pub, Fin touched her arm and Gabe jumped.

"Sorry." He tilted his head to the side. "Can I buy you a drink to say thanks?"

Gabe turned and smiled. "Sounds wonderful, but, um, do you have your wallet?"

"Oh, damn, I forgot about that." He tapped his forehead with his right hand.

She laughed. "Lost your memory along with your boat?"

"Must have."

"Well, I think stopping for a drink is a wonderful idea, and I'll pay," Gabe said, heading into the pub.

Once they had their drinks, they sat down on the lower terrace. The sun was so warm that Gabe shed her jumper. September was the perfect month, she thought, with its blue skies, warm sun and few tourists, just enough to keep the local businesses happy but the roads reasonably clear.

"Do you know everyone here?" Fin held his pint.

"Sort of . . ." She paused. "I spent much of my childhood here."

"Perfect." He glanced out towards Falmouth Bay.

"Yes." Gabe thought of the early years when her father was still around. "Where did you grow up?"

"Here and there."

Gabe frowned.

"My father was a diplomat." He traced a finger through the condensation on the side of his glass. His fingers were long, but they weren't a musician's hands. "I did spend many summers in Fowey, though, with family."

"Lovely."

"It was, yes."

"I don't mean to intrude . . ." Gabe pursed her lips, trying to think of how to ask this.

"But you will." He raised an eyebrow and Gabe noted the hints of green in the deep-set blue eyes.

"Why are you staying with us if you have family in Fowey?"

"Fair question." He sipped his beer. "They sold the house this spring when my grandmother died and the family couldn't agree on who should have the house."

"Oh." Gabe continued to study him, hoping he'd reveal more. When he didn't volunteer anything further, she asked, "And you normally live . . .?"

He rolled the pint between his hands. "You see, that's the problem. I don't *have* a normal at the moment."

Gabe tilted her head to one side, waiting for him to continue.

"Normal disappeared when my wife left me for her best friend."

"Oh!"

"Oh, really doesn't cover it." He gave a dry laugh. "I was so shocked I wanted nothing to do with my old life because it was a lie."

"I see."

"I wish *I* had," he said, shaking his head. "But enough about me." He grinned, revealing slight dimples. "You live with your grandmother?"

Gabe nodded, thinking that didn't sound very good, a thirty-year-old woman living with her grandmother.

"And she's the famous artist Jaunty Blythe."

Gabe sucked in a mouthful of air, wondering how he knew. There were no photographs of Jaunty in any magazines or papers, no interviews . . . And then she remembered that Jaunty had taken him to the studio.

Jean. *Gabriella must understand that Jean is the key.*

After my first year studying in Paris my style was improving but Jean's — Jean's was special. It was based on hard work and sound skills but somehow, despite the technical ability underlining it, her work was innocent, even slightly primitive. Under each painting was a flawlessly executed sketch but once she used paint it altered. I wish I knew how she achieved it.

She hated that she was broke, so I suggested she send her paintings to a gallery owned by a friend of my father's. They liked her work and took her on.

Jaunty stood and closed the window. Champagne. When had she last had champagne? All this thinking of the past was opening memories so long put away . . .

"I am drunk." I look out of the window to the courtyard far below.

"Me too." Jean raises the bottle of champagne and brings it close to her face. "We may need another bottle."

"We do." I turn and smile.

"It's all thanks to you."

106

I laugh. "Nonsense. The paintings wouldn't have sold if they weren't wonderful."

"Really?" Jean's face brightens. It is the first time I have seen self-doubt in her.

"Of course." I raise my nearly empty glass. "Mark my words, Jean. You will be one of the most important and sought-after painters of the century." I meet her eyes and see the tears shining there. Lifting my glass, I finish its contents, washing away the bile in my throat.

CHAPTER
SIX

After Fin had finished talking to his insurance company on the landline, they walked to the quay. Enquiries discovered that perhaps his boat had been found. A call to the harbour master from a local farmer, Steve, who Gabe knew, pinpointed its location further upriver on the south side. They walked the banks of the creek and found a few of Fin's things — well, she assumed they were his — had washed up on the mud and the tide had left them drying in the sun. A shirt hung from a low-hanging branch as if someone had done his washing, and a plastic basin was making its way out of the creek. It was a sad sight on a beautiful day. She looked at Fin. He had spoken calmly to the insurers despite the fact his "home" was in ruins. In fact, to her mind, he appeared almost too calm about it. What was going on in his head?

He turned to her. "Do you have a camera?"

"Just the one on my phone."

"Is there a way to get to the other side of the creek easily?"

"You could swim," Gabe said with a faint smile.

"Don't fancy it. You?" He grinned.

"No." Gabe laughed. Her skin should still be prune-like after last night but it wasn't and she would like to keep it that way. "You could walk around the creek. It would take about an hour at most."

"Drive?"

"Yes, but it would still take a half-hour and then the walk down to it. The quickest way would be by boat." Gabe looked at the hill behind the quay. Jaunty's old rowing boat was under a tarpaulin in the undergrowth about halfway up.

"I need photos for the insurance. They'll be sending a loss adjuster, but *Jezebel* wasn't the only boat damaged last night, it could be days or weeks before the loss adjuster comes here."

Gabe nodded then walked up the path and turned into the hillside, walking through the ferns and brambles to where she could just make out the blue plastic sheeting. Fin followed. Once upon a time this little rowing boat had been Jaunty's pride and joy. In the summer, tide permitting, Jaunty had rowed them both to Helford to collect supplies and have an ice cream, but Jaunty never went beyond Helford village. She would venture to Gweek and fish the many creeks but never out to the bay. Maybe it would bring memories of near-drowning too close. Gabe knew she had been found near the Manacles, off St Keverne.

Gingerly Gabe pulled back the tarpaulin and watched a large spider move away, then woodlice dropped down. When a slug fell on it, Gabe shook her hand and pulled back. Fin came closer and released the rope holding the tarp down. In one movement, he pulled the cover off and revealed the little white boat with its blue trim. The paint was flaking off in large chunks.

"Let's turn it over." Fin pushed through the undergrowth to the stern and Gabe took the bow. It flipped easily and despite the neglect it looked sound, but there were no oars. "Shall we take it down to the quay?"

Gabe nodded, thinking the oars must be in the shed. Holding on to the bow, Gabe back-stepped on to the path and finally on to the quay. The tide was still too far out so they would have to wait for a while.

"Shall we leave it here?" He smiled, and the sunlight caught his cheekbones and cast shadows on his deep-set eyes. Right now they looked almost navy and very guarded despite his smile. What was he hiding?

"By the way . . ." He bent to fix the rowlocks, then paused, looking up from his task. "I can't say thank you enough for saving me. And well, yours and your grandmother's kindness for letting me stay." He smiled and studied her. Gabe blushed and turned away.

"Um, yes, thanks." The less said about the rescue and its aftermath the better. The image of him standing with a small towel slung about his hips wouldn't leave her thoughts. She knew nothing about this man, yet he was making her think about desire again. But desire, want, and need had left her four years ago, and without those emotions her singing was flat, even if it was pitch perfect. To be a decent soprano, let alone the one she had wanted to be, passion was required. But fear

110

trapped her. In an act of violence one man had neutered and silenced her.

The back of her throat tickled and Gabe coughed. She hadn't been able to do her vocal exercises this morning. Because Fin was here her whole schedule had been disrupted and her grandmother was behaving oddly. He had a lot to answer for.

Jaunty walked to the gramophone. She needed music. Gabe hadn't sung this morning; there had been no scales, no arpeggios, no arias. She flipped through the records and selected *Tosca*. It was her mother's finest role at La Scala. It was also the last time Jaunty had seen her perform. Despite her shaky hand, she placed the needle sucessfully then sat and let the music flow over her while she wrote.

Milano. Mother's home. For her, singing at La Scala was the pinnacle, a greater triumph than the Met. It is also where my parents met. Father had been visiting with friends when they attended Carmen. Mother had been in the chorus then, but according to Father she shone far more than the diva and he had declared he had to meet her. It was love at first sight, much to my English grandmother's dismay. Despite my mother's aristocratic, if somewhat impoverished, background she was nothing more than a foreign singer as far as Lady Penrose was concerned. My grandfather was still alive then and Father said that he had given his blessing against his wife's wishes. They were married in a church just steps away from Lake Garda one bright July morning, and although I wasn't there I can picture it clearly: Mother in a beautiful suit and Father looking like the happiest man alive. For me, that image summed up love and I wanted the same. It is funny the way life turns out, Gabriella. Embrace it.

Love took me by surprise. I wasn't expecting it, and if I am honest I had more than a bit of my calculating English grandmother in me. I knew that "love" would free me, at least from her. Looking back, I suspect my parents stayed in Europe to avoid her and although Mother sang in Covent Garden, it was never a first choice. She preferred Milano or Vienna with its wonderful cafés. Even now, just thinking about those, I smell the coffee. Would I recognise those cities now? And what of Paris? I am sure I would not know London.

Jaunty stretched as she heard voices coming into the house. She covered her journal with blank sheets of paper as Gabriella entered the room.

"Jaunty, please can you change the music?"

Jaunty heard the words, which, though they were a request, sounded like an order. But everything about Gabriella was tense so Jaunty stood and walked to the gramophone. "Don't you like Maria Lucia?"

"No, I love her. She was one of the greats, but I just can't listen to *Tosca*. How about *Madame Butterfly* or maybe *Carmen?*" Gabriella turned and left, and Jaunty

112

stared after her. Her granddaughter was on edge. Last night must have upset her more than she had let on. In truth, Jaunty was stunned that Gabriella had managed to save a man of Fin's size in such a fierce storm. She was lucky not to have lost her own life, and just thinking about the possibility horrified her grandmother. Of all the things Jaunty had needed to teach her, she had failed at teaching her to fear the sea. Putting the record back into its sleeve, Jaunty let her fingers run across the picture of her mother on the cover.

Of all the music Jaunty could have been listening to, why did she have to pick *Tosca?* After this morning's nightmare everything was too raw. Gabe's hands shook as she went through the shed looking for the oars. Once she'd located them and propped them up outside, she called the farmer whose land Fin's boat had washed up on and arranged a time to meet him. He'd already helped two other yachtsmen with their boats. Gabe looked out of the kitchen window. The sun was still shining but Gabe could see a bank of grey cloud hanging above the north shore that looked as if it was coming this way.

Before leaving the cabin she checked on Jaunty, who was still in her room, sitting at her desk sketching. Gabe couldn't be sure, but sketching was good. Her grandmother hadn't painted in ages but maybe the desire was returning. This was encouraging. Could it be possible that a few days of proper eating had improved things? Gabe worried about Jaunty's health and wondered if Jaunty had let her health slip too far? Without a doubt

Gabe had left it too long before moving here. She should have done this a few years ago.

When she reached the quay, Fin was rescuing what he could from the holly and the mud. It wasn't much, but the tide had turned and the rowing boat was afloat. The sun shone so brightly at the moment that it was hard to believe that last night's events had happened. She could almost think that she must have dreamt that she dived into the creek in the middle of a major storm to rescue someone.

Fin waved to her and climbed on to the quay, placing some of his belongings on it.

"Was this stuff inside the boat or on the deck?"

"Deck."

Gabe nodded. Getting the mud out of the clothes would take some doing, and she wondered what state the things in the boat would be in. Rain would have poured in through the night, and possibly salt water if the waves had risen high enough, and when she had been in the river last night the swell had seemed impossibly high.

He held out his hand and took the oars from her. "I think I should be able to get across now."

"I'm coming with you."

He tilted his head to the side and studied her. "I thought you might not want to be on or in the water ever again."

She laughed.

"And on this, a beautiful autumn day . . ." he pulled the tender closer and placed the oars in the rowlocks ". . . it doesn't look so bad."

114

Nodding, she hoped his boat wasn't as damaged as they feared and he could be on his way. As pleasant as he was, he was a disquieting presence at Bosworgy. She had come here to be alone; well, alone with Jaunty. However, he had already proved himself useful by cleaning up Jaunty's dinghy while she'd been looking for the oars.

Gabe climbed into the boat and sat in the bow. Her arms still felt heavy with tiredness and her left hand bore the marks of the holly tree. This would interfere with her piano-playing for a while. Fin untied the painter and pushed off. He sat still and let it steady before he began to row the short distance out of the creek and towards his beached lugger. Gabe could hear but couldn't see the tractor in the field above. Steve, the farmer, was true to his word and his timing.

Watching the river rather than the stranger's broad shoulders as he rowed, she still wasn't sure how she could have pulled a man of his size to safety. She wasn't big or strong. Well, she had a certain level of fitness because her singing required it and her lungs were good, but even so, the more she thought about it, the more she wondered how she had achieved it. It was a miracle they hadn't both died. She watched an egret land on an outstretched branch, its white feathers in stark contrast to the hillside behind it.

Gabe turned as they came around into the next cove and approached his boat. How it had come to rest here when the tide had been going out puzzled her. She couldn't remember which direction the wind had been blowing, but it must have been an easterly.

Splintered wood sprang from where the mast had been. It was bad, but not as bad as she had imagined. She tied the rowing boat on. The lugger was upright but leaning at an angle, wedged in the rocks, and Fin climbed aboard. The boat shifted but remained stable.

She spotted the tractor and waved to Steve.

"Damn!" Fin's voice came from below.

Climbing on to the boat, Gabe nearly lost her footing on the deck, but she managed to make it to the cabin below. Then she wished she hadn't. She closed her eyes, trying to let go of the fear. Water swirled around her calves and she tried to take a slow breath, but couldn't get any air in. All the terror of last night swamped her. Opening her eyes to find her way back out she saw papers scattered all over the table. Once her head was above the hatch, she could breathe.

"Hey, Gabe," Steve called. "Is she seaworthy?"

Gabe scampered the rest of the way out. "There's a lot of water inside but that could be rainwater."

Steve clambered over the rocks, looking at the side of the boat. "Nasty gash."

Gabe saw the hole in the deck.

"Aside from some scratches the hull is intact, it appears." Steve was now at the side of the boat and he gave Gabe a hand as she climbed off and on to the rocks.

Fin emerged from the cabin. "I can't see any interior damage other than water. I don't suppose anyone has seen the masts and sails anywhere?"

"Not that I've heard yet, but the river is filled with debris." Steve shook his head. "It wasn't a clean break so I don't think the main mast would be much use to you anyway."

"True. Just wishful thinking on my part." Fin turned, pulled his phone out of a waterproof bag, and began taking pictures with it.

Steve moved around the rocks so that he could get a good look at the far side. "When the tide is a bit higher we should be able to float her off. Don't suppose you know where you want to take her?" he called.

Fin had disappeared inside the boat again, then he came out and handed Steve his phone. "The insurers mentioned a boatyard in Falmouth. Would you mind taking a few shots of the bow from down there for me?"

"No problem." Steve moved around the boat. "Lucky you weren't on the boat last night, then."

"I was. Came on deck to check things and something hit me and I was knocked into the water." He paused and looked at Gabe. "If it wasn't for Gabriella, I would be with the mast somewhere out in Falmouth Bay."

Steve looked up. "What?"

"She saved me last night."

"You saved him?"

Gabe nodded.

"Known him long?" Steve grinned knowingly at Gabe. She went pale. Surely Steve didn't think Fin was hers?

"No, don't know him at all." Then Gabe thought of the mole that sat just below Fin's navel. She shouldn't know about that at all. She might have seen him nearly naked, but despite that she knew nothing about Fin.

Steve tilted his head and winked. "Ought to be careful then. Save a stranger from the sea, and he'll turn your enemy."

A shiver went down Gabe's spine as she looked at Fin.

CHAPTER
SEVEN

Looking up from her desk, Jaunty watched the mist lift from the river. The sun hit the emerging shoreline at Groyne Point, where three herons walked the beach. She imagined the leaves were turning colour as she knew they did at this time of year, but she couldn't see it. It was lost.

Paris. I'd been there for a year studying with Pierre. I was improving. My parents, even my English grandmother, could see that. This was not what they wanted for me, but the more time I invested in my art, the deeper my determination went. It was also freedom. I knew the city well, and during my time there Jean and I would wander, painting. Nothing was beneath our notice, from the dustbins to the whores. The thought of the variety now makes my head swim.

I turn the corner and Jean is trying to hand a plate back to a waiter. I laugh. It's happened again.

"Bonjour." I come up to the table and smile at the waiter as I take a seat. I tell him I will take the salad covered in anchovies that sits

in front of her and order Jean a plate of tomatoes, cucumber and lettuce instead.

"Why do they never understand me?"

I chuckle. "Oh, but they do."

She laughs and pushes a letter across the table to me, then looks down. I don't understand how she can still be embarrassed about this now. She is so clever in other ways. I skim the contents and realise that it is the assistant at the art gallery who has written, and he has used words that she would never be able to read, such as exquisite. He has also thrown in numbers, and that would flummox her all together. I look up and take Jean's hand.

"It's all good. All your paintings have sold and they want to know if you have more."

Her shoulders relax and she smiles. "What would I do without you?"

"Well, learn to eat anchovies for one thing!"

I knew from the outset that I was in the presence of true genius. Jean was so gifted and while I had talent it was not on the scale of brilliance. I could have been jealous, but I was in awe. I excelled in portraiture and knew that after my years of study in Paris I would retreat to the acceptable position of painting society portraits. She, however, would become great.

We would roll into the studio after a morning painting and I could see the way Pierre regarded her. He too knew that she was special. Sometimes I wondered if it was the difference in our backgrounds that shaped our talent. Had mine been too soft, too loving? Had my years studying the great artists of the past held me back? She had limited exposure but so much drive.

I felt very protective towards Jean. I did all her correspondence and her accounts. They muddled her. I tried to teach her but her energy was reserved for her work. She even ignored the attentions of Pierre. Jean had a zest and an energy that glowed from within. She was all for art, while I was all for life.

The escalating cry of a curlew sounded across the water, and Jaunty raised her head. The tide was further out, exposing a tangled mess of seaweed, rock and silt. This was the noisy time, when the mud was exposed and the wading birds gathered to find food. She pushed the window further open. The fresh breeze swept through the pine needles, whistling in accompaniment to the curlew and the gulls.

A sharp spasm ran up her arm and Jaunty dropped the pen. With her other hand she rubbed her knuckles and wrist. Gabriella and Fin were out. Gabriella was cautious with Fin, and she was probably right. There was something about him, aside from his looks. He was quiet but he missed nothing, and perhaps it was madness to give him free rein in her studio. Only Gabriella had had that. Jaunty could tell that she had looked through the stacked canvases but nothing more.

Soon Gabriella would have no choice but to clear out the studio. Jaunty should have done it years ago and a bonfire would have worked nicely. Maybe it was not too late, but would it matter when she was dead? Everyone else had preceded her, no one could verify or deny what was there.

Dietrich.

No, it was too soon to talk of Dietrich. Jaunty looked at her sketch of Fin. *Alex.*

I was home from Paris and forced to stay with my grandmother. Mother was performing in New York again and I loved my grandmother's house, but not her. Her home, well, really our home, since my grandfather and my father's older brother had died, sat on the banks of the Lynher. I loved the water and the time my father spent teaching me to sail. Those were the good memories, not the time spent with the sourpuss. I hated being left with her. I longed for the lazy Augusts normally enjoyed on Lake Garda with Mother's family and her artistic friends, but in 1939 that wasn't happening because of the American performances that my mother had lined up.

When Rebecca issued an invitation to join her family near Falmouth I leapt at the opportunity. It saved me, and the summer of 1939 is as fresh in my mind now as if it was yesterday. Grandmother was pleased to be relieved of me, and it was a time of madness and magic.

From the moment Rebecca and her brother Alex collected me from the station and took me to the rambling Victorian house in Flushing, I knew my life would change. Alex wasn't there the whole time. He had joined the army after university and was working at the war office in London. My schoolgirl crush on him hadn't abated at all, but what had changed was Alex's attitude to me. He couldn't take his eyes off me — and I was the same.

I was bereft when he disappeared back to London, and spent my time being the third wheel with Rebecca and the boy who lived next door. Her mother was keen to encourage this relationship and long days were spent on the beach, walking and messing about in boats. I counted the days until Alex would be back. No one expected us to fall in love, but we had and we grabbed moments alone on the pretext of Alex teaching me to sail. Those were precious hours spent on the water, although at first it was just the brush of a hand or the connection of a tanned leg against mine.

Thoughts of Alex distracted her from her task and Jaunty shook her head. She must write down only what Gabriella needed to know in order to make some sense of Jaunty's life.

Gabe wanted to do her vocal exercises, but thus far her shadow, Fin, was always with her. They had arrived back at the cabin and he asked to use the phone. As soon as he was on it Gabe walked out to the studio. Once inside she locked the door and began the exercises to open her chest. Every muscle in her body felt as if it was curled into a tight ball. She knew that standing under a hot stream of water would help, but that brought back memories of last night, which reminded her of the nightmare she'd woken up from. After that fateful final performance and hours in the police station, she had stood under the running water for ages, but it hadn't washed anything away except the scent of him. Although that had been a start.

The big window in the studio framed the sunlight playing on the river. Gabe sighed and then pushed a deep breath out and pulled her arms back, but they only went so far. She repeated the exercise and each time her arms moved a centimetre further. She bent slowly from the waist, letting her upper body hang. Rolling up one vertebra at a time, she raised her arms above her head, poised herself on one foot — and toppled over. Nothing worked. She went back to stretching her chest muscles and when they had reached half her normal expansion she began the scales. At first her voice was hollow but with each repetition it gained strength. Had she stayed the course she would only now be coming into her voice. But she hadn't.

She opened the piano and played the scales, but the piano was off and her hand ached. What day was today? When was the tuner due? She closed her eyes. Life had stepped out of line. Somewhere, since she had been here, it had gone off track and she needed to put it back to rights.

She moved on to singing arpeggios, but she was slipping and the notes were not clean. She slowed down. Everything about her at the moment wanted to race. She counted to ten, controlling her breathing before beginning again. The notes became clearer. Flipping through the sheet music, she came to *Tosca*. Her hand stilled. She hadn't been able to remove it from her thoughts since this morning.

Maria Lucia's haunting rendition of the Puccini floated in her head. She hadn't listened to *Tosca* in four years. He had stolen that from her as well as everything else. But she could claim this back at least; she was strong enough. Closing her eyes she began "Vissi d'arte". The pain inside her flowed out into the lyrics and she visualised the words, anger, despair and pain floating in the space around as she let the song fill her and the studio.

The last note left her and she collapsed on to the floor, tears slipping down her cheeks. What on earth had made her sing that? She wasn't as strong as she'd thought. Gabe rose from the floor and looked around. To regain control of her emotions she needed to focus on the practical things. Glancing about the studio, she saw she would need to find sheets and blankets for the bed. Hopefully Fin wouldn't be here too long, because he unsettled her. She didn't know why she felt that way, but she did. The grey painting sat on the easel, blocking the view from the bed. Gabe took the painting off and placed it carefully aside. The easel folded effortlessly

125

and she put this on the floor near the window. Her piano was already standing to one side. Before closing the door behind her, she took one last look through the big window. Sunlight reflected off the water in bright diamonds. She sighed. With that view he'd never leave.

Jaunty could just make out the sound of Gabriella singing in the studio. It was *Tosca*. The emotion caught her, making it difficult to swallow. How could the child know that much pain? Her voice ripped through the defences around Jaunty's heart and she could hear her mother. She blinked. At her age how could she still long for her? Long for the stroke of a hand, a sparkling laugh, a lullaby. All Jaunty had were the old records with their scratches and distortions, but Gabriella's voice touched her.

Jaunty pushed the tears away but couldn't stop them. She moved back from the desk and walked to the window. Sunlight glinted off the wake of a motorboat heading towards Gweek, but the view of the river offered no consolation this time. Despite her internal agony, the tide would continue to turn. Why was she crying now? Surely the time for tears had passed.

There was a slight cough. Fin stood just behind Jaunty. He placed a hand on her shoulder and the small action was too much: she sobbed and gasped, unable to speak. The cries wracked her frame and she couldn't stop them. He turned her around and pulled her into his arms. She collapsed against him, taking the comfort of a stranger. The more she wept, the less strength she

126

had left and eventually he was supporting her completely.

Finally Jaunty lifted her head.

"Better?" he asked.

"No, that's impossible." She forced her legs to work and pulled back. She wobbled and he was at her side, helping her to reach the bed. His shirt was soaked with her tears. She felt for the hankie in her pocket and blew her nose. "Thank you."

"No problem." He studied her. "Was it Gabriella's singing?"

Jaunty loved the shadows created on his face from his cheekbones, so like Alex. "Yes, it broke the dam."

"A long time in the making?"

"Yes." She gave a short laugh, not quite a snort or a sigh.

"She has an incredible voice."

"She does." Jaunty paused to see if she could still hear Gabriella, but the there was only silence. "We are privileged to hear her."

"Surely that is how she earns her living?"

"No, she composes ditties for commercials." Jaunty pushed herself off the bed. "I need tea."

"Let me."

"Thank you, but I need to move." She walked to the door and turned back to see him looking on her desk. She hesitated. "Actually, would you make the tea?"

He looked up. "Of course." He smiled at her and she went to her desk after he'd left the room. She viewed what she'd left out, wondering if there was anything there that could expose her — but wasn't that what she wanted?

Gabe left the studio and walked away from the cabin, which was snug enough with two of them living there, but with three it would be far too small. And Fin altered the atmosphere. He was like the east wind, which cleared the skies but ruffled the waters. Was it his testosterone or was it just him? He was intense. He'd said very little about himself, certainly hadn't given enough information to give him a bed for more than a night. How did they know they could trust him? He could be a reporter, Gabe fretted. After all, a few had tried to get interviews with Jaunty over the years.

Gabe walked the lower path along the creek. She couldn't walk as quickly as she wanted to because the way was still treacherous with wet, fallen leaves, making it slippery. She should have taken a different route to where the hillside was filled with ripe damsons and blackberries.

Near the creek she climbed down the bank. Gabe picked up a stick and chucked it into the water. It swirled around before catching a current and making its way out towards the river. Right at this moment she felt like that stick, being pushed and pulled by the current, unable to stop the forward motion to the wider waters ahead. She was in control of her own fate, but she knew only too well that sometimes life took control. And when it did there was nothing she could do. That wasn't the case right now. She could tell Fin to leave. It was simple: take him aside and ask him to go. She turned and walked back to the cabin.

The problem was that he was too attractive. But she couldn't place just what it was about him that made him so appealing. His features on their own were handsome, but not extraordinary, except for the knowing eyes and the full mouth. Gabe blinked. No, she didn't want to think about him at all. Just this slight digression raised her temperature.

In the distance she could see Fin standing with a phone to his ear. Moving closer, she could hear his voice.

"Enough, Patricia! I gave you the flat and you took the cat and the car."

Gabe hid behind a tree, wondering what to do. She might know nothing about him and want to know more, but eavesdropping wasn't the way to go about it. Retracing her steps down the path, she realised there was something familiar about him. He was like an itch that she couldn't reach.

She stopped walking when she couldn't hear his voice, then turned around and headed to the cabin again, hoping he had finished his call. She saw Fin spin, looking as if he was going to throw his phone into the creek, but he brought his arm down again and slipped it into his pocket. He took three deep breaths, then walked slowly back into the house with his face revealing none of the emotion Gabe had just witnessed. How could he control his feelings like that? Gabe could only do that if she didn't allow them in the first place.

★ ★ ★

Jaunty relaxed. There was nothing on the pages that Fin could have seen that would have told him anything. Maybe he hadn't been looking at the diary but at the sketches. She laughed when she studied her nude drawing of him. How would he feel about that? Somehow she didn't think it would bother him.

In the kitchen, she found the back door open and the tea made, but no Fin. The deep timbre of his voice was audible but not the words. Jaunty poured herself a mug of tea and walked back to her desk. She felt a new spring in her step and knew it was because of having this man about the place. She also knew that underneath she was still weary, so she must make use of this burst of energy and get the truth down.

Jaunty stopped and looked at her sketches of Fin. This is what Alex would have looked like had he made it to his thirties. His cheekbones would have become more pronounced, like Fin's, and maybe the blond hair would have darkened.

The day before I was due to leave, and despite the all-present talk of war, Alex and I sailed around to the Helford. The sun warmed our skin and we anchored in Frenchman's Creek. We shared a picnic and our kisses became heated. Before long we had tied up the boat on an old quay and climbed the bank to a cabin. Blackberries were in abundance on the hillside and we gathered the ripe ones as we climbed. We called hello around the cabin but no one was home. Finding a sunny spot between the pine trees, we fed each other the bittersweet fruit. Dreams . . . How we shared dreams. We would buy the cabin and it would become ours and ours alone.

He looked at me with such longing — and I knew I loved him. With blackberries still staining out lips, we kissed and before long innocent caresses had moved beyond the point of no return . . .

Alex proposed to me and I accepted. We'd sat on the bank looking upriver and made plans. I could see our future so clearly. He wanted me to finish my final year in Paris. We knew the war was coming, but looking out on the Helford in the sunshine we still thought it far enough away from us. We agreed that next summer we would be wed and we would keep our secret until I was home at Christmas, then tell the families.

Tears flowed down Jaunty's face. Oh, such lovely dreams.

At the sound of Gabriella and Fin talking in the kitchen, Jaunty put her pen down and hid the notebook. She did not want it found before the time was right. Most importantly, she did not want to talk about it. That would be too hard. If Gabriella could read the truth after Jaunty was gone and then digest it, that would be enough. Jaunty couldn't bear the thought of seeing the disappointment on Gabriella's face, because the way Jaunty had actually lived went against everything Jaunty had taught her granddaughter.

There was a tap at the door. "I've made some dinner." Gabriella stood in the doorway, not coming into the room. Jaunty frowned. This wasn't normal.

"Lovely. Are we eating outside?"

"If you'd like."

"Yes." Jaunty levered herself out of the chair. Her hip joints had stiffened while she'd sat. Gabriella was still standing in the doorway watching her. It was almost as if her granddaughter was seeing her for the first time — and maybe she was. Jaunty felt she was doing the same, seeing herself for what she was: a liar and a thief, and more.

Gabe steadied Fin's boat as he climbed aboard. It was going to be towed to the boatyard in Falmouth for repair. She handed him the empty plastic shopping bags and waited while she heard him move about the cabin. Something about this whole thing was wrong. Not the part about helping out someone in need — he didn't appear needy. He was well spoken, owned a boat, and appeared to be in control of everything, except maybe his ex-wife. Didn't he have a job he needed to go off and do?

He walked on to the sloping deck and handed several bags to her. "Just a few more things and the rest should be fine to leave on the boat for a while."

"OK." Gabe took the bags and carefully placed them in a dry spot on the dinghy. Fin disappeared again and Gabe debated looking into the bags. What would the contents tell her about the stranger in their midst?

Gabe checked to make sure that Fin was still inside the boat and began to rummage through the bags. It was mostly clothes and the odd book. His reading choice was intriguing. John Le Carre, Dorothy L Sayers and Shakespeare. She closed one bag and peered in another one, but stopped when she heard his footsteps.

"That should do it." He held several more bags and a laptop in a protective case. Gabe wondered why he hadn't moved it earlier. She wouldn't have left hers unattended in a boat. She looked to the field above. It was filled with cows ready for milking. OK, maybe she was being hard on him. He was a man who had happened to chat to Jaunty and then had had the bad luck to have been caught in a storm and nearly drowned. She should cut him some slack. She didn't have to look for the worst in everyone; she had been doing that too long.

The bags safely stored, Gabe went to the far side to balance the boat as Fin stepped in, smiling.

"Thanks for the help."

He had a grin that made a mockery of her fears, transforming his serious face to one that was almost childlike. She smiled back. "No problem," she said, then looked away. It *was* a problem, but she was going to try and be grown up about this. It was time she moved on, even just a bit. She could be gracious. It was in her somewhere. Well, it used to be.

They set off. Above, the sky was dark blue as the last of the colour of the sunset disappeared, and this evening a wind blew in from the mouth of the river, whipping the surface into little waves. It worked against them. Gabe watched his back while he rowed and a feeling stirred inside her. She tensed. She might be willing to tap into her once-pleasant self, but she wasn't willing to go to the place of attraction, the place where she made herself vulnerable again. It was that vulnerability which had destroyed her and all her dreams.

CHAPTER
EIGHT

Sunlight broke through the clouds and highlighted the bank of oak on Merthen Wood. The light made it appear closer than it was and Jaunty raised her hand, wanting to touch it — a bit like these memories. Rolling her shoulders back made them ache but Jaunty felt time running away from her. Fin's presence here was a gift, a gift from the sea. He was bringing the memories back into sharp focus and he could help her if she could trust him.

Telling this tale was never going to be easy, Gabriella. Maybe that is why I have waited so long. I don't know how much you need to know but I will continue with my memories as they come to me.

When I think back to how naive I was, it frightens me.

I went back to Paris filled with dreams and I left Alex with my heart full. He placed his signet ring on my finger and we stole back to the cabin one more time before I left on the evening train.

The water laps at the stone quay. Alex ties the boat on and flashes me a smile. I swallow

down the excitement building in me and grab the picnic basket. I am not hungry for its contents. Alex is what I need, not food or wine. Now that we have broken the restraints I think of nothing else.

He takes my hand and we run up the hill. The cabin is still empty and we spread the blanket on the pine needles. I lie back, seeing the blue sky through the branches, and feel Alex's hand as it travels up my thigh.

Jaunty shivered. A sleepy wasp came through the window and rested on the edge of her mug. Summer was coming to an end. There was a chill in the wind despite the sun's warmth, and she must focus on writing for Gabriella.

It hurts even now to think about it, knowing what I know. We lost so much time. But back then my step was full of joy. I placed Alex's ring on a chain around my neck so that my grandmother wouldn't question it when I passed through to say goodbye on my way to Paris.

My last meeting with her had been less than pleasant. She had been dismissive of Alex's family. They were merchants. She almost spat the word out. I just let her talk. Her plans for me were for next summer: the season. But I had no intention of being a debutante. I was too old. Nor was I intending to go along with her plans to marry me to a lord.

Alexander Carrow would be my husband and my miserable grandmother would just have to live with it.

And so, despite long-distance pleas from my father, I returned to Paris just two weeks before war was declared . . .

"Jean, Paris will be OK, won't it?" I look up from my canvas.

"The Nazis wouldn't dare, or so the Parisians say and have been saying all summer." She walks around to look at my work. "My God, he's well built."

I hit her with my brush. I can't get Alex out of my mind, nor do I want to.

"I can tell what you were up to on your holiday."

I giggle.

"Are you in love?" Jean takes up the paintbrush and dabs it in the cobalt. She dots it lightly at the knee joint. The painting is instantly balanced and I am in awe.

"Yes — and how do you do that?"

She laughs her deep throaty laugh. "Simple. Step back from your work. Half close your eyes and all will become clear."

I do this but nothing is obvious.

"You are looking too hard and trying to hold it close. You must let it go."

But Paris was fine, I thought. The French felt the Nazis wouldn't dare. Jean had spent the whole summer in Paris working. She assured me that all was well. I don't know why I believed her. Her mastery of the language was such that she had trouble ordering a meal, so how could I trust she would know anything? But I did. I stayed put and began to work very hard. I needed to make a name for myself. When the war was over, Alex would be a barrister and I a society portrait painter. That was our plan.

However, my summer of playing and very little painting showed up badly against Jean's hard-working one. She had moved on in leaps and bounds while I was away. I helped her to send more paintings to the gallery in London. Something had altered her vision, and it was stunning.

We settled down to life again, both painting and working with Pierre. My work moved more and more into the abstract and hers remained realistic. Egging each other on, we painted from life and were challenged by the changing face of Paris. Her work became stronger while I was pulled towards portraits from my memory. In secret I kept sketching Alex, trying to keep him close. His ring hung above my heart and his letters became less frequent and told me nothing, which in a strange way told me everything.

After walking up the track to get enough signal to receive her emails, Gabe was quickly reminded by the influx that she had been neglecting her job. They needed the money, so she couldn't let work slide or the commissions she relied on would dry up. Her piano was in the studio and that was where Fin was, and she couldn't move it into the cabin, she knew that, but her keyboard would fit in her bedroom, just.

She brushed against the bay hedge and stopped to enjoy the aroma. Some places didn't smell of anything much, but here at Bosworgy there were so many scents and the individual fragrances vied with each other to be the dominant one. The time of day and the heat of the sun seemed to aid some more than others and now, as she moved closer to the studio, the scent of pine erased the bay. A heron, startled by her footsteps, flew from its perch on the fallen branch below. Gabe started. Her nerves were on edge. As much as she didn't want to think about it, she wasn't happy to be around men any more, and she understood this was a natural response — the therapist had told her so. But it wasn't convenient when half the population was male, and having one take up residence in the studio wasn't good.

The door was slightly ajar. She found herself inwardly shouting, "Why are you here?" But if she didn't vocalise the question Fin could never answer it. She knocked.

"Come in."

Gabe walked in to find Fin putting on a shirt and looked quickly away from his bare torso.

"I've just come to collect my keyboard."

"Do you want to work here?" He did up his buttons.

Gabe watched the deft fingers at their task. "No, it's OK. My computer is set up in the bedroom so I'll just take this and get to work."

139

"Do you need a hand?"

"No, thanks. I can manage." But Gabe fumbled when she unplugged the keyboard and collapsed the legs. Fin grabbed the console before it hit the ground and his arm brushed hers. She backed away.

"Thanks."

"No problem. I'll just carry it for you." And before she could refuse he was out of the door, leaving her to gather the cables and follow. A gull screamed just outside and Gabe wanted to do the same.

She made her way back to the cabin, expecting to find Fin in her room, but he had left the keyboard on her bed and was nowhere to be seen. He might be with Jaunty. Gabe frowned. She didn't like the amount of time they were spending together.

The scent of Fin filled her bedroom and Gabe shut the door. It was no longer her space. After setting up the console she put on her headphones, blocking out the world. Before she looked at her brief, she took a deep breath, then regretted it: lemony aftershave.

Pulling her shoulders back, Gabe held the position and lowered them, opening her chest. She felt her spine click and brought her arms forward slowly before pulling them back again just a bit further. She felt better. Her fingers hovered above the keys. The pain in her left hand from the holly cut stilled her fingers. Gently she played some slow chords then tried a Chopin mazurka from memory. She missed a few notes by hitting the wrong keys but the scabs held. Still, it did mean that her reach was limited, and her playing would be as well until her hand had fully healed. She played

"Twinkle Twinkle Little Star", letting the childhood tune soothe her. Only then did she read the brief for a second-hand car salesroom outside of London that needed a chirpy tune for a radio advert. She sighed and went to work, playing with sounds until she hit what she felt would fit the remit. That done, she connected her computer to the keyboard and downloaded the tune. Once on the computer she added the other instruments to the composition and scratched her notes down on sheet music. This was never what she imagined her life would be like.

She pushed through the sheets of music beside the keyboard. A keyboard was fine, but right now only playing on the real piano was going to chase her demons away. She found her own work, something that she had begun a few weeks ago. It was not for a commercial, not for the public; it was a symphony, a symphony of loss, but as yet it was incomplete. Picking it up, she set off towards the studio, hoping Fin was still somewhere else.

In the sitting room she looked for Jaunty, but she wasn't around. She popped her head into the bedroom and Jaunty wasn't there either, but on the desk were sketches, sketches of people. Gabe wasn't sure what she was more surprised about: that they were of people or that they were of a naked Fin and a portrait in charcoal that looked like Fin but not quite. It was of a younger man. Jaunty had captured Fin to perfection. Desire swelled up in Gabe and she looked around, hoping that no one could see her ogling the nudes. Her fingers ran down the outside of the sketch collecting the gritty remains of charcoal on it. She pulled back and swallowed. She had no place for desire in her life.

The dreams of the night drifted away as Jaunty watched Fin's head disappear from view down the bank. She put her hand to her heart: *Alex*. She looked to the sky. Rain was moving in from the north. It was a changeable season, fruitful and frantic yet strangely peaceful on the river. At this time of year it was more like it had been in the past. Few boats cruised by the point and the sounds filling the air were of the birds and the cows.

Yes, each year as the autumn moves on to winter the Helford goes back in time. It is more how I remember it. It is only of late that the loud powerboats fill the creek at high tide and the reckless young power around in circles when they should take it slow.

When I came here the second time, I was a young mother, wet behind the ears. I had left the security of Mrs Bartholomew's bed and breakfast. She had been a woman of few words, but she saw my fear, my loneliness and ineptitude. In the quiet time, before Philip was born, she taught me to cook, to wash and to clean. Gabriella, life here in this part of the world was not as you know it now. There was no electricity or running water.

The boom of an air cannon went off on a nearby field and scattered the river birds, setting them off low above the water until they rose on the air currents, complaining all the way. Jaunty listened to the increasing sound of a helicopter from RNAS Culdrose. She couldn't see it yet, but before long it would be in view.

The war had begun but Paris thought the Nazis would never make it that far. My parents were in panic and when spring came my father began to pull strings because he was determined to get me out of Paris. He had left Mother in New York and come back to serve but I was reluctant to leave. I hadn't heard from Alex. His last letter had told me to trust him and to pray. I did both. There was no point in heading back to London. Alex wasn't there. But Father became insistent and even I realised I would need to leave when the Nazis were just outside the city.

Father made arrangements for me to depart on the Lancastria out of St Nazaire. I packed what few things I could, consigned my paintings to the concierge, and readied myself to go, but there was one problem: Jean. She had no connections to get her out. I told her to pack and come along. There was no way that they would leave a British citizen in occupied France, or so I thought.

Nothing had prepared me for the chaos of the port. The numbers of civilians and soldiers trying to return to England heightened the combustible atmosphere. I tried to get her name on the lists, but it didn't work. I didn't stop at the first attempt or the fourth.

"Go." Jean pushes me into the crowd but I cling to her hand. We are moving along with the flow and she tries to free her hand but I won't release it. Tears flow down her face and I feel her fear. My stomach is in knots. I can't leave her.

The cold grasp of the water took Gabe's breath away as she slipped into the creek. The river was strangely still and she set off across it. Again her dreams had been filled with thoughts of the competition and its aftermath. When she woke sweat poured from her as if she had run a marathon, and her limbs were bound with the twisted sheets. Now the deep thump of an engine reverberated in her ears. She paused to check for the boat. They wouldn't see her in the low morning light. She kicked harder until she had reached the safety of the north shore. She panted as she looked back towards the cabin. It was almost invisible behind the trees. If she didn't know it was there she wouldn't find it. However, she did, and she could just make out Fin walking from the studio.

She began a more leisurely breaststroke for the first part of the swim, but the further she reached the more she thought of her nightmares. She changed to the butterfly to try and eliminate them from her mind. She almost lacked the strength to climb up to the cabin when she had reached the point but physical exertion always helped.

After showering, Gabe went into the sitting room. No sign of Jaunty. She peered into her grandmother's bedroom and Jaunty was sitting at her desk at the end of the room. Her head was down and she clutched a pen in her hand. She didn't look up. Gabe tensed, then crept up to her to make sure she was just sleeping. Looking around, Gabe wondered what she had been writing but saw no paper. Backing out of the room, she crashed into Fin. His hands grabbed her shoulders and Gabe sucked in a mouthful of air. She pulled herself together and walked past him to the kitchen. He followed.

"Do you mind if I use the shower?"

"You don't have much choice as there isn't one in the studio." She wished he'd just do it without asking. She didn't want to think about him.

"Thanks. I won't be long."

"Is that you Gabriella?" Mrs Bates called from outside.

"Yes." Gabe walked to the door.

"I was passing and just wanted to be sure you were settled in all right. I hear you have a strange man staying."

Gabe pushed down her shoulders as the tension rose in her. "We're fine, and yes, we have a man staying with us. The one whose boat was wrecked."

"The one that was with you in the shop? So good-looking." She wiggled her girth and stood straighter. "But you need to be careful of strangers. You know nothing about this man."

Gabe nodded, agreeing with her, but at the same time feeling the urge to tell her to piss off. "Wise words, Mrs Bates. I'm sure he won't be here for long."

"I hope he will be." Jaunty had come up behind Gabe without a sound.

"You're looking well, Jaunty. Having Gabriella here has lifted you I can see."

"Nonsense. I was fine on my own." Jaunty moved to the kitchen and placed a cup in the sink, and Fin walked into the room dressed only in a towel. Jaunty grinned and Gabe swallowed. "But it's good to have a man about the place."

Mrs Bates blushed and colour rose in Gabe's face.

"I'm sorry. I didn't expect anyone here." He nodded to all three women and eased out of the back door. "If you'll excuse me . . ."

"I say!" Mrs Bates turned and watched him walk to the studio.

You would. Gabe was most interested in Jaunty's reaction. Her eyes were smiling and less sadness pulled at her face. "Thank you for dropping by and checking on us, Mrs Bates. I'm afraid we can't stop any longer as Jaunty has an appointment, so if you will excuse us?"

The woman left with no further questions.

"I don't have an appointment." Jaunty turned to Gabe.

"You're right, you don't."

"You've changed." Jaunty turned on the tap to fill a glass.

"Yes." Gabe walked into her room and shut the door. She needed to work and this was her only space. But she had forgotten that Fin had used her shower and the room smelled of him.

146

* ★ ★

The journey to the studio took longer than Jaunty remembered. She had to stop frequently to fill her lungs, but while Gabriella was occupied she must act. She almost lost her nerve but moved forward to the door, as there was no time to waste. "I gather from the way you look at paintings that you know a thing or two about art." Jaunty leaned against the doorjamb to the studio. Fin was pulling a shirt over his head and again she was jolted back in time. It was here, where the studio now was, that she and Alex had first made love.

"I'm an art dealer and historian." He looked at the paintings about the room. Some of them were her best and some her worst.

Jaunty swallowed. "I thought as much." Doubt filled her, but his profession might work in her favour.

He cocked his head to one side just the way Alex had. Alex had always questioned her assumptions. He was good for her. Dietrich had simply loved her.

"You have been trained to look at a work, assessing each of the aspects, from brushwork to colour to perspective and so on, as if you were reading a text. Other people look at art, and my work in particular, and just *feel* something, but they are not sure quite how or why they do." Jaunty turned to him. "You read the painting first, then step back and, I hope, feel it."

He laughed and a shiver ran over Jaunty's skin. It was the caress of a memory. One so long buried that now, out of its hiding place, it made breathing difficult. A waft of pine scent blew through the door, the pleasure of her lover and the pain of the prickly needles against her skin all wrapped in the scent. How had she suppressed it for so long?

"Who do you work for? What's your area of speciality?" Jaunty moved to her armchair. Her first instinct had been to go to the stool in front of the easel. But it and the easel had been moved. Instead she slipped into the overstuffed chair. It was still in her favourite position. If she turned her head to the right she could see the river and directly in front lay the mouth of the creek.

"Who do I work for? Good question." He sat on the edge of the bed. "Before the divorce I shared my business with my wife. Now she owns it all and I owe her nothing. I am free."

"Hence drifting around the Helford on a boat."

"Well, yes." He looked Jaunty directly in the eye. "You see, my grandmother died and left me *Jezebel*, some money and a few prized possessions of my great-uncle who died in the last World War — in fact, he drowned off the coast of Cornwall, not too far from here."

Jaunty gave a dry laugh. She knew where this was leading even if Fin didn't. "Who was your great-uncle?"

"Alexander Carrow."

Her heart stopped for a moment, hearing his name spoken. "So you came to discover more about the man who left you a legacy?"

"Yes. The legacy included a beautiful painting of the mouth of Frenchman's Creek and the cabin."

Jaunty's hand flew to her heart and he leapt to his feet.

"Are you OK?"

She knew the watercolour. She had painted it just after that fateful visit and given it to him as a gift before they parted. It was a promise. "Do you still have this painting?"

"Yes, I salvaged it from *Jezebel*."

"May I see it?"

He rifled through some things at the side of the bed and pulled out a framed watercolour. Jaunty's chest tightened again. There was no doubt. He handed it to her and she could see her emerging style. But unlike the work that she was now known for, the landscape was obvious, whereas since the war the water was all. If there was land in the painting it was merged into the water to become part of it.

She had signed it with her first name only. It was odd to see it on the bottom of the paper. She looked up to find Fin watching her. He knew, but he didn't know. She turned the painting over in her hands. It was in the frame she had put it in and the original tape was still on the back, damaged but there.

"It's lovely."

"Yes, it is." He paused. "It's been bothering me." He walked to the window facing the river and looked out. "It has been knocking away at the back of my mind, saying this style is familiar but . . ." He turned around and looked at Jaunty, waiting.

"Yes, I see what you mean." She got up and placed the painting on the bed and left the studio.

CHAPTER
NINE

Jaunty sat at her desk. The afternoon was grey with no breaks in the clouds. The river reflected the flatness. She had passed Gabe on her way out to the studio. She looked as if she was about to speak but had said nothing in the end. Life was passing her by before it had even begun. Jaunty had had life but then retreated into survival mode. But had she had any choice? No. Today it would be different, but back then there were very few choices available to her.

It was chaos in St Nazaire. Panic ruled and it became clear that Jean wouldn't get on the boat. Things were dire. The Nazis were bombing and we were, well and truly, in the terrifying midst of war. I looked at the fear in Jean's eyes. She would never survive in France and I knew what I had to do. We were similar enough in appearance that the photograph in my passport could be her. Once the boarding began I thrust my ticket and my papers into her hands and grabbed hers.

When she began to protest, I put my finger over her mouth. I told her what she already knew. I had a chance of survival here in France and she didn't.

I told her I would find a way back to England. She was to let my father know I was alive and that I would do my best to get home. Her eyes widened and before she could do or say anything else I fled into the crowd and began to make a plan. I knew staying in a large port was not going to be safe.

Jaunty took a breath. Her chest was tight. She could smell the harbour, the scent of seaweed and rotting fish. She sat back and shook her head. She should remember the smell of burning, but no, it was fish she could smell. How Jean had hated fish and Jaunty had sent Jean to her death in the sea. She closed her eyes. What else could she have done? Jean, even if she'd survived the attack on the *Lancastria*, just before 4 o'clock that afternoon, couldn't swim. Jaunty had prayed for a long time that Jean had been killed instantly and hadn't drowned.

Jaunty did not want to think of drowning. She must continue writing.

I was alone with someone else's passport in an occupied country. I had some money and a bit of jewellery along with a set of watercolours. Not exactly the best tools for survival. However, I knew I needed to become someone else and not someone English. Part of it wouldn't be difficult. I was fluent in French and I knew Paris like the back of my hand.

There is much I could say, but I find I'm reluctant to dwell on some parts of the past. But you, Gabriella, need to know at least the minimum to understand how I came to be the woman you know as your grandmother. One night in a café, I met a Frenchman who was willing to help me and had the connections needed. I am not proud of what I did in return — just thinking about it makes me feel ill. However, after handing over my body, most of my jewellery and the watercolours, I had French papers. As quickly as I could, I left the port and headed to the coast of Brittany where I felt I had the best chance of getting back to England.

Eventually I found work and accommodation in a village on the coast. It was simple to be an art student from Paris because that is what I had been, although that part of my life suddenly felt very far away. Before those dreadful days I had never realised what a sheltered and protected life I had lived. Although life in Paris was wild and I had thought I was the most sophisticated woman, a few weeks travelling alone through occupied France changed any view I had of myself. I was simply a naïve young woman of nineteen who longed to be safe with my mother in New York or even dodging bombs with my father in London. Anything would have been preferable to being someone else in an occupied country with no idea of who to contact or how to leave France. A month before I would have laughed at myself. Then, I foolishly thought I had all the connections in the world and they would save me.

I kept to myself and no one questioned me. I got a job working in a bar and rented a box room from a fisherman's widow. It was the closest thing I could do to become invisible — hiding in plain sight. At night I would lie awake and pray for my parents, for Alex and for Jean. My parents would be grieving for me, believing their daughter had been lost with the other 4,000 souls on the Lancastria and I had no way to contact them. Each day I would visit the church and pray. The young curate would try and engage me in conversation but I always managed to slip away. I worked on the basis that the fewer people I allowed near me the safer I was, although the whole time I listened to every conversation, including that of the Nazis, when they arrived in the town. The more information I had, the safer I felt.

In the bar, I would chat with the soldiers grudgingly — or so I made it appear. It was a fine balance. I was fluent in German but told no one, knowing that that way the soldiers would talk freely in front of me and I would hear things. Slowly it dawned on me that some of the information I was overhearing could be useful to the allies.

By that time I'd been working in the bar about a year and knew all the locals. It was the hub of the village and I guessed that a shopkeeper, Richard Mauvieux, was the man I should contact for the resistance. The whispers I'd heard proved to be

153

correct. He was the local leader and I began to feed information through him.

A stiff breeze howled through the pines as Gabe walked to the studio. The door was halfway open and, stopping just outside, she peered in and saw Fin flipping through the canvases stacked against the wall. She froze. What on earth was he doing? He had no right. She marched in.

He looked up and smiled. "Jaunty is an outstanding artist."

Gabe took a step back. "Yes. Yes, she is." Of course, she thought, what human wouldn't be curious about the paintings of a famous artist if they were sleeping among them? Why must she always think the worst of people?

He glanced at the music in her hand. "You'd like to use the piano?"

"Yes, please." Gabe hovered near the doorway.

"No problem. I'll get out of your way." He picked up a file and his phone and Gabe backed out of the studio to let him pass, but his arm still managed to touch hers. She held her breath until the feeling aroused had passed. She closed the door firmly behind her and sat at the piano. She played scales, checking to make sure the tuner had done his job and that her hand was up to something more rigorous. She then launched into a Scriabin Etude.

When she was finished she dropped her head on the piano and let her mind go blank. She wasn't sure how long she had been sitting there when she heard a tapping on the door.

"Come in." She sat up.

The door opened and Gabe prepared to face Fin. But it was Max Opie.

"Hi."

She blinked.

"I asked about you in the shop," he said, stepping tentatively through the doorway.

"Ah."

He cast a glance around the room and stopped at the view. "You're no amateur."

Gabe shrugged. She was in no-man's-land. "Not a professional either, really."

"Interesting." He turned to her.

"Not interesting at all." Gabe stood up and turned over the score that she had intended to work on once she had warmed up. He had been staring at it.

"If you say so, but no amateur plays Scriabin like that." He smiled.

"I am only a professional musician in that I compose music for ads."

He leaned against the piano. "It pays the rent?"

"Well, yes." Gabe pushed the stool under the piano. "How can I help?"

"I need a soprano." He smiled and hooked his thumbs into the pockets on his waistcoat.

Gabe shook her head. "Well, you've come to the wrong place."

He stood straight and pushed his satchel behind his back. "I haven't."

"Look, I'm not some lost Cinderella looking for her place in a choir." She walked to the window and watched the cormorant dive into the fast-flowing surface.

"I googled you."

Gabe's eyes opened wide. "Surely you are not that short of sopranos in Cornwall."

"No, there are many wonderful voices, and up-and-coming ones like Hannah. But I am composing an opera and I need a fully fledged professional soprano so that I can listen to it being performed the way it should be."

Gabe looked at her fingers. To sing, to sing something new . . . Her hands began to shake. She looked up. The river's surface was disturbed and the swell still lingered from the storm. The tide was on its way out and the east wind was blowing in the opposite direction. She felt like the water, being pulled and pushed into two different directions. To sing again, joy.

He joined her at the window. "You wouldn't be singing in front of anyone but me."

His hand touched her arm. She recoiled. No.

"Sorry," he said. He took a few steps back.

Max wasn't the man who had raped her. He looked like a little boy, so eager. She took a deep breath. "Can you leave the work with me and let me think about it?"

He smiled. "Of course." He picked a pencil off a shelf and scratched down his number on the score. "Give me a call in a few days." He began walking out but then stopped and turned. "What an amazing studio. I've always loved your grandmother's work."

"Thank you." She watched him leave and when he was out of sight she picked up the piece. Her fingers ran over the notes on the first page. She could hear it in her head. Before long she was humming and then singing. The piece could have been written for her. She sat at the piano and played the score.

Random notes reached Jaunty, then drifted away on the breeze. She squeezed the pen between her fingers and watched the blood drain away. She must hold on to her thoughts. Clarity. Just tell the facts. But Jaunty wasn't sure what was fact and what was fiction. Things were slipping from her even now.

I had begun to pass information on to the resistance. It had taken a year but they had begun to trust me. I didn't socialise at all and made sure that no one had any reason to pay attention to me. As much as possible I was simply the woman who worked at the bar. For another year this is how I survived. Then, having provided good information, I became more a part of the team and eventually I was asked to meet Alain, the area coordinator. Everyone always spoke of him in hushed tones.

Gabriella, I thought he would dismiss me. But my small role had become so important to me. It made me feel less awful about Jean and about the pain I knew my parents must be experiencing.

The room is filled with cigarette smoke. I breathe deeply and rub my hands on my skirt. I long for one as I practise what I will

157

say to Alain. I look up when I hear a knock and my breath catches. I am paralysed. Alex stands at the door. Blood drains from his face.

He doesn't move but continues to stare. Our eyes lock. I will myself to move but nothing happens. He closes the door. I find my feet and I am in his arms. I taste him. I feel him. I am against the wall and he is in me. I am complete.

Thank God no one was with us to witness my reunion with Alex. I was alive. He was alive, and for the moment that was all that mattered. After that meeting, my role increased. I would like to say it did because I was good, but truly it was so that Alex and I had reasons to be together and those infrequent reunions kept me sane. It became harder to pretend to myself and to others that I didn't have joy when I was so full of love. But it was vital for me to remain invisible, boring, the sort of woman no one takes any notice of.

In a world that was so wrong he was my joy, my passion. When I wasn't with him I trained myself not to think about him. It was so important. No one knew that we knew each other outside of France and we never spoke in English and we never spoke of home. All that longing went into our lovemaking.

Forgive me, Gabriella, I have wandered off again. I do want you to know that I did do something useful during the war because I fear that you will look on my life and see only its lies. At least then it was more than the lies, or maybe it was then that the lies mattered the most.

Jaunty lifted her pen when she heard a car on the track, but it didn't turn down the drive. Gabriella. Jaunty understood loneliness because it was all she had felt after the war and soon became all she craved. By the end of the war she had loved too much.

Love, promises, desire . . . gone . . .

Jaunty looked up when she heard Fin tap on her door. She put the book aside and called to him to come in.

He stood by the window looking out at the water. He turned to her. "Those pre-war paintings aren't yours, are they?"

Jaunty placed her fingers together. She could lie but she had done that enough. She stood. "No."

A slow smile spread across Fin's face. Jaunty knew that she had solved his puzzle. But now that he had an answer what would he do with it? There was a knock at the door.

"I'll get it." Fin disappeared.

Jaunty walked through to the sitting room, considering what should happen next. Above all Gabriella must not be hurt. Jaunty looked at her paintings on the sitting-room wall. The deception had been obvious for years for anyone who really wanted to see it. Jaunty felt a twinge, reached for the door handle, and fell to the ground.

★ ★ ★

Gabe sang the scales quietly, building until her voice began to work properly. The score was brilliant and her heart begged her to sing it. The libretto was based on the story of the Lovers of Porthgwarra. She remembered reading the tale years ago in an old book of Jaunty's, *Popular Romances of the West of England* by Robert Hunt. Max had captured the lovers' anguish at being forced to separate and the parents' anger and prejudice beautifully. On the keys her fingers flowed through the opening bars, then she sang.

She lost herself in the music. She was Nancy, the maid of Porthgwarra and her lover, William, was across the sea. They had promised each other to remain true, that they would be together in three years, no matter what. Gabe forgot her location, the time — everything was gone and she sat on the rocks above the sea while the incoming tide swirled around her, taking her life but bringing William to her. The slow sound of a steady clapping broke into her trance. Spinning towards the sound, Gabe found Fin and Max standing by the door.

"Sorry to interrupt but the doctor is with your grandmother."

Words of anger that were about to spill from her mouth died and she ran, pushing past both men. How long had she been singing? She had no idea. It had absorbed her totally.

Reaching Jaunty's bedroom she found the doctor speaking with her grandmother.

"Ah, there you are, Gabriella." Dr Winslade looked up from where he was sitting on the side of the bed. "Your grandmother has had a minor heart attack."

160

Gabe stopped moving.

"Don't worry. It's happened before and she refuses to have any treatment for it. She and I have had this battle many times and I will give you *your* chance to argue with her — but in truth there is little that we can do now other than to make sure she takes her medication and doesn't over-exert herself." He stood and picked up Jaunty's hand.

"Listen to Gabriella even if you won't listen to me."

Gabe looked at her grandmother. The bed seemed to have absorbed Jaunty into it. She could barely be seen under the eiderdown and Gabe knew that whether she wanted it or not, Jaunty was slipping away from her. "Thank you, Dr Winslade."

He nodded and left them. Gabe sat on the edge of the bed.

"Don't Jaunty me," her grandmother said.

"I didn't say a word," Gabe said gently, pushing a strand of hair off Jaunty's cheek.

"You were about to." Jaunty smiled tiredly. "But I am old, Gabriella. Let me go . . ."

Gabe swallowed but didn't answer. She turned away and saw Fin in the doorway. He must have called the doctor. She had been lost in the world of the music and her grandmother could have died. From now on she must stick with the music she got paid to create, not waste time and energy on stuff that didn't belong in her life any more.

"You look tired." Gabe placed a glass of water on the bedside table.

"I am." Jaunty's voice was a whisper.

"Get some rest."

Jaunty closed her eyes and Gabe prayed it wasn't for the last time. She stood, looking about the room, and her glance was drawn outside to the trees, which seemed to hold the room in their embrace. Tonight the wind rushed from the north, roaring through the pine needles and rattling the windows. She could feel the draught. She pulled the curtains closed and walked into the sitting room. Fin and Max were sitting on the sofa with the teapot in front of them, looking well acquainted.

"Thought you might need tea." Fin picked up the pot and poured.

Gabe took a step back, offended. This was her home, not his. But then immediately she knew she was being ridiculous. It was tea and he was right: she needed a cup. "Thanks." She sat opposite them. "Thank you for acting so quickly, Fin. I should have been here."

"You can't be here all the time and, besides, I was." He handed her a mug.

Gabe bit her lip. This was true. Maybe she did need help, but it didn't have to be him. She turned to Max. "And you?"

"I was walking down the path when I heard Fin swear."

"Ah." She sipped the tea. "Thank you for your help."

"No problem. Happy to." He nodded. "You totally got the music."

Gabe closed her eyes. She had forgotten that. They had heard her. They had stood and listened while Jaunty was with the doctor. Her muscles tensed and her

162

toes curled. "Yes, well, it's a beautiful piece but I don't think I can help you."

Max looked as if he was about to drop his cup. "*What?*"

Fin put a hand on his arm. "Max, she's in shock about Jaunty at the moment and I'm sure she's wondering about her care and so forth. Maybe now isn't the time to talk music."

Gabe relaxed and cast a glance at Fin. A hint of a smile played on her face. "Do you two know each other?"

"Yes, we went to prep school together." Fin smiled. "Took a few minutes to realise why I knew the face — or I should say the hair?"

Gabe looked at the deep auburn colour of Max's hair. She had wished for years that hers had been that dark instead of a brighter, not-to-be-missed red. She had dyed it but that had proved to be too much work and now it was back to its beacon shade and she just scraped it back and hoped no one really noticed the colour. "So you two go back a long time?"

"Aged five, but we'd lost touch about thirteen when we went to different senior schools," Max said. "I was surprised to see Fin here, but he's brought me up to date." They looked at each other and Gabe wondered if Fin could move in with him instead of occupying the studio.

"Funny that after all these years we end up in the same place. I'm here using my aunt's cottage while I'm on sabbatical and she's off sailing in Greece."

As if reading her thoughts, Fin spoke. "Shame he hasn't a room free for me. Max tells me that every bedroom in the house is filled with china that his aunt collects."

"Yes, the other bedrooms are filled floor to ceiling with pink lustre. It's one of the reasons I was asking for your help. I had originally planned to have a soprano I know come down, but I can't put her up." His eyes opened wide with a pleading glance and Gabe laughed. He didn't do the puppy-dog look very well.

"Maybe in a bit? Once things have settled with your grandmother?" He tried the eyes again and she smiled but shook her head.

"Enough, Max, you haven't changed." Fin stood and walked to the window. Rain was now lashing down and beating against the glass. The sky and river were the same grey and it was hard to distinguish between the two. "Did you drive here or walk?"

"Is that a subtle way of telling me to be on my way?" Max asked.

Fin raised an eyebrow.

"I take that as a yes and will head out and walk home in the rain."

"I can give you a lift." Gabe jumped up, suddenly wanting to be away from Fin. At least with Max she knew what his motives were.

Jaunty opened her eyes. The sound of the rain had been playing a tune in her head. She knew she had to tell the truth, not just to Gabriella but to the world. Fin's appearance had made that clear and it was as if the thumping of the rain on the roof was the sound of time running out. But how could she achieve it all? The racket of voices provided the answer. Fin could help her. He had his own agenda but she was sure they could work together. She couldn't wait any longer. Her hand rested over her heart. There was still so much to say and to do and there were the hidden paintings too.

"You're awake." Fin stood in the doorway.

Jaunty nodded.

"You gave us a scare."

Jaunty laughed. "I'm ninety-two and I won't last for ever, nor do I want to." *Just a little bit longer.* That's all she needed. She mustn't waste time.

"Can I get you anything?" He came closer.

"Where's Gabriella?"

"Just taking Max back to the village."

Jaunty sat up in bed. "Max?"

"Max Opie, a musician. He's Pam Harper's nephew."

Jaunty tilted her head, then smiled. She knew Pam, slightly mad but a great lover of art and pottery. "Can you hand me the notebook in the desk drawer? The key for the drawer is under the ink pot." She could not squander a single second.

Fin moved swiftly and unlocked the drawer. He handed the notebook and the fountain pen to her. "May I ask?"

Jaunty looked at him. If she closed her eyes halfway, as she did when she was trying to assess her subject, she could make him Alex; but what good would that do? Fin was a thirty-five-year-old Alex and she was ninety-two. "You may, but I'm not telling today. Maybe tomorrow."

His eyes sparkled as he smiled. "I can hope."

She nodded. "Definitely. And now I'd love some weak tea with lemon."

"Coming right up."

Slowly unscrewing the top of the pen, feeling her joints complain with each twist, Jaunty wondered where to begin now, because she had to shorten this to make sure that she would get the important parts down. She could come back and fill in the gaps if she was able.

Dietrich. Jaunty looked at the page. The writing was almost undecipherable. What had she written last? She didn't know. She must forge ahead no matter how much the memories hurt.

As far as the locals were concerned I was from Paris, an art student at a loose end, so my cover was sound and I was safe until Dietrich von Hochsbrinck walked in. I'd last seen him when I was fifteen but recognition happened in a second for both of us. His eyes met mine and he knew, and I knew. The captain with him ordered wine and I turned away, my heart racing, my face flushed. Would he say anything? I had to keep my head.

My hand shakes as I place two glasses on to the tray with the bottle of wine. I feel sweat breaking out on my forehead. The glasses clink against each other as I move across to their table. Dear God, don't let Dietrich

speak to me or even look at me again. If he speaks to me I am dead. If he says my name I am dead. I place the tray down and ask them if there is anything else they want. Dietrich looks me in the eyes again as the other man waves me away.

My legs barely function; I hope they are not watching me. I fall against the wall in the back room, gasping for air. Dietrich didn't betray me. What should I do now? Sitting out there in a German lieutenant's uniform is the boy I'd spent my summers with on Lake Garda, the boy with whom I'd practised kissing. His mother is one of my mother's best friends and now he is the enemy.

In this whole crazy mess, I hadn't thought of Dietrich or his family. I certainly hadn't thought, that of all the people I knew in Europe, it would be Dietrich who would appear in Brittany. I had no idea what to do. Where could I go? People were relying on me. Alex was counting on me.

I inhale. Think! I need to keep my thoughts clear. I need Dietrich on my side. I rub my temples. I will do whatever I need to do.

Dietrich had been keen on me for years. I needed to spin him a tale of sorts. Tell him some of the truth and enough of a lie to keep him quiet. I would simply do what I needed to do. That was all.

"Shall I put the tea on the table?" Fin stood beside the bed. She hadn't heard him come in. "Gabriella has just arrived back."

Jaunty nodded and closed the book. She wasn't ready for Gabriella to know. The shame still ran too deep.

CHAPTER
TEN

Gabe hesitated, watching the steam fill the shower. She knew she was being foolish. It was all a long time ago. She had changed the course of her life and she would never have to see or face Victor Justin again. A ball formed in her throat and wouldn't move. She had left his world and he walked free. The mist swirled about her feet while she battled with her thoughts. Max's request had been an innocent one but it had opened wide the hole inside her. "Sing for me," Victor Justin had said. How many times had she heard those words before? And all it took had been saying yes for all her hope, all her ambition to end. He had done it to others. She had been warned but she hadn't listened, hadn't believed. It was her fault. She had chosen to go to his room.

Throwing her robe on to the bed, she walked under the spray. She was in charge of her life now. *He* hadn't stopped her singing. Her own guilt had done that. It had strangled her vocal chords. She had stood by the piano two days later at a tutorial and not a sound emerged when she should have been basking in the glory of winning first place. But all she felt was that if she opened her mouth he would do it all again. And

169

everyone had looked at her with knowing eyes. That was the worst part. They had all guessed what had happened. They had seen them walk out of the party together.

Gabe hadn't been the last, she was sure. And that hurt almost as much. She hadn't done anything to stop him from doing it to someone else. The water ran over her body. She hated herself and she hated her voice. She rolled her shoulders back to relax the muscles. This wasn't good. She had moved on. She could sing. She sang every day, just without an audience. She had sung in front of Hannah. Now, without thinking, she began to warm up her voice. The words of the love song she had sung yesterday bounced off the walls and the glass panels. Throwing her head back she let her voice rise.

I am thine,
Thou art mine,
Beyond control;

In the wave,
Be the grave
Of heart and soul

She leant against the shower wall. She couldn't tell if she was crying but she thought she was. She could taste salt on her lips and all this emotion was why she didn't sing in front of people any more. It made her vulnerable.

Reeling out of the shower, she shut the water off. He wouldn't win. She might never sing publicly again, but her voice was not dead. She roughly dried her hair and twisted it in a tight chignon at the nape of her neck. With one of Jaunty's old Guernsey sweaters on over a pair of leggings she felt ready to face whatever the day brought. She just hoped that it wouldn't be any more heart attacks or new works of music, although she couldn't get Max's opera out of her head. Its beautiful melody kept weaving in and out of her thoughts, and the lyrics had wound their way around her heart.

The morning sun caught the fields and foreshore of Calamansac. After the rain of the night, the morning sparkled and the pine needles continued to send water drops down with the gentle wind. Pulling the notebook out Jaunty began to write.

As I watched them leave the bar together I knew it wouldn't be long until Dietrich sought me out. It was in his eyes as he left. I was compromised — but I had key information to relay that night. It had to be done. Alex and his team were relying on me. I cleared the glasses and washed them up, willing my brain to think of a solution. I walked out of the kitchen into the cool November air. It had all been so simple up to this point but now everything was wrong.

Why was Dietrich in the army? He is a pianist like his mother. He didn't belong here, but nor did I. I had never expected to be a spy, but I am one.

I take a drag of the one real cigarette I'd saved. It calms me. I need to think. How do I handle this?

"Little one, you were the last person I'd thought I'd see here." He speaks to me in German.

I jump. Think fast. I hand the cigarette to him and he takes a drag. He hands it back to me and I know what I must do. But what are the right lies to tell? I look about to make sure no one is watching us. To be seen talking to him would ruin my cover.

"Why? Or should I ask how?" Dietrich touched my sleeve. Icy fingers cover my skin. I shiver. Fear. I scan the area. I am a spy. I will be shot if I am discovered.

The moment is still so clear in my mind. Maybe that is what that sort of acute fear does to you or to your memory.

"It's a long story." I hand the cigarette back to him and smile.

He nods.

"You know I was in Paris."

He stares at my mouth. I watch his breath in the cold air. It fills the space between us. "My mother mentioned it." He speaks in French. I sigh. He understands.

"Well, I didn't think the war was really coming and I got caught in Paris. It wasn't the place to be so I escaped to the country and found work here."

He steps closer. I see so much in his eyes. Loneliness, fear, desire. "I've missed you."

I look into his tiger eyes. They are so beautiful. And when he strokes my cheek I feel the old emotions creeping back. This is not going to work. He is a friend. He is the enemy. He leans forward and kisses me.

My eyes close. It is different from those first tentative kisses in the boathouse on Lake Garda. Sometime in the intervening years he has learned a bit more about kissing and so have I.

Gabe tapped on the door and came in carrying a tray. "Morning."

Jaunty closed the book and slid it under the pillow. "Did I hear you singing?"

"I hope not."

"It was music I am unfamiliar with. What was it?"

Gabe swallowed. "It's a new composition by Max, the man who helped when you had your turn yesterday."

"Max?" Jaunty rubbed her temples. Dietrich's brother's name was Max. She looked out of the window.

"He's a musician who lives in the village in his aunt's house on Vicarage Lane. He's there while she's sailing."

Max. He was much younger and not musical at all. He caught us kissing in the boathouse and had run to tell everyone. Jaunty smiled.

Gabe plumped the pillow behind her. "Jaunty, where are you?"

"Max who?"

"Max Opie. Fin told me they went to prep school together." Gabe poured tea and handed the delicate cup to her grandmother, then sat on the side of the bed.

"What do you know about him?" Jaunty blew on the surface, vaguely remembering Fin talking about him.

Gabe sat back. "Well, he's made quite a name for himself in the choral world. He's originally from St Austell and he went to Truro School on a scholarship."

"Not him." Jaunty puckered her mouth. "What do you know about Fin?"

Gabe shook her head. "Not much."

"Have you asked him?"

Gabe looked out the far window. "No."

"He's very good-looking." Jaunty studied her granddaughter, noting the slight flush on her cheeks.

"Yes, you could say so." Gabe stood and pushed the curtain fully back from the nearest window.

"You don't like him."

Gabe turned and looked at Jaunty. "No, I wouldn't say that."

Jaunty laughed. "I like him."

"I know." Gabe frowned again. "Why him?"

Jaunty sipped her tea. Why him? Could she say that he was like her lost youth? That he reminded her of happy days? No, she couldn't. "It suits me."

"Fair enough." Gabe stood and kissed her cheek. "I have to go in to Helston this morning. Fin will be around and Dr Winslade will come by at some point."

Jaunty watched the straight back of her grand-daughter as she walked to the door, then she pulled out the notebook and began again.

"Why doesn't she sing any more?" Fin scooped Jaunty up and placed her gently down on the chair on the terrace.

"I don't know." Jaunty pulled the blanket closer around her shoulders. Although the sun was shining, the breeze from the north was cold. Fin went back inside and grabbed another blanket for her legs, along with her notebook and her pen. She wondered if he had looked inside. He didn't hide his curiosity and she knew he had figured out part of her secret, but there was no way for him to discover the rest unless she told him.

"She should be on stage." He pulled up another chair.

"I know, but she hasn't been on a stage in years and she has never said why." Jaunty sighed. "I only hear her sing or play when she doesn't think I'm listening."

"She has real talent." Fin put on sunglasses.

"I know." Jaunty thought about Gabriella's musical lineage.

"Max has been raving about her voice."

"I wish I'd heard it too. But I think she may have been singing it in the shower this morning."

Fin stared at the creek. "Max was always brilliant, always focused on what he wanted to achieve. It was clear from early on he was a kid who was clever and good at rugby."

"What about you?" Jaunty studied him.

Fin's mouth twitched into a lopsided grin. "Boring."

"Doubt it."

"You know I'm divorced and I'm an art historian and art dealer. Not very interesting."

"On the contrary." Jaunty stroked the cover of her notebook. "Most interesting on many accounts."

He turned to her. "You are far more interesting."

"No." Jaunty frowned.

"Yes. Famous, reclusive, prolific. No interviews."

Jaunty smiled. "It's good, isn't it?"

"Very, but why?" He leaned forward, resting his arms on his legs. "The paintings of pre-war Paris are renown. You should have been at the centre of the art world and not living the life of a hermit."

Had Alex survived, life would have been so different and she might well have lived a life of launches and society parties. But that didn't happen and it was far too late to think of the "what ifs". Jaunty looked at her watch. It was noon. "Would you pour me a whisky?"

He stood. "Are you sure the doctor would approve?"

"Absolutely." Dr Winslade was a sensible man. He had been looking after her since he had left medical school and both of them knew that her days were few — she had lived well beyond the threescore years and ten supposedly allocated to her.

"What about Gabe?" he called from the kitchen.

Jaunty snorted. "No, she certainly wouldn't approve, but she worries too much."

She opened the notebook. She was halfway through, she believed.

"Do you want ice? Or water?"

"Neat."

Fin coughed. "Mind if I join you?"

"Not at all." Jaunty held out her hand and took the glass from him. While he was pouring himself one, Jaunty swirled the whisky around, remembering the colour. Now it was seemingly bland and clear without much variation but she knew it wasn't. She sniffed it and was grateful that she still had that sense in full. She looked up at Fin. "What colour are your eyes?"

Fin frowned. "Blue. Why do you ask?"

"Because I can't tell." She rolled the glass between her hands.

"How long?"

"Almost a year." A year without the one thing that had held her together all this time. If she could still paint she would want to carry on.

"Is that why you stopped painting?" He took his sunglasses off and studied her.

"Yes." Jaunty sipped her whisky. "Do you resemble someone in your family?"

"They say I take after my great-uncle. His eyes in particular."

Jaunty's gut clenched. She knew, then, just the shade of blue, the cerulean blue of the Cornish sky on a clear summer day with a hint of Hooker's green running through the iris.

"I'm named after him and my mother's father."

"She's Irish?"

Fin smiled. "Her father was."

"What do you know of your great-uncle?" She looked out on to the creek. It was almost at the point were it would fill quickly and all the exposed mud vanish in what seemed like seconds.

"Alexander died in the war. He was in the SOE."

Jaunty nodded.

"I've done some research since my grandmother left me his things."

"Yes?" She studied him again.

"He died returning to England. He drowned when the fishing boat he was in was hit by another vessel in thick fog and his body was never recovered."

"How terrible." Her heart twisted.

"Yes."

Jaunty could see the questions in his eyes. She looked down into her glass when she heard Gabriella's car. Now was not the time to talk.

Jaunty could hear Gabriella and Fin in the kitchen. Gabriella still treated him with caution, but when she thought no one was looking, Jaunty had seen the gleam in her granddaughter's eyes when she watched Fin. Those eyes said more than Gabriella knew.

I lived the life of a widow and a reclusive painter. Each day passed much as another. I only went as far as I could walk, although I had a car. The car was only used to collect Philip and to get supplies. I spoke to as few people as I could and made my business my own. The only real contact with the world was the gallery, and that was by post and phone. Thankfully, I painted what I chose and people bought it. I painted the river, the water, because my heart was buried in the sea with Alex. Each turn of the tide brought him closer to me and took my love back to him.

I was a mess. I'd kept up my double charade. I was a spy; I was a lover and another man's fiancé. I was good at lying but that was about all. Although I was stopped and questioned a few times, Dietrich protected me. The community were suspicious but had no proof. We were very discreet — only the trees could tell tales.

Becoming his lover had been easy and I loved him. Yes, Gabriella, I loved him. It was simple to forget the war and the lie I was living and remember Lake Garda and the endless summers. I shudder now, thinking about the men I'd slept with to reach this point. It had always been about their pleasure, never mine. That was never the case with Dietrich. He was always a kind and generous lover.

But I betrayed him daily. Sometimes I wonder if he knew. His life was always in jeopardy because of me, and when Alex would come to town I would fly into his arms. Two lovers, one heart, one child.

Would Gabriella understand? Did she herself understand? Had Gabriella known such love? Maybe that wasn't the point. She was doing this so Gabriella would know who she was.

My lovemaking with Alex was different. The hunger in him and me could have set the world on fire. Sometimes now, as an old woman, I wonder how a simple act could be so different. For some it is no more than the scratching of an itch, a biological urge. Yet the same act to another is a declaration of love and, in those days, the seeking of peace in a world that was wrong. Dietrich should never have been a solider. His soul was too delicate, too gifted. Those tiger eyes could hide nothing from me and I saw his need.

But Alex . . . Alex was almost born to espionage. I didn't know all he did for he kept it from me, but I saw the respect others showed him. Our lovemaking was so fierce, so hungry, I could almost forget the fumbling beginnings on a sun-drenched hillside. But I forget myself, Gabriella, you do not want to know about the sex life of your grandmother.

Jaunty put the pen down. Gabriella was singing the haunting lines *I am thine, thou art mine, beyond control* . . . The emotion carried on the wind and came through the window. *Alex.* Jaunty stood. Despite Gabriella saying she didn't want to sing, she was. Her genes were pushing her to her destiny. Jaunty walked around her room. It took such effort but if she didn't move then her legs went dead. She laughed. It would not be long before all of her did the same.

180

When I discovered I was pregnant I knew I couldn't continue with this charade. I didn't know what I could do, but staying in France wasn't an option. Once my pregnancy was discovered then assumptions would be made, so I had to get back to England. I was engaged to Alex but I had no idea whose child I was carrying.

He knew the nature of my relationship with Dietrich. It was a secret I couldn't keep, just like my pregnancy. He knew that Dietrich protected me more than he himself could, so he chose to ignore the relationship. When I told him of the pregnancy, Alex, of course, said that the child must be his. He blocked out the other possibility and made plans to get me home.

"Alex, are you sure?" I clench my hands. Not wanting to but knowing I must say what is in my heart. "What if the child is Dietrich's?"

His body stiffens but he turns and pulls me into his arms. "It's mine. You are mine." He kisses me, parting my lips with his. Hunger ignites us and I grind against him, forgetting the future and thinking only of my need for Alex.

What I would do in England I didn't know. My parents believed me dead and how could I return to them pregnant? But I would have no choice. They might disown me but it was a risk I would have to take. I knew what my grandmother would say, that I was a disgrace to the family.

In the dark of night, a week after I had broken the news to Alex, he took me to the young village curate and we were married.

The clouds slide across the moon as we race to the kitchen door of the rectory.

"Quick, before you are seen." The young curate looks at us and I flush under his scrutiny. We stand together under the single light bulb in the kitchen and the room smells of onions and cabbage.

"Follow me." He leads us through a dark hallway, then stops us from following. "Wait."

In the darkness Alex reaches for my hand. "I love you," he says and we kiss.

"Come quickly." We follow the priest through a door into the church. Only the sacristy candle is alight, which casts shadows across the tabernacle and altar. Fear settles in my stomach. Outside the wind rises and the windows rattle.

"Are you sure?" the curate asks me.

"Yes." I nod.

"Good. You are making a promise before God." Alex and I reach for each other.

It was never recorded because it couldn't be. Alex promised me we would do it again once we were back in England so that no matter what, the child was his.

Gabe stood by the door. "Jaunty, do you feel up to dinner?"

"Yes."

"Shall I bring it to you or would you like to eat at the table?"

"Table." Jaunty thrust the notebook under her pillow.

"I'll just lay it, then I'll give you a hand."

"Fine."

As soon as Gabriella was gone Jaunty wedged the book under the mattress and went slowly out to the sitting room. She didn't need help. Fin was opening a bottle of wine and Gabe was putting a casserole down. It should really just be the two of them having dinner, Jaunty thought, and turned round, but Fin was at her elbow. "Have you forgotten something?"

She looked at him. He knew. "No, I don't think so."

"Good." He led her to the table and pulled out her chair. When had a man, or anyone for that matter, last done that for her? Jaunty swallowed. She had given up so much. Could she have done it differently? She shook her head. It didn't matter now. It was done.

CHAPTER
ELEVEN

Gabe was in the car park at the top of Helford. She had come to use the WiFi in the café to send off her latest composition but she needed to get Bosworgy connected, and soon, if she was to make living here work. Using a public network was so slow and unsecure — not that anyone would want to steal her latest masterpiece, she thought ruefully.

The old chapel above the village housed the thriving café for part of the year and even now, in mid October, there were enough tourists around to form a queue for coffee. Gabe stood looking at the tempting cakes on offer.

"Hello, Gabe." Hannah, the young singer, was putting scones on a plate.

"Gosh, they look good." Gabe smiled. "How are you?"

"I'm good."

"Sorry I didn't make it to the concert. The tickets were sold out. Did it go well?" Gabe's glance fell on the cakes again. Could she resist? No.

"Brilliant. I wish you'd been there." Hannah dashed out to deliver the scones and clotted cream.

"Hello, my lovely. What can I get you?" Gabe didn't know the woman at the till.

"What's that divine-looking cake?" Gabe pointed.

"This one?" The woman lifted a plate.

"Yes."

"It's rhubarb and ginger."

"Yes please, and a black coffee." Gabe handed over the money.

"Shall I have Hannah bring it out to you?"

Gabe nodded and walked slowly away from the till, admiring the old chapel's vaulted ceiling. She remembered, from her childhood, hearing that its bell had come from a shipwreck. At the time a shipwreck had sounded romantic but now Gabe shivered at the thought.

Gabe walked into a woman as she went through the door.

"Hello, Gabe. God, it's been a long time."

Gabe stood back and exclaimed, "Jenna Williams!"

"Yes and no. Jenna Tregonig now." They both stepped outside to let a group into the café.

"Congratulations."

"Well past that. I've been married for eight years." Jenna laughed. "You can see my brood sitting with Mum at the far table."

Gabe saw Mrs Williams talking with four children. She looked at Jenna. "You've been busy."

Jenna smiled. "I have. Have you ordered?"

Gabe nodded.

"Well, you remember Mum. Grab a seat with her and let's catch up."

Gabe thought for a second about just disappearing. There would be questions.

"Where are you going to sit?" Hannah came out with her coffee and cake.

Gabe smiled and accepted defeat. "Just over there with Mrs Williams. Hannah, do you know the WiFi code?" She mustn't forget why she was here.

"I'll bring it to you."

"Thanks."

"Well, if it isn't Gabriella Blythe." Helen Williams patted the seat beside her. "I'd heard you were back, looking after Jaunty."

Gabe smiled as Helen picked up a toy car from the ground and handed it to the second youngest child. No sooner did he have it in his hands than he threw it down.

Bending to collect it again, Helen asked, "So how is Jaunty?"

Gabe frowned. "As well as can be expected."

"She's a good age." Helen waved to a woman at another table then turned and focused again on Gabe. "And how are you, my dear? Haven't seen you in what feels like for ever."

Although Gabe had been back frequently, it had always been for short visits just to see Jaunty. "It's been a while, and I'm good. How's Mr Williams?"

"Oh, JC is just fine. He's still fishing and still talking about retiring."

Jenna joined them at the table with a tray filled with drinks and cakes. Her kids all had their hands on them before she could sit down. "I should be cross but I know they're starved. We've just been on a long walk." Jenna poured her mother some tea. "So don't tell me you've told Mum all your news."

"Most disappointing — she hasn't told me a thing." Helen chuckled.

"Well, you can see my life." Jenna waved her hand towards the children. "But what have you been up to in the last ten years. Last I knew you were at the Royal Northern College of Music."

Gabe nodded, wondering how to make this simple. "Yes, I finished there. I got my masters and now I'm a composer."

"Not singing? Thought that was your real love."

Gabe shook her head.

Helen looked up from cleaning the youngest one's face of chocolate cake. "More important than that is her love life; last I remember she was mooning around me at Pengarrock, all love struck with Tristan."

Gabe blushed. She'd forgotten that.

"Don't think he's up for grabs any more," Jenna said, smiling.

"I'm sure Gabriella's got some lovely man tucked away that we don't know about." Helen sipped her tea and winked.

The image of Fin walking in front of Mrs Bates in a towel flashed in Gabe's mind. Word did spread fast here. Never mind that he wasn't her man at all.

Jaunty couldn't find her notebook. She didn't remember where she had hidden it but near to hand was the sketchpad she had used to draw Fin and Alex. That would have to do.

The storm that brought Fin reminded me of the night before we crossed the Channel, coming home. I was the only one to survive and to this day I'm not sure how, except I knew I was carrying another life and I owed it to the child inside me to hold on. I deserved to die, but the child had done no wrong. Only Alex knew I was pregnant and I had only told him after he found me suffering from a bout of morning sickness, and at that point I didn't know if it was his child or Dietrich's. Indeed, I wouldn't know for almost forty years. Funny how genes will out in the end. Philip, physically, could have belonged to either man, and based on his skill with numbers I had assumed he was Alex's son, something I could hold close to remind me I was once worthy. But then you, Gabriella, showed me the folly of my belief. You, dear child, had Dietrich's tiger eyes. Only then did I know how much I had betrayed the man I loved, but by then the betrayal of everyone connected with me had gone so deep that it didn't matter. It was just another nail in my coffin and my life that had been spent accumulating those hand-hewn nails. With each brushstroke and each signature I made another one.

Was I wrong? What could I have done? It was a different time. There was no one I could turn to and it wasn't Philip's fault. He was the reason I survived. I couldn't kill another soul.

Jaunty coughed. Her chest tightened. She must focus.

All was well. We could see the Cornish coast in the moonlight. The war wasn't over but it was for me. I would be home. Alex and I would marry quickly and quietly, and while I knew he would have to head back to France I was confident that life would be good. The war would end and he would return to me. We could live our dream.

"Is that Orion's belt?" I point to the star-filled sky above us, listening to the waves splash against the bow.

"Yes," he whispers close to my neck. I shiver and his arms close around me. "There's a shooting star. Make a wish."

"I wish to be in your embrace for ever."

"Silly Jeanette — now it won't come true."

"But I'm living it now."

"True." He kisses my neck as the boat rocks. His thigh slips between my legs and I wish we were alone. "Tomorrow or the day after I will marry you again."

"Are you planning on making a habit of it?"

"Nothing would give me more pleasure."

My hand slides up his thigh. "Are you sure about that?"

"Oh, most definitely, Mrs Carrow. Most definitely."

As we lay on the deck, peering at the stars and holding hands, we made plans for the future. I longed to hold him properly but it would have to wait until we reached Cornwall. He knew the church he wanted us to be married in for the second time. He told me of sailing up to it, St Anthony, in Gillan Creek. There, in the candlelit church, he wanted to make me his wife officially.

The boat was under sail and the winds were perfect. The only sound was the splash of the waves on the bow — and then a sudden bolster fog rolled around us. I turned to Alex, frightened, but he assured me that it would be fine. The captain made this trip nightly. It would be OK. And so, lulled to relax by the motion of the boat, I dozed — and woke to the sound of crushing wood. I was thrown out of the boat into the icy water and I called out to Alex again and again, but he never answered. Swimming to a piece of wood I looked around, but could see nothing in the fog except nearby debris and heard nothing but the throb of an engine fading in the distance.

Through the window she could see the clouds crack near the horizon, and colour, or what she knew would be colour, bled through, tinting the sky. Within seconds the sun had dropped below the horizon and the surface of the river reflected the pale sky. Her heart ached as she wrote. Even after all the years she could feel the cold and the despair. Was she remembering it all? She was sure there were key things she was leaving out.

Cold. My limbs twitch and convulse. I kick my legs hard, raising my body up, but I can't see. The fog conceals everything. I grab a piece of wood. "Alex!" My voice doesn't travel. The fog holds it close. "Alex." I release the plank and stop kicking. It is pointless. I slip under. Salt stings my eyes. My stomach turns and I think of the life inside of me. I kick to the surface.

The water was so cold and I knew if I didn't move I would die of exposure. I called out for Alex long after the rumble of the engine had faded, but no one replied. Swimming, I found a piece of the boat large enough for me to get out of the water. Splinters lodged in my hand as I scrambled on to it. I had no idea where I was and the thought of death enticed me. I was frozen through and shivers wracked my body. There was no spare flesh on me but my hand travelled to my stomach and I knew I had to hold on for that scrap of life. It hadn't done anything to deserve a watery grave, even though, without Alex, that was what I wanted. Part of me prayed that he too was alive and adrift on a piece of wood like me, but I didn't dare to hope, and as dawn broke I could barely move. The mist was rising. Turning my head to the side, I saw rocks. A voice boomed out and, dazed, I looked towards it. A fishing boat, not far away. My arm felt too heavy to lift but eventually I waved it, rocking the bit of boat that was holding me. I don't know whether I had slept or passed out, but the next thing I knew I was in a hospital room. I heard voices on the other side of the door saying I was lucky to be alive.

Jaunty looked up when she heard a tap on the door.

"Hello, Jaunty." Dr Winslade put his bag down on a chair. "You're looking so well I may be able to turn you over to the nurse."

"Indeed."

"But if I did I wouldn't have the pleasure of your company." He sat and held out his hand for Jaunty's arm. She obliged, thinking he was a good man. Before long he'd checked her pulse, her lungs, her heart and her blood pressure.

"Well?"

He tilted his head. "I won't lie. I'm worried."

Jaunty nodded.

"I'd be happier if we could bring you in for tests."

"No, there are better ways to spend my tax money than running a bunch of tests on me. I'm old. I'm dying. It's my time."

"I don't agree."

"I know. And I thank you for your care."

"A pleasure. Is there anything else you want to tell me?"

"No." Jaunty smiled at him then took his hand. "Thank you." He stood and gave her hand a squeeze as he left. Jaunty could hear him chatting with Gabriella, and picked up her pen.

A doctor examined me and finally I spoke to an officer. I would not tell anyone my name. I simply asked to speak to Major Penn because I knew Alex reported to him. Eventually another officer entered the room. He said he would take me to him. He drove us a short distance to a house on the north shore of the Helford River.

Out of the window I see the cabin. So close to a place of such happiness I want to cry. Tears are all I seem to have and I wake each night calling out Alex's name.

Major Penn stands by the window. "Why did you want to see me?" He turns and studies me. I touch my hair and smooth it.

"I am J —" I stop. Who am I? Who am I to Major Penn. I blink. "I am Simone Dubois. Operation Vent."

"Ah, Jean Blythe." His brow lifts and he comes closer and takes a seat beside me. "I am so sorry about Lieutenant Carrow."

I hold my breath. I can do this. "Thank you."

"What happened?"

"I'm not sure. A collision in the fog, I think." I twist my fingers tight, holding back the tears. "I fell asleep on deck and woke when we were hit."

He nods. "That's what we'd gathered."

"Has anyone else been found?"

"No, local fishermen found you and bits of the wreckage." He stood. "I don't suppose you know where you were when you were hit?"

"No, sir." I look down. "We'd left the Scillies and had been sailing for maybe a half-hour at a guess." I am puzzled. "What do I do now?"

"We could still use you in France."

I shake my head. "I'm pregnant. I thought Alex had told you."

"No."

"May I use your phone and call my father." It is my only option.

"Your father?"

I forget they think I am Jean and she had been an orphan.

"Someone who was like a father to me."

He frowns. "Who?"

"Lord Penrose."

He glances out of the window. "I'm sorry to tell you, but Lord Penrose is dead. He died in the blitz."

I suck in air. What of my mother? "Lady Penrose?" I ask.

"It has been reported that she died of a broken heart having lost her daughter and her husband." I close my eyes. That only leaves my grandmother and there is no way that I can turn to her.

Jaunty coughed. Just thinking about all of this brought the pain too close.

The Major gave me money for a ticket to London, and his sister's name and address. I could stay with her. I sat on the train to London knowing that I was a married woman, but I couldn't prove it so I couldn't go to Alex's family. They would be worried sick about him. How could I say I was his wife and I was pregnant with his child when I didn't know whose child it was that I carried? I couldn't — no, I wouldn't — turn to my grandmother. As the train slid past the lush English countryside I knew I had to remain Jean, but how?

Gabe left Fin patching a hole in the shed roof. He was handier around the place than she would ever have imagined, and he seemed determined to earn his keep. The week had passed quickly and she was thankful that he had been with Jaunty when she'd had her attack. Walking down the path towards the cabin she could hear the deep throb of a boat engine. She looked out over the creek but couldn't see the source. The breeze came from the west and it felt warmer than a summer's day.

"Don't want to hear any more reports of any more illness," a male voice said.

Gabe heard Jaunty laugh.

"That's an order. I'll just put the fish in the sink." Mike Gear came strolling out of the kitchen.

"Hello, Gabe."

She grinned.

"I won't give you a hug." He looked down at his fish-smeared overalls.

Gabe twitched her nose. "Yes, I'll take a rain check."

"I was just dropping some monkfish cheeks off for Jaunty. I know she loves them." His phone rang and he delved inside his pocket and pulled it out. "Hello, darling. I'll be home in about a half-hour. I just popped by Bosworgy to check on Jaunty." He smiled at Gabe and she could hear his wife, Sue, on the other end. "Yes, I remember the folk group is at the pub tonight."

Gabe watched gulls circle and knew it was because of Mike's boat below. He must be tied up to the quay.

"There's an idea. Come to the pub tonight, Gabe. There's a men's group singing. It'll be like old times."

"Sounds great." Gabe bit her lower lip, thinking of nights with her father at the pub, where he and others would sing. "But I can't leave Jaunty."

Mike nodded. "Hadn't thought of that. Shame."

"Enjoy it for me."

"No worries there, and put the fish in the fridge if you aren't going to eat it tonight." Mike waved when he reached the bend in the path and shortly after she saw his boat pull out into the river.

Gabriella, my head is muddled. I can hear your voice and memories of you and Philip fill me. I do not need to share those memories with you; you have your own of your father. He was so different from me. If I had been him I would have resented you for taking my love away but he, dear sweet soul, loved you more.

Jaunty rubbed her temples. She must push onwards.

I walk through the gallery door just before five. This much I know. I have to do this. I am Jean Blythe. I pray she will understand. Jeanette died on the Lancastria. I can do this.

I scan the room and see three of Jean's paintings on prominent display. The price listed is triple what her first painting sold for. I spin around and I spot two more. They were painted one sunny morning sitting by the Seine and these paintings are sold.

A man in a dark suit walks up to me. "Hello. You have wonderful taste. Her work is brilliant, so collectible. I wish we had more but these may be the last ones." He shakes his head. "I haven't heard from her since the invasion of Paris." He frowns and looks me up and down. I am concious of my tatty clothes.

"I wish I could tell her how acclaimed her work has become." He seems sincere.

My heart races. "Peter Knowles?"

"In the country; the bombing wasn't good for his dickey heart."

I breathe. I must do this. I look heavenward and ask Jean to forgive me. I would rather she

was alive and we would survive together. "I'm Jean Blythe."

The man claps his hands together. "Someone who has made it through this awful war! I cannot tell you how happy I am to meet you. I'm Paul Nichols. We've corresponded."

"Yes." This at least is true. I had written all Jean's letters. "A pleasure." I change the shape of my mouth slightly. Jean was from London. I picture her in my head and affect her mannerisms.

With no choice left to me I have come to the gallery as Jean, hoping she will forgive me for taking her name, her fame and her money.

Leaving the gallery I wander the streets of London, go past our old house. A bomb has wiped out the terrace. From there I walk to the Brompton Oratory and in its cool, dark interior I light a candle for my mother. I have no idea where she died or where she is buried. I pray for my parents. I pray for Alex. I pray for the child growing in me. The flame flickers in the draught and I think of my grandmother and debate if I should turn to her and just be me, Jeanette. It is not too late to stop this subterfuge. But as I look up at the statue of St Francis I know I can't do it. She will throw me out and then I will have nowhere to turn.

The confessional beckons and I long for forgiveness.

"Forgive me, Father, for I have sinned. It's been four years since my last confession." I take a breath. Where should I begin? "I have returned from France. I . . . I can't say why I was there."

"What you say in here is safe."

I nod but I hold back. I can no longer trust.

I knew that I couldn't risk staying in London; someone from my past might recognise me. So I made a plan to move to Cornwall. I was unknown in the west and I would be close to Alex. Before I left London I went to a hairdresser and had my hair cut short. It changed my whole look; I was someone else now and always would be.

CHAPTER
TWELVE

Gabe was handing Fin the last glass to put in the dresser when Mrs Bates appeared at the door. "Good evening, Gabriella."

"Yes?"

"You look surprised. Didn't Jaunty tell you she rang and asked me to come over?"

Gabe shook her head and looked at Fin, who shrugged as Jaunty came into the kitchen. "Keziah, come and sit down." Jaunty took Mrs Bates's arm and walked through to the sitting room. "Gabriella, would you make us a pot of tea before you head to the Shipwrights?"

Gabe shook her head and grinned. Obviously Jaunty had overheard Gabe's conversation with Mike. "Fin, fancy a drink at the pub? There's a local folk group singing tonight."

"Sounds great. I'll just grab a sweater."

Gabe made the tea and took it to the two women. Jaunty entertaining anyone was odd, but Gabe knew her grandmother was worried about her move here, didn't want her to be alone, but Gabe had left London to find solitude and instead she was being pulled into the social whirl.

Mrs Bates came to the kitchen. "Don't forget your torch, dear. The nights are drawing in." She leaned closer to Gabe and whispered, "No need to rush back. Have a lovely evening out." She patted Gabe's arm as Fin appeared on the terrace. "He's a looker."

"Thanks, Mrs Bates." Gabe dashed away from Mrs Bates's knowing look, well meaning though it was. Once they were well away from the cabin, Gabe turned to Fin. "Thanks for all your help with the shed and, well, everything really."

"Not a problem, it's the least I can do."

"Well, yes, you could strim the field and help me harvest the apples." She cast a sideways glance at him and a smile spread across his face.

"I suppose I could, but I had the impression you wanted me gone?"

Gabe pursed her lips. "Might have done, but you've turned out rather handy."

"Have I now?" They paused and turned to see the sun set behind them. "I would never tire of seeing that," he said.

"Me neither." They picked up the pace and reached the pub just as the group began singing. The harmony of voices rang out with "Haul Away Joe".

Fin leaned close. "This time I can buy you that drink."

"Pleased to hear it. I'd love a cider."

"As you wish." He disappeared into the throng at the bar as Gabe spotted Jenna across the terrace and made her way to her.

"Who is the dishy guy?" Jenna pointed at Fin.

"He's Fin."

"Fin who?"

"Fin Alexander."

Jenna raised an eyebrow. "I like the five o'clock shadow he's sporting."

Gabe looked at Fin standing chatting at the bar, then turned to Jenna. "Yes, I rather like it too."

"He kind of reminds me of someone from the telly, but I can't think who." Jenna studied him.

Gabe didn't know what he did. What if she'd been right and he was a journalist?

Someone tapped Gabe's elbow and she swung around to find Max. "Hello."

"Great to see you here." He smiled at Jenna and Jenna sent a knowing glance at Gabe. Gabe rolled her eyes.

"Max, have you met Jenna?"

Max extended his hand.

"No, we haven't met but didn't you organise the wonderful concert?" Jenna asked.

Max nodded.

"It was brilliant and you raised a few thousand pounds, which is fantastic. Well done," Jenna said, beaming.

The singers began again and Max whispered, "Have you thought about the opera at all? I'd love to hear your comments?"

"Are you sure?" Gabe studied him. He seemed sincere.

"Yes, please. I really would."

"I'll take a look, but I won't sing."

He tried the wide-eyed look. Gabe laughed and shook her head. She turned to watch the men who had begun "Shenandoah". Her eyes met Fin's as he scanned the crowd. A smile lit up his face and a feeling she had put away ran through her. She took a few shallow breaths. This was very dangerous.

Gabe hadn't had a swim in days. Sitting on a tree stump, cradling her coffee, she looked down at the rocks below. The water was clear and among the weed swam hundreds of minnows. They moved together like an Olympic synchronised swimming team, first with the tide and then against it, covering the same area.

Climbing down to the bottom step, Gabe placed her foot on the rock below. The wind blew around her. She would need her wetsuit before long, but the water was warmer than the air at the moment. If she hesitated any longer she would never do it. Taking a shallow dive, she hit the water and kicked past the weed out into the middle. Strong strokes took her into the haven of the creek. She slowed and took time to see the trees reaching out to her. As a child, depending on her mood, they had been both welcoming and threatening. Today they were neither.

Since she'd arrived the leaves had begun to turn and the holly was covered in berries. Switching to breaststroke, she stopped when she heard a splash behind her that was far too big for a fish. Turning her head, she glimpsed another swimmer. It must be Fin. Since her father had died she had never had anyone swim in the creek with her and with each stroke she pulled harder, but he was catching up with her. Their unofficial race would come to an end soon as the water was becoming too shallow for proper swimming the further they went.

"Morning." Fin came up to her. "When I saw you dive in, I thought it seemed a good idea."

Gabe didn't reply but turned over on to her back to let the water carry her away. It was strangely intimate to be in the creek alone with Fin. The distant hum of a boat engine coming down the river provided the backbeat to the cry of a curlew and the screech of the gulls. The sky was pale blue behind the fast-moving clouds. If she focused on these things, and not on the man beside her, the world was good.

Voices carried on the wind and Gabe flipped over. A boat was about to break their solitude by turning into the creek. She pointed to the side and Fin nodded. At full throttle the powerboat approached and only slowed when the driver spotted them in the water. The raucous laughter was not followed by an apology, as it should have been. Even though it was out of season, speed restrictions should still be respected. The boat ignored Gabe and Fin and motored on.

"That was close."

Gabe nodded and maintained a slow breaststroke back towards the mouth of the creek. Being in the water with Fin was a perilous experience.

"I'm sorry I disturbed you."

Gabe turned to him. He did disturb her, but she could handle it. It was good, in a way, to feel attraction, and it was safe. He wouldn't be here for ever. Beside her, the surface of the water was covered with an armada of fallen leaves setting out to sea on the tide. She smiled, then splashed him. "Race you!"

A steady thumping noise flowed out of Gabriella's bedroom. It sounded like a beat of some sort but Jaunty wasn't sure. Gabriella must be working. She had muttered something about a zoo before she shut the door to her room after breakfast.

A sharp shower had begun and Jaunty rose to close the windows. The terrace was covered in puddles and the river and sky merged together, but if she looked east the sky was clear. She left her room and found Fin sitting in an armchair reading a book on illuminated manuscripts. He was waiting for her, Jaunty sensed, and she too was ready, but Gabriella was near. Even though Jaunty knew Gabriella would be wearing headphones the risk was too great.

"Can you help me out to the studio?"

Fin looked up from his book. "Of course." With care he marked the page and came towards her. She was unsteady on her feet now and with the path being wet he might have to carry her, but she couldn't talk to him with Gabriella so close. He took her arm and they made it to the door.

"I had better let Gabe know where we are so she doesn't worry." He smiled then dashed off to Gabriella's room.

"True." Jaunty held on to the dining table. He was a good soul. She was right to trust him. He would do as she asked and there was information that she wanted now. He would help her find it.

A man walked up to the door carrying a toolbox. "Morning. Is this Bosworgy?"

"Yes."

"Excellent. I'm here to connect the Internet."

Jaunty's eyes widened. The Internet? She opened her mouth to speak, but Gabriella came up behind her and put a hand on her shoulder.

"Wonderful. Come in out of the rain."

Jaunty took a few steps backwards. She knew what the Internet was but she didn't know why they needed it. The phone was intrusion enough. Fin took her arm and with his other hand held an umbrella above her head. It kept the rain off her, but he was drenched by the time they reached the studio. Each step was an effort for Jaunty. She sucked breath in great gulps but it didn't seem to fill her lungs any more. Time was racing away like the tide at the moment. From here she could see the mudflats and across the river the beach at Calamansac looked large. The landscape became alien during these extreme tides and this evening the water would cover the quay, erasing it from the terrain.

After they entered the studio, Fin swiftly tidied the bed and took a towel off the back of the door to dry his hair and shoulders. Jaunty hobbled to the armchair. This was not going to be comfortable, but she must be brave. She could still remember how.

Fin filled the kettle and turned it on. He would make this easy for her. She just needed to begin. It didn't require a preamble but she might. How to start?

"Is camomile tea OK?"

"Yes, thank you." He moved confidently about her things. She reached into her pocket and pulled out a key. When he handed her the mug she gave it to him.

"What's this for?"

"I need your help." Jaunty tried to breathe. Her chest tightened, but not like the other day. "I have a secret and you have guessed that already."

He nodded.

"Well, I know the truth needs to be told but —" Jaunty stopped and closed her eyes as she brought her hands together. "I have realised that it needs to be told not just to Gabriella as I had thought, but to the world."

"Yes." Fin sat on the edge of the bed.

"Promise me you will do as I ask?"

"How can I promise when I don't know if I can comply?"

Jaunty laughed. "True." She looked at the camomile tea in her mug, then back at Fin. "All I'm asking you to do is to not reveal the truth until I am dead and that you do it as soon as I die."

Fin frowned.

"It sounds mysterious but I must do this my way. In the past I thought no one needed to know and the secret could go to the grave with me, but in recent years I have come to understand that Gabriella needs to know, that it might help her in some way. And now, as the end approaches, I realise the world has a right to know the truth." She took a sip of tea then began.

"Behind the head of the bed is a concealed door to a false wall. That key opens it . . ."

The engineer departed and Gabe smiled. She wouldn't have to go out to send her work off now and life would become easier.

Fin and Jaunty were still out in the studio. Jaunty was becoming very close to Fin, and Gabe didn't want to resent it, but she did a little. For years she had been the only other person to feature in her grandmother's life, but now there was someone else. She walked into the kitchen and pulled out the ingredients for sandwiches. When had she become possessive? She hadn't been as a child. Was it all connected to one event? She ripped bits of lettuce off the head and laid it on the bread, then remembered that she hadn't buttered it. Why, after all this time, did it still shape her life? Wasn't that letting him win?

She knew that answer and didn't like it. Opening a tin of tuna, she pushed him to the back of her mind and began humming the tune from Max's score. It was stunning; somehow the music had captured the Cornish landscape with its quiet moments followed by bleak passages that portrayed the moors with such heart-breaking beauty. The lush refrain brought the wooded river valleys to her mind. Even without the words this piece of music evoked Cornwall. As the heartbroken man travelled the length of the county looking for work, the music conjured the varied landscape and in her head she heard the swift notes and saw the light dancing off the turquoise water before it fell to the drumbeat of the waves hitting Lizard Point. Desolation.

The sandwiches in front of her were far from a work of art. She must do better if she was going to entice Jaunty into eating more than a mouthful. Gabe glanced out the back door. The rain had softened but she would still get soaked on the way to the studio if she tried to carry a tray. Maybe she should just go and get them? But what if Jaunty was actually working? Not likely, but if she was happy in the studio then she should stay.

Gabe could wrap up the sandwiches and take them out — it would disguise their dull appearance for one thing. She laughed. She was deluding herself and she had become very good at doing that.

"Hi." Fin dashed through the door shaking the rain off like a dog. "You read my mind."

Gabe smiled. "How's Jaunty?"

"Good. She's nodded off in the chair so I thought I'd make some lunch and take it to her, but you beat me to it." He grinned and looked all boyish.

"Great minds or something like that." She cast him a sideways glance, loving his grin.

"Are we connected to the world now?" He looked through to the sitting room.

His broad shoulders were soaked and his shirt clung to him. She took a deep breath. "Yes."

"Did you get any work done?" He picked up a baby plum tomato and ate it.

"No, not while he was here." Gabe sighed.

"Much to do?"

"Unfortunately yes."

"Well, don't worry about Jaunty. I'll keep an eye on her."

Gabe flinched slightly at the thought, but knew she was being ridiculous. It was good to have someone around to share her worries with. She should count Fin's help as a blessing not a curse. "Thanks."

He packaged up the sandwiches and put hers on a plate, then went and grabbed his book, which he tucked under his arm.

"Get the work done and then we can take Jaunty out if the rain stops." He looked heavenward. Sunlight showed through the clouds and a rainbow crossed the river. Its end appeared to be in a yellow field surrounded by green ones.

"OK, but I'm not sure where we could take her."

"She wants to go on the river, so I thought we could row her down the creek this evening if the weather improves."

"OK, OK."

He dashed out the door and Gabe stood still, realising she was relying on him. But she mustn't. Who knew how long he would be here or even who he was.

Jaunty took a pencil off the table and a piece of paper. Each moment must be used.

I made my way to Truro where I stayed in a rooming house until Philip was born. When he was a year old, I went to Helford, where I had known such happiness, however briefly, and discovered the little cabin was for sale. The owner had died in

210

the war. I bought it immediately despite it being too remote and totally impractical for raising a small child. There was no electricity, no running water and no near neighbours.

The local population knew me only as a slightly mad war widow. That was how I came to live a remote life and began painting again. During Philip's naps I painted, and all I could see in my head and around me was water. At night I dreamt of the sea and that was what came out on to the canvas.

The rain had stopped and the clouds had parted to reveal patches of, what Jaunty knew, was ultra marine with a touch of cyan. The tide had turned and the herons made the most of the riverbank while they could access it.

I made a papoose, American Indian style, and would walk along the creek with Philip close to my heart. I loved him without reservation, although even after his birth I was no closer to knowing who was his father because he was the image of me. I prayed he was Alex's and that I had at least a part of him with me, and the rhythm of our days was long walks and me painting when he slept.

Oh, Gabriella, I was weary. It shames me now to think about it. I know I wasn't as loving as I should have been but at times there was nothing left in me. I had to survive, which meant that there was no time for self-pity or even to make friends.

But I owed it to Jean to survive. She had lost her life because of me and I had stolen her identity. I had to make something of it, something she'd be proud of. Her voice was forever in my head, telling me to add that touch of cobalt, to lighten the brush stroke or to step back from my work and actually see.

When the colour left me months ago, Jean left me. I see that now. And I am hollow.

Jaunty looked at the river. It was her conscience. It was her love. It kept her focused. She owed it to Jean. To Alex.

These early canvases I sent to Paul, fully expecting that there would be no market for them. But I was wrong. The demand for Jean's work had grown. Apparently he had told collectors that I'd been so scarred by the war and what I'd seen that I could only paint the sea. Paul was always an excellent salesman.

So my paintings sold, and sold well.

A helicopter from RNAS Culdrose flew overhead and Jaunty stood to watch it. Soon it disappeared and a motorboat towing a yacht made its way towards Gweek, the sunlight catching the bright paintwork on the hull. Jaunty sighed and began again.

And so the lie grew and I accepted that I was Jean Blythe — or, rather, I was Jaunty. In Paris another

English student had nicknamed her Jaunty because of her happy attitude. She had loved the idea of being a mystery so she called herself Jaunty, and when she was in a rush, the Jaunty became simply a J. So when I began painting again I signed my paintings with a J, mimicking her bold strokes.

Oh those carefree days in Paris!

It would have been impossible to imagine back then that I had to become the happy person that she had been. I had been very happy once but I had never had her exuberance, and now, with an empty future ahead of me, it was harder to hold on to what little I could conjure. Each day I woke and I thought of Alex and what I had lost and it was only Philip that kept me going. He was a joy and a trial and there was no one I could to turn to. I couldn't let anyone close.

Jaunty stopped. No one but her knew of the lie. Fin had guessed but he only knew that she hadn't painted those Parisian works.

It was, and is, just me who carries the truth and the lie. As each breath seems harder to take, the lie becomes heavier.

She stopped and stood. Her fingers ached. Canvases lay stacked in this, the perfect studio. When she had chosen the spot she knew the northern light would be superb, for she had lived in the cabin for two years by then. And of course, this spot held her memories of Alex.

Jaunty shifted through the paintings and sketches. There was so much. She looked up when Fin came back in.

"How is she?" She straightened.

"I've told her to finish her work so that we can take you down the creek when the weather clears and you've woken from your nap."

Jaunty chuckled. "You're wicked."

"Possibly." He handed her a sandwich. "Now, the price for my complicity is that you eat the whole sandwich and not just two bites, because I see how your lack of appetite worries her."

"I know. She has always been a worrier but it has become worse."

"Well, it's hard."

Jaunty looked at him closely. "Why did your wife leave you?"

"Just because you are sharing your secrets doesn't mean I have to reveal mine."

"True." She took a bite of her sandwich and waited.

"Patricia left me because she was in love with someone else and had been for a long time." He walked to the window. "I should have seen it. I should have seen it before we were married but we were business partners and lovers and it all seemed to work." He laughed, but with no pleasure. A self-deprecating smile remained on his lips. "It's funny how we see only what we want to."

"How long were you married?"

"Ten years." He turned around. "I should have noticed something was wrong." He stopped.

"You don't need to say more. I can fill in the blanks."

His full mouth twisted into a grimace. "Yes, the less said the better. Now, what do you want me to do about all these paintings?"

Jaunty watched his glance rest on the second-to-last portrait she had painted of Gabriella. Although she could no longer see the colour, in her mind she knew that the glory of Gabriella's hair was displayed against the backdrop of the dense woodland on the opposite side of the creek. The myriad of greens balanced the burnished glory of that hair but the light in her granddaughter's eyes had vanished now. No longer did hope visit them. They were now focused but not happy.

"She's beautiful." He picked up the canvas and put it on the easel.

"Yes, she is such a mix of the past, but the most startling feature is her eyes. They are special."

"Incredibly. I've never seen any eyes like them and with her hair it is such a striking mix."

Jaunty sighed. Dietrich had been blond and Gabe's eyes were almost identical to his, but the addition of her red hair brought out the depth of their colour.

Fin finished his sandwich and washed his hands in the sink. "I think I had better put these paintings away if you really don't want her to see them now."

Jaunty nodded. There was so much there. She had forgotten how much she had painted. "Will these have any value when the truth is out?"

215

Fin carefully picked up some watercolours. "Yes, I think quite a bit, but it's hard to say." He looked at her. "You have only told me part of the story and the rest of it might be the part that impacts the value of your work, as you know."

Jaunty nodded, and knew she was right to trust him.

CHAPTER
THIRTEEN

With the composition safely on its way, Gabe took out Max's opera. He expected some sort of response from her and she had dreamt of the lovers and their plight last night. The imagery was so clear in her mind. The tale was perfect for an opera, love thwarted, an old crone, magic and myth entwined. Max had enlarged the story with the baritone, the parentally approved suitor, trying his utmost to woo the maiden with comic results.

The call of an egret broke into her thoughts. That was what was missing from the score! He'd captured so much of Cornwall in the music, but he had neglected the birdsong that was the soundtrack of everyday life. Now a stonechat was singing.

Her fingers ran over the keyboard before she began picking out notes that mimicked the birds. Then she introduced them to the beach scenes where the maiden looks out to sea, longing for her lover. Yes, it definitely added a layer of resonance to the music. She played it again and recorded it, and then, standing up, she sang the new arrangement. It was better, but she longed for feedback from the great soprano, Georgina Piper, whom she had last worked with. Gabe knew that she wasn't using her voice fully, that it lacked depth. She paced the room. The only way to improve was to train and to perform so she should expect nothing else. She couldn't do it alone and she wouldn't perform because if she moved into that world again *he* would be there.

Why was she worried about her singing anyway? What did it matter if she reached her potential or not? There was no point in striving to be the best if you had an audience of one. She put the score and her notes away.

"Hello." There was a tap at the studio door before it opened and Max stepped inside, talking. "Fin, I wanted to let you know I figured out where I'd seen Gabriella before. It was at the World Opera competition. She sang 'Vissi d'arte' in the final and she was spellbinding. She won. But I did a little digging and it appears she hasn't sung since." He stopped chatting when he didn't see Fin.

"Did your digging say why?" Jaunty noted the surprise on his face.

"I'm so sorry. I thought Fin was here."

"I am." Fin rose from his knees.

"Oh." Max looked between them. "I'm sorry about investigating your granddaughter's career."

"No need to apologise; I'd like to know what you've found out." Now Jaunty remembered. There had been an excellent write-up in the *Telegraph* regarding the win.

Fin pointed to the kettle. Max nodded and perched opposite Jaunty on the stool. "Unfortunately I found nothing else. The competition should have been the start to her career, but . . ." He shrugged.

"So there was nothing you found out?" Jaunty studied Max. He was what she would call a snazzy dresser with his brocade waistcoats and polished brogues.

Max looked at Fin and Fin nodded. "There were rumours about something happening after the performance."

"What?"

"Well, one of the judges was known to prey on women."

"And?" Jaunty could see he knew more than he was saying.

Max looked to Fin again.

"What happened?" Jaunty clenched the arms of the chair.

"I don't know."

Jaunty sat forward. "Was she attacked?"

Max shrugged again.

Fin walked to the window and looked out. Jaunty thrust herself out of the chair. Fin came to help her but she pushed him away. The river was still, or appeared so, yet Jaunty knew the changes were always happening below the surface. She didn't know why Gabriella had never told her about what had happened, why she'd buried whatever it was.

"You know it's not too late for Gabriella to sing again." Max spoke softly.

Jaunty saw her own reflection in the glass. "I know that with work it could happen. But she has lost years of training." She shook her head. "She sings every day but it's not the same, and who knows if she could or would ever step on a stage again." Jaunty had held the secret too long. She had left it too late to help her granddaughter.

Fin carried Jaunty down to the quay. The sun was low in the sky and a gentle breeze stirred the water. Gabe steadied the boat as Fin helped Jaunty to get in. Despite careful handling, Jaunty nearly fell and Gabe wondered why they were doing this. However, the smile on Jaunty's face spoke of happiness, so Gabe didn't say anything, just settled her grandmother on to the cushion she had brought for that purpose.

Fin untied the boat and began to row. The tide was high and the low-slung branches that lined the creek rested in the calm waters. Jaunty was alert, watching everything, then suddenly she stilled and stayed looking at the right-hand side. Gabe couldn't read her expression and she stared in the direction of Jaunty's glance, but saw nothing apart from the trees. The creek was quiet except for the splashing of the oars and the calm surface mirrored the evening sky above.

Gabe turned and looked in front of the boat. A thin mist shrouded the surface of the water ahead and a shiver ran up Gabe's spine as the banks reached towards each other and trees almost touched. The character of the creek transformed. Any sense of civilisation had disappeared with the thickening mist. Jaunty's expression altered and years seemed to disappear from her face.

Fin stopped rowing and let the momentum take them along. He pulled out a basket from under his seat and produced a bottle of champagne and some plastic flutes. The pop echoed around them and Gabe frowned.

He handed the first glass to Jaunty. "Happy Birthday." Gabe couldn't see his face, but his deep voice carried clearly on the dense air. He turned and handed a glass to her, then smiled. How had she forgotten it was Jaunty's birthday? She had been too wrapped up in her own thoughts.

"Thanks." Gabe raised her glass. "Here's to you, Jaunty." Fin placed a leg over the seat so that he could see both of them. He took a sip and then pulled a loaf cake out of the basket. "Lemon drizzle seems appropriate considering the changeable weather conditions." He glanced towards the river. A bolster fog had moved in and erased the view. They were alone and the world felt very far away. Even the birds had stopped and an odd silence filled the air.

"Thank you. Birthdays at my age are not something you really want to remember, but if you are going to, this is perfect." Jaunty smiled and lifted her glass. As she waved her empty hand, Gabe noted how bent the fingers were, as though she was holding a brush.

"I love this creek." Jaunty's eyes filled with tears. Gabe watched her compose her face, trying not to show emotion, but it wasn't working. Her grandmother reached for the necklace she always wore. It was a long chain that held a ring by her heart. Gabe assumed it was her wedding ring. She'd once asked but Jaunty had never really answered her. Gabe couldn't remember

221

now what she'd said, something like "It was a promise." Yes, those were her words.

"Shall we sing?" Fin looked to Gabe and held a knife above the cake.

Gabe could hear a different question in his voice. It was more, will *you* sing? Of course she would sing happy birthday to her grandmother. She had not become that precious.

Gabe began and Fin's solid baritone followed her lead. The tears that had been pooling in Jaunty's eyes fell down her face. She clapped her hand as best as she could with her cupped fingers. "May I ask for you to sing the song your father loved, the Scottish ballad 'Ailein Duinn'?"

Gabe looked at her grandmother and could see the longing on her face. How could she refuse? She nodded and took a sip of the champagne. She closed her eyes and sang.

How sorrowful I am
Early in the morning rising
Ò hi, I would go with thee
Hi ri bhò hò ru bhi
Hi ri bhò hò rinn o ho
Brown-haired Alan, *ò hi*, I would go with thee

If it is thy pillow the sand
If it is thy bed the seaweed
Ò hi, I would go with thee
Hi ri bhò hò ru bhi

Hi ri bhò hò rinn o ho
Brown-haired Alan, *ò hi*, I would go with thee

If it is the fish thy candles bright
If it the seals thy watchmen
Ò hi, I would go with thee
Hi ri bhò hò ru bhi
Hi ri bhò hò rinn o ho
Brown-haired Alan, *ò hi*, I would go with thee

I would drink, though all would abhor it
Of thy heart's blood after thy drowning
Ò hi, I would go with thee
Hi ri bhò hò ru bhi
Hi ri bhò hò rinn o ho
Brown-haired Alan, *ò hi*, I would go with thee

The last note hung on the mist and in the distance the sound of farm machinery carried from the shore. Jaunty sighed and shivered at the same time. A soft rain had begun to fall. Fin looked directly into Gabe's eyes before she could put away the emotion the song had stirred. A look of understanding flashed across his face and then, without a word, Fin began to row back to the quay.

Jaunty was up and dressed when Gabe came out of her room at seven. Gabe blinked when she saw her grandmother putting yoghurt into a bowl.

"Good morning."

"Indeed it is." Jaunty smiled. "Can I do one for you?"

"Not awake enough to eat yet." Gabe yawned.

Jaunty sat down. "Ah, but I heard you singing."

"Just exercises."

"Thank you for yesterday."

"No problem." But of course it was. Her heart had opened up and she'd looked at Fin before she closed it. That was the difficulty. She could not sing without making herself vulnerable. Well, that wasn't quite true. She could sing "Happy Birthday" or "We Wish You a Merry Christmas", but not truly sing. For that she had to open her heart, and he had seen. He had touched her arm but didn't say anything as he left last night and she could still feel his hand.

She opened the back door and came face to face with him.

"Morning." His hair was askew as if he'd just run his fingers through it and there was a shadow of stubble across his face, which just served to highlight the good bone structure. She must not have closed her heart again totally last night, for it raced inside her.

"Yes."

"May I use your shower?" He looked at the towel thrown over his arm. His shirt wasn't buttoned and she stared at his chest before blushing and turning away.

"Sure." Two large steps took her to the fridge where she dug inside to find the grapefruit juice. When she stood up he had disappeared, but she could hear him singing in the shower. It was "O Sole Mio" and Jaunty caught her glance. They both laughed.

"It's best he never seeks a career on the stage."

"Quite." She took a sip of the juice and frowned when the sour taste hit the sides of her tongue. "I'll just dash out and pick up my music on the piano while he's here."

The dew was heavy and the rising sun caught the beads of moisture. The wind came from the north, bringing a distinct chill but also clearer skies. There was a little fog lingering on the river which would quickly burn off as the sun rose. Gabe's mood lifted.

Inside the studio she stood in front of the piano. Her fingers reached out to the keys. Her hand had healed almost totally now. Checking that she was still alone, she sat down and played Max's music and then began to sing, this time letting the emotion of the piece build fully in her. Her voice opened as it hadn't in years, and when the song finished she found she had stood at some point, knocking back the stool.

Fin stood in the doorway wrapped in nothing but a towel. "I didn't want to disturb you."

"Sorry." Gabe righted the stool and collected the sheets of music.

"Apology not required. In fact, I'd love to ask for more." He stepped fully into the studio, close enough to her that she could see the goosebumps on his arms. She didn't dare look at anything but his arms. Even letting her eyes stray to his throat was playing havoc with her equilibrium. She felt raw and exposed from singing and yet high at the same time. Seeing a near-naked Fin wasn't helping.

225

She glanced down and saw a large expanse of thigh. Colour rushed to her face, which was ridiculous. She was a grown woman. As she walked past him, she looked up and caught his glance. Her feet refused to go any further and Fin didn't move. She could see flecks of green in his blue eyes and a damp curl fell on his forehead. His mouth formed a half smile.

Gabe finally managed to find her voice. "I'd better go and check on Jaunty."

"Yes, she was finishing her breakfast and enjoying listening to you in the distance," he said. "She loves hearing you sing."

"She has always loved music."

"You can tell. Have you thought about singing her Max's work? Maybe take her to Manaccan."

Gabe chewed her lip. Jaunty might really enjoy the outing. She'd coped well with last night's trip and seemed so much brighter for it this morning. "It's worth considering."

"Good." His glance met hers and she couldn't move. "I'm full of good ideas." His mouth lifted into an enigmatic smile. Gabe tore her glance away from his mouth and it fell on to his bare chest, then down to where the towel sat very low on his hips. She swallowed then fled down the path, thinking she must find him a larger towel.

Jaunty looked at Fin and at Gabe. Something had changed and the atmosphere around the table almost sizzled.

226

"I've spoken to Max and he says to come at any time." Fin passed Gabriella the salad.

Gabriella turned to her grandmother. "Jaunty, would you like to come to Manaccan to Max's to hear me sing?"

Jaunty dropped her fork, then quickly picked it up, hoping her mouth wasn't hanging open. Leave Bosworgy? It had been so long since she had even gone as far as the supermarket. She looked around the room knowing she would be leaving it for ever soon.

"Maybe it would be too much." Gabriella exchanged glances with Fin.

If she didn't go now then Gabriella would find a way not to go. "I would love to," she said firmly.

Gabriella looked at her closely. "Are you sure?"

Jaunty wondered if she was. She was safe here, but she must teach her granddaughter that being safe wasn't everything. "Yes. I would like to."

Gabriella nodded. "OK, after lunch then."

"I'll let him know." Fin went to the phone in the kitchen.

Jaunty studied her granddaughter. Her hair was not pulled back quite so tightly and a stray strand had escaped, framing her oval face. She didn't look as gaunt as she had done, and her glance kept darting to Fin when she thought she wasn't being watched. This was all good, but Jaunty wanted to know what had changed her mind about singing. This was a seismic shift. Last night when she'd sung it was if an angel had come from heaven. The voice wasn't as rich as it should be, but then singing in a foggy creek was not exactly ideal.

Jaunty remembered how her mother complained about various conditions affecting her voice.

Jaunty stood and Gabriella rushed to her side. "I'm fine. I just need the loo, which I can manage on my own."

Gabriella stepped away. "Have you finished eating?"

Jaunty turned. "Yes."

"Tea or coffee?"

"No, thank you. I'll be ready to go when you are." Jaunty made her way into her room. She hadn't heard Gabe sing properly in too many years and she had never seen her on stage. A whole life wasted in fear that someone would discover her secret, and now she was going to tell everyone. Had the secrecy been worth it?

Jaunty gasped as she walked through the door to Max's sitting room. Above the sofa hung a large canvas she had painted twenty years ago. It was all in yellows. *Philip and Gabriella, summer.* She had never seen her paintings anywhere else but her own domain. The room swayed a bit, but Fin took her elbow and steadied her. He whispered in her ear, "I own several of your paintings. Sadly, they are in storage at the moment."

She turned to him.

He leaned closer to her. "No, I didn't let the ex take them."

Jaunty frowned. Seeing her work on someone's walls shouldn't surprise her. After all, she had been selling paintings for years. The J was painted in burnt umber. *J. Jean.* Jaunty blacked out for a second.

Fin guided her by the elbow to the big sofa under her work and Jaunty turned her head for one last look.

"Can I get you anything?" Max asked Jaunty as he led Gabriella to the piano.

"No, thank you. Please forget I'm here." She turned to Fin, who was sitting next to her.

"Same here." Fin glanced quickly at Gabriella then back to Jaunty.

Max waved his hand. "Make yourself at home."

Fin nodded.

Jaunty watched her granddaughter. The vitality that had shown in her eyes this morning had vanished. Another strand of hair had fallen down, softening the features but not hiding her fear. Even from this distance Jaunty could see the small pupils.

Max sat down at the piano. "I would just love to hear you sing this first section, to let me see how you have interpreted it. Is that OK?"

"Could we do a warm-up first?"

"Of course! I'm sorry I'm so eager. I had the youth choir I'm working with singing parts last night, but I'm just desperate to hear *you* sing it."

Gabriella's mouth lifted into a half smile then she swallowed. Jaunty noted her hands were clasped tight.

Max ran through some scales to flex his fingers then hit a note when Gabe indicated. She worked through some vowels. Her voice grew with each repetition.

Max shifted through some music. "How about Hahn's 'À Chloris'?"

"Good."

Max began to play and Gabriella sang. Jaunty closed her eyes. She knew the song well. Her mother used to sing it all the time.

Arpeggios . . .
Dietrich's long fingers run across the keys.
Mother looks to him and he begins.
Bright hot sun reflects off the lake, bouncing on to the ceiling. A fly circles my head and Dietrich's shoulders flex. He's so handsome. His mother sits beside me with her wrist in a bandage.
Mother finishes. The last note fades.
"You will go far, Dietrich. The world will be yours." My mother kisses the top of his head as if he is a toddler and not fifteen.
Dietrich.

"That was perfect, Gabe." Max shuffled some papers.

"I wouldn't go that far. Where are we starting?" Gabriella's speaking voice had dropped.

Max pointed. "If we begin here where Nancy has been parted from William and then sing straight through to here?"

"Are you sure?"

"Yes."

Max played and Jaunty let the new music carry her away. She didn't want to look backwards, but the sadness in the opening movement chipped away at her reserve. Gabriella sang of lost love and her voice wrapped itself around Jaunty's heart. Jaunty closed her eyes.

Alex's warmth seeps into me. His body meets mine from shoulder to ankle. The stars sparkle.

"I love you." He kisses me and I feel desire but sleep is calling me. Alex holds my hand.

Jaunty grabbed her heart and fell on to Fin.

Part Two
Gabriella

Monday for danger,
Tuesday kiss a stranger,
Wednesday for a letter,
Thursday for something better,
Friday for sorrow,
Saturday see your lover tomorrow.
Sneeze on Sunday morning fasting,
Enjoy your true love for everlasting.

CHAPTER
FOURTEEN

Gabe paced the waiting room. They'd been there an hour and Fin watched her from the far side of the room. He was still clutching the white plastic cup from the vending machine and Gabe wondered why waiting rooms in hospitals had to be so dreary.

Fin's phone rang and he stood and stepped outside. She studied him through the glass door. The sun shone, but that cold north wind blew and it pushed his curls to one side. He'd been a rock. When Jaunty had collapsed he'd been on the phone to emergency services in seconds. His quick actions with CPR had kept Jaunty alive while they waited for an ambulance.

When Fin walked in a doctor came with him.

"Miss Blythe?" The doctor looked at her.

Gabe stood. "Yes."

"Your grandmother is in a coma."

Gabe nodded.

"She has also had a stroke."

She held her hands together, trying to read between the lines. "What does it mean?"

"They may not be connected. She had a minor heart attack last week and she is also diabetic; her blood sugar had dropped too low and we are correcting this, but thus far it has had no effect. Did she hit her head or suffer any other trauma recently?"

She shook her head. "I don't think so."

Fin coughed quietly, then said, "I don't know if this is important but she told me she had stopped seeing colour a year ago. I looked it up and it said a possible cause could be head injury."

Gabe frowned, wondering what else Jaunty had told him that she hadn't told her.

The doctor said, "Perhaps. It's possible that she may have had a minor heart attack a while ago and blacked out, hit her head but did nothing about it."

Gabe sighed. That sounded so like Jaunty, never drawing attention to herself.

"It could be that a blood clot had formed and it moved to the brain. At this point it is all guesswork." He paused. "I suggest you head home. She is stable for the moment and we'll call if anything changes."

"May I see her first?" Gabe swallowed. She wasn't ready for this. There was so much that she hadn't said or done.

"Of course. Follow me."

Gabe turned to Fin. He held out his hand. She took it and they walked down the corridor to ICU.

"Would you like me to drive?" Fin asked as they came to the car.

Gabe looked at him. She was wrung out so it would be wise to let him drive. "I'm not sure I want to go, Fin. What if she wakes?"

238

"They'll call. And it only takes fifty minutes to get here."

"True." Gabe looked at her watch. It was already seven in the evening. She opened the door and slid into the passenger seat.

"Don't blame yourself." Fin adjusted the rear-view mirror.

"If only we hadn't taken her to Max's. Maybe it was all too much." Gabe stared at her hands.

"Nonsense. She loved it. I could see it on her face."

Gabe turned to him. "Are you sure?"

"She was very happy." He took his hand off the wheel and touched hers.

"If you say so." Gabe looked out the window at the darkness. The only lights were those of the oncoming traffic.

Fin touched her hand again. "I do. Your singing gave her tremendous pleasure. You should make a recording that they could play to her."

Gabe frowned. "Really?"

"Yes. It could help her recovery."

Closing her eyes, Gabe tried not to think about the inevitable. Even if Jaunty woke up she might not be fit enough to come home. What would they do? There was no way that Jaunty would go into a nursing home. Could Gabe take care of her? She would have to get help, which meant reworking finances. She rubbed her temples.

Fin switched on the radio and a violin concerto by Mozart came on. Gabe began humming, then woke with a start when the engine was switched off.

"Sorry to wake you."

"Well, you couldn't leave me here in the car all night."

"True. Would you like company or would you like some time alone?"

Gabe paused before she shut the car door. The cabin sat in darkness and suddenly she wondered how Jaunty had lived here on her own for all those years.

"Company, if you don't mind."

"It will be a pleasure."

"Thanks." Gabe led the way down the path. She needed to install some security lights that would switch on when you came past. She nearly lost her footing but Fin caught her before her feet went from under her. He was like her guardian angel at the moment, and boy did she need one.

At the door she fumbled for the key and felt foolish as tears appeared. If she was going to cry it should have been at the hospital, not here, not now that she was home. Fin's breath caressed her neck and she wanted to lean back against him, let him take the strain, because suddenly she didn't feel up to it.

Unbelievably tired of fighting, she knew she needed to rely on someone else, but that was more frightening than relying on herself. She brushed her tears away with the back of her hand and fitted the key into the lock.

Gabe woke to the sound of someone in the house. She sat up, grabbed her robe and rushed out of the bedroom to find it was only Fin making coffee.

"Did I wake you?"

240

Gabe's heart felt like it was about to escape from her chest. "Yes."

"Sorry. Can I make it up with a coffee?" He smiled and made an attempt at Max's puppy look.

Gabe nodded, not sure she could speak. After a bowl of soup and a whisky she had gone to bed leaving Fin sitting and reading. It should have made her feel unsafe, but it had had the opposite effect — and now she was happy to see him. She had never thought she would feel that way again.

"I rang the hospital and there's no change. Jaunty is stable so they are moving her to another ward." Fin handed her a mug. It was what she should have been doing, not sleeping. A glance at the clock on the wall told her it was already nine thirty. She'd slept for twelve hours.

Gabe walked through to the sitting-room window. A soft veil of rain fell, muting the autumn colours and softening the edges on everything outside. She noted the pillow and blankets folded up on the sofa and turned to Fin.

"I slept in here last night in case you needed me."

Needed him? Looking at the stubble on his face, the full mouth and bedroom eyes she *wanted* him. The realisation that she was allowing herself to feel this caused the hair on her arms to stand up. Her armour had been broken and she must tread very carefully because he would be gone shortly. He couldn't stay here for ever. It was fine for now because she did need him, but that would pass, as would her wanting him. That was normal. He was good-looking and helpful, a winning combination, but she knew nothing about him. She didn't even know what he did.

"Fin?"

"Yes." He looked up from his book.

"What do you do?"

He gave her a lopsided smile. "A funny time to ask."

"Yes, I meant to but never got around to it." She felt foolish she hadn't found out more about him before.

He put his book down. "I'm an art historian of sorts."

Fin's phone rang. "Hello." He turned from her and walked out of the back door where the reception was better. Gabe was surprised it rang in the cabin. The wind must have changed. She topped up her mug and looked in the fridge. She would need to shop after she visited Jaunty, and Fin's suggestion of making a disc of music for her grandmother might not be a bad idea.

Putting her coffee down, Gabe walked into Jaunty's room and went to the old record player. Beside it was a basket holding all Jaunty's beloved albums. They were almost entirely opera, with the exception of a few collections of piano concertos. Flipping through them, Gabe took a trip through memory lane. This all used to be in the studio and Jaunty would listen while she painted. She would hum but never sing.

"Sorry about that. Shall I make an omelette?"

Gabe jumped. "That would be lovely." She selected what she was sure was Jaunty's favourite, a collection of arias by Maria Lucia, and put it on. It began with "Habanera" from *Carmen*. Carmen was a role that Gabe had longed to play and had never done so. She wouldn't touch it now. As she walked through the bedroom she put her hands on her hips and lip-synced the words. As soon as she reached the sitting room where she could possibly be seen she dropped her hands and Carmen's attitude.

Fin was grimacing as he mixed the eggs when Gabe came up to him. "Are you OK?"

He shrugged. "Just the ex-wife."

"Problem?"

"Money. Always money. It always has been." He sliced a tomato. "When we were students she was forever struggling with her overdraft and when we were married I never let her near the finances. Since the divorce she has to do it and she's made a mess of it." He put the tomatoes in the pan with the cheese. "Her partner is no better and it appears that the business is already in trouble in just the six months that she's had it on her own."

"This is the business you began together?"

"Yes." He expelled a sound that was half sigh, half laugh. "By the end of the year the business will be bankrupt."

"And this worries you?"

"No. What bothers me is that she still thinks she can come to me for help." He turned the cooker off.

Gabe wondered what had happened. He was helpful and kind; the way he turned the omelette out on to plates was skilful; the man could cook — what was not to like?

"Fin?" Gabe paused, wondering how to ask and even if she should. It was none of her business. "Why did you divorce? Was it money?"

"If only." He shook his head and turned from her. His shoulders slumped. "Money I can deal with, but betrayal was a lot harder to take." He handed plates to her. She placed them on the table and poured him a glass of wine, longing to know what the betrayal was. As she gave him the glass the pain in his eyes was obvious. In the time he'd been with them he had never revealed so much of himself as right now.

"I suppose it shouldn't hurt and in a way it doesn't any more, but Patricia left me for her best friend, Joanne." He gave a bitter laugh. "It wasn't that she left me for a woman that hurt, really. It was that the affair with Joanne had been going on the whole time I'd known her."

Gabe put her hand on his arm, trying to imagine what that sort of betrayal felt like, and she couldn't. "I'm sorry."

He laughed. "Yes, me too for the wasted years."

Looking at the self-deprecating grin on Fin's face, Gabe understood too well about wasted years.

After a couple of hours sitting at Jaunty's bedside, Gabe yawned. There was nothing she could do but watch the machines that monitored the state of Jaunty's tenuous hold on life. Having mindlessly chatted away about nothing in particular, she felt so helpless. The nurses were lovely and had said that talking to Jaunty would be good, so she had. Now Gabe sang. She sang the Scottish ballad that Jaunty loved and she sang a lullaby. Her grandmother appeared to breathe easier and she could have sworn she felt her hand squeeze gently.

However, Gabe noticed the nurses pausing to listen by the door of the ward and the visitor for the other patient in the room was in tears.

"That was so beautiful, my dear. So beautiful." The woman blew her nose. "She'll love that. You know, you should be on the stage with your gift. You have the voice of an angel."

"Thank you," Gabe said, then she shuffled out past the nurses who were all smiling at her. "If I brought in a CD of music and a small player could it be played quietly for my grandmother?"

"What a lovely thought. Would it be of you singing to her?" the staff nurse asked.

Gabe nodded.

"Such a wonderful idea! I'll just check with my manager but I don't see a problem."

When Gabe walked out into the grey afternoon, it was only four, but with the heavy cloud cover it felt much later. She called the number Fin had given her and arranged to meet him at the superstore. He had come in to Truro with her, but after a quick visit with Jaunty he had headed off to the library to do some research, he said, which seemed odd, but what did she know about him or what he did?

She had a full basket and was staring at the meat section when she looked up to find Fin coming towards her with a sparkle in his eyes. It took a second before she could find her voice. "A good day?"

He held out his hand to take the basket from her. "Yes." He peered in it. "What are we having for dinner?"

"Don't know." All she had been thinking about was what songs to record for Jaunty. When she'd sung, Gabe could have sworn she had felt Jaunty's hand move in hers.

"I'll cook tonight," he said. "How does a chicken and mushroom risotto sound?"

"Divine." Gabe looked up at him.

"Good, why don't you grab a cup of tea in the café and let me sort the shopping." He gave her a gentle nudge in the right direction and disappeared down another aisle. Gabe thought he might be too good to be true, but right now she wasn't complaining.

In the café, Gabe stood beside the counter and stared at the takeaway cup, trying to decide if she wanted or needed to put sugar into it. Her mind was all over the place. She needed to make the recording for Jaunty so that the nurses could play it to her quietly when Gabe wasn't there. Anything that could reach her grandmother was to the good.

Fin walked through the door into the café and Gabe's heart skipped a beat. His face lit up with a smile and she reminded herself that she was not in the market for a relationship. But that was not what her body was saying. Although she had imposed famine conditions on it for years, it was more than ready to come out and feast. Instead of feasting, she made herself look out of the window at the sudden sun that had appeared rather than watching him.

"A glorious end to the day." Fin was beside her and she jumped.

"It's mostly been a beautiful October so far." Gabe turned from the window and looked at the man beside her.

"Shall we sit down?" Fin waved a file that he held in his hand in the direction of the tables and chairs.

"Why not?" She walked to an empty table and then noticed that Fin hadn't joined her. He was talking to a man who had just walked in the door. The man looked vaguely familiar and Gabe wondered where she had seen him before, but she couldn't place him.

Fin came over with the man.

"Gabe, let me introduce you to an old friend — Sam Marks. He was down here on holiday when his wife's appendix burst."

"Is she OK?" Gabe asked.

"Doing well, thanks to some fantastic care, so I've come to do a bit of shopping. Fin tells me your grandmother's in hospital too. What's wrong with her?"

"She's had a stroke." Gabe was careful not to say Jaunty's name. If people were interested in art at all then they knew of her. She glanced at her watch. "In fact, I'll dash off and have another few minutes with her, if you'll excuse me." She looked back before she went through the door and saw they had occupied the table she'd left, their heads together as if they were sharing a secret.

Gabe dialled Max's number. She wasn't sure about asking for help but it would be quicker if Max would accompany her for Jaunty's recording. "Hi, Max?"

"Gabriella! How's Jaunty?"

"Stable, and that's why I'm calling. I need to ask a favour."

"Ask away."

"The other day Fin suggested I make a recording so that they can play it to her." Gabe took a big breath. "Well, today I sang to her and I think her hand moved in mine."

"Wonderful. I'm happy to help."

"Great. By any chance are you free tonight?"

"Yes. I'll come round in about a half-hour. Does that work?"

"Yes." She looked to Fin. He was wearing Jaunty's black and white striped apron and creating the most divine smells with garlic and onion.

Fin waved to get her attention. "Ask him for dinner."

"I heard that. And yes."

Gabe smiled as she put down the phone, but then her chest tightened as the reality of what she had decided to do hit her.

Fin came up to her. "It will be wonderful." He placed a hand on her shoulder and looked in her eyes. "She'll love it."

Gabe swallowed. These past four years she had done everything to become invisible and now she was destroying it all. However, if it helped Jaunty she would do it.

"Thanks. I think I'm going to have a look through Jaunty's records again for more ideas." She took a step back so that his hand fell away and immediately regretted it, wanting his touch again. "Unless you need help." She risked a glance at Fin's face.

He held out his hands and puffed out his chest. "Don't think I'm up to the job?" He grinned.

"Well, I'll see how you manage tonight." She laughed.

"Ye of little faith."

Gabe grinned as she went into Jaunty's room feeling light-headed. She'd been flirting. *He'd* been flirting. This felt very strange. She was out of her depth.

Sitting cross-legged on the floor, she flipped through the albums and put on a recording of Maria Lucia singing the part of Violetta from Verdi's *La Traviata*. Tucked inside the sleeve was a newspaper cutting from the 1960s, regarding the rerelease of Maria's arias. Gabe scanned the yellowed paper and felt a lump in her throat. It was such a sad story. She had died of complications following a battle with pneumonia. It said she had lost the will to live following the death of her only child and of her husband during the war. A draught blew in from the window and Gabe shivered. She heard the sound of the gravel on the track. Max must be here, and early too. She picked out the album mentioned in the cutting and put the rest of the records in a neat pile, then she stood and found Max standing in the bedroom door.

"Maria Lucia?" He smiled.

"Yes. Jaunty has the full collection from what I can tell."

Max tilted his head to one side. "Yours is a sort of similar voice. Your training is very different but there is a quality of tone, I think."

Gabe smiled. "That is a big stretch of imagination, but if it's meant to put your soprano at ease it just might work."

"Excellent." He stepped back from the door. "So tell me what you're going to sing and what we are using to record you while we lay the table." Gabe followed him out of Jaunty's room, wondering if she could really do this.

Lying in bed, exhausted but unable to sleep, Gabe rolled over again. It was now approaching two and they had finished recording about half past midnight. Despite feeling like a wrung-out dishcloth, with eyes that were burning, her mind wouldn't calm down. The music had stirred her too much. There was no sense in fighting it any longer. She might as well get up and have a cup of herbal tea.

Once she was out of bed, she made her way to the kitchen and switched on the kettle, then stopped when she realised the idea of hot chocolate appealed more. She was reaching for the tin when she heard Fin's voice and nearly dropped it on the floor. She'd forgotten that he was staying on the sofa.

"Enough!"

Gabe crept over to the sofa and peered at him. He was sound asleep but arguing with someone.

"Verdi." He turned over and the pillow came out from under his head and he rolled off the sofa and landed with a thump.

Gabe raced into the kitchen and put the milk on. She didn't want him to find her watching him while he slept. She would be mortified if someone watched her when she was having her nightmares. Her heart went out to him.

"So I'm not the only one who isn't sleeping well."

Gabe turned to him. He was dressed only in his boxers — and she wasn't sure how his wife could have preferred anyone but him. She didn't know where to look. "Hot chocolate?"

He rubbed his chin. "Perfect."

"Won't be a minute." Gabe turned back to the hob. She'd been staring. But it was OK to find him so attractive. Because he was. She hadn't had these feelings in years and now there was a gorgeous, mostly naked, man standing less than a foot away. She wanted to turn around and kiss him. He was attractive, more than attractive. OK, who was she fooling? He was sex on legs and she was way out of practice.

"There's quite a draught coming in through the back door." He walked over to it, checking it was fully shut. Gabe sneaked a peek but then turned away quickly when he walked back to the sitting room. Gabe took a calming breath. This was fine. It was perfectly normal to feel attraction. She was thirty, but she just wished her hormones hadn't woken up so violently. She didn't react this way with Max, who was just as good-looking, but there was something in Fin's eyes and that full mouth . . . She swallowed and took the milk off the heat.

She carried the mugs into the sitting room. Fin had thrown on a V-neck cashmere sweater and disappointment swamped her. Her eyes travelled to his thighs. She was behaving like someone starved, feasting on the view of all his beautiful flesh. She handed him a mug and sat on the chair opposite. Sitting next to him, on the sofa with his blankets bunched, would have been too much.

"What was keeping you awake? Was I talking?" He raised an eyebrow.

Gabe smiled. "You were talking, but I didn't hear that until I was in the kitchen."

He rolled his eyes. "I hate to think what I was saying." He blew on the surface of his cocoa.

"Oh, nothing too revealing." Gabe kept a straight face. "Or too compromising."

"Oh, do tell." He grinned.

"No, I think I'll keep it to myself."

"Tease."

Gabe looked into her mug and felt the blood drain from her face.

"Are you OK?" Fin spoke quietly.

She nodded. He hadn't meant anything by it. She must let go. Looking up, she pointed to his upper lip and laughed. He had a chocolate moustache. Fin licked it off and Gabe closed her eyes as she took a sip. The combination of chocolate and Fin was almost too much. She had to pull herself together. Maybe she needed to get out more after all, if one scantily clad male with a kissable mouth reduced her to a mass of desire.

"What woke you?" Fin put his mug down.

"Wasn't a case of waking but of never sleeping." Gabe turned the mug in her hands. "I think singing stirred up too many emotions that couldn't be shut down easily." She looked up at him. "As you gathered, I haven't sung many of these pieces in a long time."

"May I ask why?"

Gabe sat upright in the chair then pulled her legs under her. May he ask why? She looked at him and something inside went click. Jaunty liked him. Gabe liked him. She swallowed then said, "It's a long story."

"To stop such a talented artist it must be."

A rueful smile crossed Gabe's face. "I'll try to make it as short as possible, if I can." She stopped. Her stomach clenched in spasms. "After a competition, a big one, there was a party where much alcohol was consumed." She frowned, struggling to find the words. "I was being hailed as the next big thing and I was walking on air, but I realised that I wanted to go to the hotel. I needed to be away from so many people, to let it all sink in." Gabe closed her eyes. She could do this. "One of the judges offered to walk me back because it was about two in the morning, and I agreed." She thought about the conversation. They had spoken about how well it had gone and the future. He had taken her hand and she had thought nothing of it. When he asked her to his room for a drink she should have said no but her ambition overruled her sense and the warnings she'd received. Even now she still felt it was her fault, despite what the counsellor had said. If she hadn't said yes . . . "When we reached the hotel the bar was shut so he invited me to his room for a nightcap." Gabe swallowed. "I said yes. I didn't think I could say no to him because he was one of the most renowned opera critics in the world. One good word and my career would be made." Gabe's throat constricted. "He asked me to sing for him, and when I came to the end of the song . . ." Gabe took a deep breath. "He raped me."

Even now Gabe wasn't sure what haunted her most, the rape or living through being photographed, questioned and examined afterwards. No, she thought now, it was the guilt. The guilt that she had gone to his room. The guilt that she did nothing and he walked away to do what he'd done to her to others.

Fin rose and came over to her. He placed his hand on hers. "Did you go to the police?"

Gabe nodded.

"What happened?"

"Nothing."

"What?"

"No, it wasn't them. They were supportive but I couldn't press charges because I was at fault. There were so many rumours about him and I knew better than to be alone with him. It was my ambition. It was my fault."

"It's *never* a woman's fault." He lifted her chin. "No woman asks to be raped. No woman deserves to be raped. He was wrong."

Gabe closed her eyes.

"I wish I could believe you, and part of me does. My head says what you say is true and if I think of any other woman I agree, but . . ." Gabe looked at Fin. "It doesn't matter. It's history and it changed the course of mine, that's all." Gabe closed her eyes briefly.

"No, he was wrong in every way." He knelt beside the chair and as a tear fell he wiped it away, which just made them fall faster.

CHAPTER
FIFTEEN

It was noon when Gabe finally set out for Truro. Everything about her felt raw. Fin had left a note on the table saying he had caught a lift to Falmouth with Max to see how the repair of his boat was going. She wasn't sure if she was relieved or not that he hadn't been there when she woke. How could she have told him all of that last night?

The car park was full and she had to circle for five minutes before someone left. Leaving the car, she grabbed the CD. The laughter that took place while making it seemed a lifetime ago and not a matter of hours. The staff nurse gave her a beaming smile as she approached the desk to get an update on Jaunty's condition.

"Have you brought the CD?"

Gabe nodded.

"Excellent. We've received permission and the woman in the room with Jaunty has said she has no objections, although she admitted she would rather have you singing live!"

Gabe's eyes opened wide.

"Yes, in fact we were chatting yesterday after you left, wondering if we could tempt you to sing to the patients in a few of the other wards. It would lift their spirits no end."

Gabe frowned. Things were moving out of her control.

"Unlike your grandmother, many don't have any visitors."

"I'm not sure. I haven't sung in public in years. I'm not very good."

"How can you say that!" The nurse took her hand and led her down the corridor to a large ward filled with elderly patients. "They're not critics, just people in need of a bit of joy. Your singing would bring *anyone* happiness."

Gabe swallowed, then smiled at the curious glances she was receiving. "I'll think about it."

"Please do, and if you sing to Jaunty today, belt it out so all of us can enjoy it, please."

Gabe nodded and quickly escaped to the chair beside Jaunty's bed. Her head was swimming. This was all too much at once. Jaunty's condition hadn't changed. Gabe took her grandmother's bent hand in hers and stroked the gnarled fingers. In her heart she knew it wouldn't be long. She couldn't and shouldn't do anything to prolong Jaunty's life. Her body looked so frail lying there with tubes coming out of her.

Gabe began to hum a lullaby, the one that Jaunty used to sing to her when she was scared and missing her father. Jaunty's hand clenched hers with some strength and when Gabe began to sing softly the fingers curled tighter. The lullaby finished and Jaunty's hand relaxed. Without pausing, Gabe began Jaunty's favourite aria. She didn't stop to think about other people, only reaching her grandmother. She stood with Jaunty's hand in hers and let the words flow out. Jaunty's fingers held hers and Gabe wasn't imagining it.

As the final note finished, Gabe looked down and Jaunty's eyes were open and the patient in the bed next to hers was clapping and shouting, "Bravo, encore!"

Fin walked through the door. He must have been standing there the whole time. "Jaunty . . ." Gabe wrapped her arms around her ". . . you haven't left me yet."

Jaunty blinked.

"I'll get the nurse." Fin disappeared as quietly as he had arrived.

Gabe stroked Jaunty's cheek. She couldn't believe her grandmother was back with her.

Gabe rummaged in an old chest of drawers looking for a decent nightgown or set of pyjamas for Jaunty. Gabe knew she wasn't at ease in the hospital gown and she had already placed some clean knickers and a hairbrush on the bed. In the bottom drawer she found a nightgown she had given Jaunty at least fifteen years ago and clearly it had never been worn. Gabe shook her head, then her fingers encountered a hard edge. An old notebook. It was an odd place for a book, but then Jaunty did things like that all the time. She pushed it back to where it had been and rushed to put everything into a bag. Fin was going to drive her to the hospital in a few minutes. He needed to borrow the car so he would drop her off.

The doctors had been very encouraged by Jaunty's progress yesterday. Gabe hadn't wanted to leave and it was odd to do so to the sound of her voice singing. The woman in the bed next to Jaunty's had been most appreciative and her grandmother had fallen asleep with a smile on her face.

Even with all of the excitement of Jaunty waking up and a more positive prognosis, Gabe knew in her heart this wasn't for long. Jaunty was ninety-three and had been holding it all together on her own for a very long time. It couldn't have been easy raising Gabe's father alone and then getting lumped with a granddaughter, but Jaunty had never complained. She had done it. She was remarkable in so many ways and almost her greatest achievement was that she was famous but unknown — no mean feat in today's world.

Gabe picked the bag up off the bed and went to meet Fin who was changing the bin liner. He looked up and smiled. "Ready?"

She was still exhausted from the lack of sleep the night before, yet he appeared totally rested. "Yes." She looked about the kitchen and saw the post in a neat pile on the counter. At the sight of the bills Gabe sighed. This week, now that they had the Internet, she would switch all of Jaunty's bills over to paperless ones. She knew it was silly but bills seemed less lethal on a screen, somehow.

Fin carried the rubbish up the hill then held open the passenger door for her. With music on she nodded off on the journey. She couldn't remember when she had felt this safe with someone. Maybe she never had . . .

"I'll pick you up in two hours."

"Thanks." Gabe dashed to the front doors and made her way through the hospital to the ward. There was a new nurse on duty and Gabe stopped to ask how Jaunty was before she disturbed her.

"She's been asleep all afternoon." The woman smiled. "Are you going to sing to her again? I've loved listening to the CD you made."

Gabe blushed. "I'll see how she is and if Mrs Smith minds."

"No need to worry about Mrs Smith; she went home this afternoon. She did ask if she could have a copy of the CD."

"Oh." It felt mean to say no but she wasn't ready for other people to listen to her and certainly not to take "her" home. When studying, all she had thought about was music and making it to the top. Everyone was the same. Despite the cliché, they lived for the music and strived for success.

Gabe stopped at the end of the bed and sucked air into her lungs. The sight of Jaunty in the hospital still hurt. How much time did she have left? Would she wake again?

Sitting on the side of the bed, Gabe took Jaunty's brush and tidied her up a bit. She began singing "Quando M'en Vo" from Puccini's La Bohéme and Jaunty's eyelids fluttered. Gabe stopped singing. "Hi."

Jaunty blinked.

"Do you want me to sing some more?"

Jaunty's eyes fluttered again.

Gabe considered some arias until she chose Mozart's "Ruhe sanft, mein holdes Leben". Suddenly another voice joined her. She turned to find Hannah in the doorway and nodded for the girl to come into the room properly. Together they made their way to the end.

"Where did you come from?" Gabe asked.

"I'm here doing community service."

Gabe frowned.

"It's a school thing. You either do cadets, dogs or grannies." Hannah smiled. "I don't do guns and we have a dog, so grannies have become my thing. I was visiting the ward next door when I heard you sing."

"Oh." Gabe was awed at Hannah's energy.

"Can we sing 'The Evening Prayer' from *Hansel and Gretel* next?" She pulled some crumpled sheets from her bag. "I'm working on it at the moment and it would really help to do it with you."

Gabe watched Jaunty look at the girl before she closed her eyes with a hint of a smile on her mouth.

"Let's give it a go. I think I can remember it."

Hannah began and then Gabe joined her. The smile on Jaunty's face grew and, at the end, there was applause from the nurses at the station.

The ongoing parade of boats being taken to Gweek for the winter had begun to thin out. As each day passed the river became emptier. The tide was high and no one visited the creek except the birds. At the moment there was only a solitary egret watching the water from the opposite shore. Gabe turned away from the window and began the search for one of Jaunty's favourite books. Today she wanted to read to Jaunty rather than sing. The singing was becoming too much. She was out of practice, but a soft voice in her head said this *was* practice. Gabe told the voice to shut up. The problem was the audience. Each time she opened her mouth the spectators grew. It was embarrassing. Gabe sighed. Hannah's delight at yesterday's impromptu performance was sweet. The girl had potential, if that was what she wanted to do. Gabe wasn't sure. By the time she'd been Hannah's age, seventeen, Gabe had known and she had worked hard to be ready for her audition for Chetham's School of Music in Manchester for sixth form. Fortunately the work paid off and she received a place. Those years were fun and hard at the same time, because Manchester had been so far from home.

Gabe sat on the edge of Jaunty's bed. She had no intention of continuing to do this. She was no longer a singer, but a composer, she reminded herself, then she bent down to find the book. On the shelf of the bedside table, Gabe scanned the titles looking for *Gaudy Night* by Dorothy L Sayers. Jaunty frequently reread that one and, sure enough, the book was there along with a few Agatha Christies. The corner of a sheet of paper stuck out from under the bed and she pulled it out. It was Jaunty's writing.

At your christening, when you were six months old, I knew who Philip's father had been. The answer to the question that had haunted me for years was in your eyes, but also in the impossibly long fingers that curled around my own. Sadness filled me as I held you, tiny as you were. You, like your father before you, would grow up with the love of only one parent. But in the end you had far less than he had. You had only me.

Gabe dropped the sheet of paper. What was this? Was she writing a novel or something? Her great-grandfather was Oliver Blythe and Blythe was Jaunty's maiden name. She had kept it because of her painting, and because Gabe's grandfather had died in the war before Philip had been born and Jaunty had registered him under her name. Jaunty had explained, many years ago, that it simply made life easier rather than trying to juggle with two surnames.

Gabe picked the paper up and turned it over to see if anything else was written on it. As she did she glanced at her fingers, which were still long. They were the hands of a pianist and had been from an early age. Before her love of singing came the love of playing the piano, and for a while she had thought that was what she would pursue. She laughed. As of today these hands were the hands of a creator of a song for a theme park. A far cry from what she had once worked towards.

Gabe walked from the car down to the cabin and stood staring upriver in the mizzle. Water beaded on her sweater and she wondered if it would clear or turn into proper rain. The landscape in front of her was nothing more than indistinguishable shapes. She knew the view because it was etched in her mind, but if she didn't she would wonder what she was seeing.

Jaunty had not responded at all today, not to the reading and not to the singing. Fortunately, this time Gabe hadn't been dragged to other wards to perform as she was on previous days. The consultant was doing his rounds and she was excused, or that was how it felt.

The scent of cooking onions wound its way from the kitchen, tempting her in out of the wet. Her mouth watered and she stepped inside, expecting Fin, but he wasn't around. In the sitting room there was a bottle of red wine on the table with two glasses. She poured one for herself and walked to the window, then stopped in her tracks when she saw Fin come out of Jaunty's room.

A strange look crossed his face and then he smiled. "I didn't hear you arrive."

"The weather must have dampened the sound of the car." She bit her lip. There was no possible reason that she could think of for him to be in Jaunty's room. She shook her head. She was being silly: he might have been using the loo. She had no reason to be suspicious of him.

"I've made a beef casserole," he said easily.

"You're spoiling me."

"You're housing me — it's the least I can do." He moved to the table and poured himself a glass of wine.

Gabe watched him, wondering what was going on in his mind. She still knew so little about him.

"Max called. He'd heard about Hannah's performance with you."

"She's got great potential and she's a good kid." She put her glass down and wandered into Jaunty's bedroom. Fin followed.

"Missing her?"

She nodded and ran her hand over the end of the bed, straightening the eiderdown. "I wish she could speak."

"You know she is listening."

"True, but . . ." Gabe paused. "I just don't think she'll come through this. I don't think she'll be back here."

"You could ask if you could bring her home." He came and stood beside her. They were so close but not touching.

"Do you think so?" She looked up. It was a mistake; his glance was so intense.

"Yes. My grandmother came home and died with the family around her." He put a finger under her chin. "She'd be happier at home and I'd help."

"Thank you, Fin. Tomorrow I'll ask." She stretched up to press a kiss of thanks on his cheek but he turned his head and her mouth connected with his. Instead of jumping away she wanted to fall into him. He kissed her back, then leaned away enough to tuck a wayward strand of hair behind her ear. Gabe couldn't move. Fear wrapped itself around her while Fin stroked her cheek with the back of his finger.

"Shall we have dinner?"

She nodded. He understood. As he took a step away, she let air back into her lungs. She had just kissed a man and he was stepping away, but not far.

★ ★ ★

264

Max was drinking coffee with Fin when Gabe came out of the bedroom. She thought she'd heard voices when she stepped from the shower, but then dismissed it because it was only eight. But obviously it hadn't been the radio.

"Morning, sleepyhead." Max grinned.

"Hardly. I was up at six making used cars sound sexy and exciting." Gabe eyed the cafetière. There wasn't enough in it to squeeze another cup out. Maybe she would have tea, but she had had that at six. "What brings you here so early?"

"A request from Hannah."

Gabe raised an eyebrow.

"She's singing at a christening in Manaccan this week and yours truly has been roped in to play the organ. She was wondering if you would sing 'Jesu, Joy of Man's Desiring' with her."

"I don't think so." Gabe frowned. "I thought a christening consisted of a few hymns and a quick exit before the little tyke uses its lungs to deafen everyone?"

"She gave me this note for you."

Gabe opened it and read:

Dear Gabe,
I know you don't like singing in front of people. I can't understand why when you have the best voice ever. But you see I'm scared stiff to sing this on my own. This is the christening for my stepmum's baby — long story. Here's the short version: she was married to my dad but he died and she remarried — bit awkward really but it's

265

cool cause Mark, her new husband, is great — and I really want to make it special for her and Mark and baby Toby. You see, they are my family though I'm kinda on the outside but I am the godmother. And I want to give this to them all from me. Well, at least I thought it was a good idea until now. I don't want to blow it and I know that after singing with you I wouldn't, or if I did you could carry it off.

Please, please, please think about it.

Love,

Hannah x

Gabe took a big breath. What could she say to an appeal like that? There was so much more unsaid than had been said.

"It's a big deal for her." Max looked so solemn that Gabe nearly laughed.

"I can tell." She turned from the men and walked out to the terrace. A cold wind blew from the north and Gabe wrapped her arms tightly about herself. The sun was high enough that the clear sky was becoming blue, adding its tint to the water, and the low rays of sunlight picked out the autumn colours on the oaks of Groyne Point. It would be a beautiful day. Gabe sighed. This was important for Hannah — and so many people had helped Gabe on her way. She could do this, couldn't she? After all, she had kissed a man last night, and that was something she had thought she would never do again.

She took a deep breath and went back inside. "I'll do it."

Fin placed his arm around her shoulders and pulled her to his side while Max said, "Hannah will be over the moon. I'll tell her later today when I'm in Truro working with the chorus." He slid a piece of paper across the counter. "And I've brought you some changes I've made." Gabe noticed his Adam's apple move up and down. "If you have time to look through it . . .?"

Gabe looked at the score on the table and smiled slightly. It was another case of reaching out and helping someone else.

Fin glanced at his watch. "We need to make a move if you are to be there at the start of visiting hours."

"True, but Fin you don't need to come. I can face this one on my own."

He touched her arm. "You just want me to stay behind to cement in the loose stones on the steps." He smiled.

Gabe laughed. "Absolutely."

"It's a good day for it." Max stood. "I'm off. I'll touch base with you later."

Fin turned to her. "Are you sure you don't need my support at the hospital?"

"Thanks, but no." She smiled at him. This she could do alone. She needed to ask Jaunty what she wanted to do before she set the wheels in motion for her to return home — because Gabe knew in her heart that when Jaunty came home to Bosworgy that it would be the end.

CHAPTER
SIXTEEN

Gabe sang the whole way in the car to Manaccan church. She didn't want to do this, but reminded herself again of all the people who had helped her over the years. Especially Georgina Piper, the soprano who had been coaching her when Gabe had pulled out of the opera world. Gabe could still see the sadness in Georgina's eyes and her last words to Gabe had been, "I understand, but you will regret this and I am devastated."

Gabe swallowed and parked the car. Sun broke through the clouds as she walked up to the church. The last time she had been here was the previous Christmas for midnight mass. She and Jaunty had slipped in late and exited early so Jaunty wouldn't be forced into chatting. Gabe hadn't understood, but had always gone along with Jaunty's eccentricities.

Sounds of the organ greeted her as she climbed the steps to the graveyard that surrounded the church. Poor Hannah was terrified, and that Gabe could understand. Pulling open the heavy church door, she reminded herself that she was only a prop. This was Hannah's chance to shine.

Gabe glanced at the altar and was nearly thrown off her feet by Hannah running to her and wrapping her in a bear hug.

"Hi."

"Oh, thank you for coming." Hannah's eyes filled with tears. "I couldn't do this without you, Gabe."

"Nonsense. You could, but I'm here, so let's get on with it." And she led them to the side chapel where Max was playing the organ.

"You're here. Excellent." He smiled. "Now we can settle down. I've never known Hannah so twitchy. Let's run through this." Max played the opening notes of "Morning Has Broken". Hannah looked at Gabe and she nodded. They sang together, but Gabe knew that it would sound far better with Hannah alone. Gabe's voice was too big for it. So without telling Hannah she dropped out on the last chorus. Max looked at her and winked.

"Why did you do that?" Hannah asked, glaring, when she finished.

"Your voice is perfect for it, mine is not — and you know it."

Hannah frowned and Gabe took her hand. "It will be fine, I promise you."

"But you will sing 'Jesu, Joy of Man's Desiring'?"

"Yes."

"Let's go through it now before we run out of time." Max began before either of them could say a word. Hannah's voice grew in confidence as they progressed and Max went through it one more time before swiftly reviewing the other two hymns for the service.

★ ★ ★

Pulling into Trevenen, Gabe shook her head. She had made it through by pretending she was just singing to Jaunty not to a congregation. Her stomach was still in knots though and she really didn't belong at this gathering but Maddie Triggs, Hannah's stepmother, wouldn't take no for an answer. She had to come back to the house and wet the baby's head because she couldn't thank Gabe enough for helping Hannah.

Gabe parked so that she could make a quick exit. Other cars were filling in around her and she had recognised many of the people in the church but hadn't seen most of them since she'd been a teenager.

"So pleased to see you." Tamsin Polcrebar came up to her and handed her a tray from her car. "So lovely, you and Hannah singing. I'd forgotten about your wonderful voice."

"Um, thank you." Gabe followed Tamsin, whom she remembered vaguely. Gabe had often wondered about this house but had never been inside.

"Let's put this in the dining room and go and get a drink." Tamsin turned to her. "You remember everyone, don't you?"

Gabe nodded and thought it best to say no more. Instead she stared at the beautiful home, with whitewashed walls filled with exuberant paintings.

"Everyone will be in the sitting room." Tamsin took her by the hand and led her down the slate-flagged hallway to the crowd.

"Gabriella, I'm so pleased you could join us. Thank you so much for singing with Hannah." Mark Triggs handed her a glass of champagne and Gabe went tongue-tied. She suddenly remembered she'd had the biggest schoolgirl crush on him when she was twelve. Now she just smiled and moved into the room looking for Max or Hannah. Gabe took a sip of the champagne and suddenly Mrs Bates was at her elbow.

"Such a beautiful service and your singing was just lovely."

"Thank you." Gabe looked down. "But Hannah and Toby were the stars."

"How's dear Jaunty?"

"Improving."

"Pleased to hear it — and how's the stranger?" Mrs Bates gave her a sideways glance.

Gabe smiled. She hadn't thought of him as a stranger in a while. "Fin is well."

Toby, who had been silent through the whole service, broke into an ear-splitting howl. Hannah quickly handed him to Maddie and came up to Gabe.

"He's gorgeous, really, but when he screams I have no idea what to do."

"When you have your own you'll learn quick enough." Mrs Bates patted Hannah on the arm and wandered away.

"Thanks again." Hannah bit her lip.

"You were great."

"Nah, you were great, but I wasn't too bad." Hannah grabbed a glass of champagne from Mark. "You were right about 'Morning Has Broken'."

Gabe smiled.

Tamsin came around with a tray of food. "Hannah, do you want to grab another plate and pass it round?"

"Sure." Hannah rolled her eyes when Tamsin couldn't see her and took Gabe's hand, dragging her through to the kitchen.

"I really wanted to say thank you again." Hannah took a swig of champagne and Gabe flinched, thinking it was a waste of a good wine.

"Well, it was important to you."

"Boy, was it ever! But 'nuff about me. Tell me about the hunk at your place."

Gabe opened her mouth and shut it. There wasn't much she could say.

"Is he your boyfriend?"

"No."

"Shame." Hannah filled her glass from an open bottle and looked over her shoulder. "I'd work on that if I were you."

It was over a week before the medical team felt it was safe for Jaunty to come home. The doctor had looked at Gabe with knowing eyes and she'd had to turn away. He wanted her to understand that taking Jaunty home meant the end, if not immediately, then soon. It was clear to everyone that in the ten days since the stroke Jaunty had diminished. She still couldn't speak, but was awake more of the time and she communicated with small squeezes of the hand and blinking. Truthfully, the whole thing was completely overwhelming, and Gabe felt totally unprepared for what was coming in terms of looking after her grandmother and beyond.

272

Now she was in the back seat of the car, clutching Jaunty's hand with one of her own, and the instructions in the other, as Fin drove carefully back to Bosworgy and Jaunty swayed beside her with each turn and roundabout. If Gabe sneezed, Jaunty would fall over. Her grandmother's eyes were overlarge in her gaunt face and though she constantly looked as if she wanted to speak, that ability had been taken from her. However, she could walk with a walker and that was a blessing. Without being able to do that Gabe didn't think they would have let her come home. The only option then would have been a hospice and that sounded so final. But who was Gabe fooling? This, too, was final.

They bounced through the ruts in the lanes and Gabe watched her grandmother grimace, but then, as the pain passed, she smiled and her head swung from side to side as if she was seeing everything on the journey for the first time. What must it have been like when Jaunty bought Bosworgy, back in 1945? Probably not much different from now, with the exception of utilities and maybe fewer houses on the other side of the river.

Fin parked the car and came around and opened Jaunty's door. He helped her to stand, then scooped her up in his arms while Gabe raced ahead to open the door, thankful that Fin had sorted the loose steps.

Earlier in the week she had found some beautifully faded hydrangeas with their flower heads still intact, and she'd brought them into the cabin to brighten it up. As a bonus, the sun was shining today, the river sparkled, and nothing else was needed. Jaunty was back.

Jaunty's armchair sat next to the French window so that she had the best view, and on the table beside it were her books and a sketchpad. Gabe put the kettle on while Fin settled Jaunty then went out to retrieve the walker from the car. Her grandmother frowned when she saw him carry it in. Gabe knew what Jaunty was thinking, but without the walker Jaunty wasn't stable enough. It was just one of the things Jaunty would have to learn to live with in order to be here at home.

Although the bed was made and the studio tidy, Gabe felt Fin's presence even though she knew he was in the cabin with Jaunty. It must be his scent, the fragrance of fresh soap and toothpaste, that hung in the air. Gabe looked at Max's revised score. Something still wasn't right. She played it from start to finish and then suddenly she knew. She picked up the pencil and began making notes on the score. Max was brilliant but he wasn't using the musical motifs of the sea shanty. She began to weave it through and then played it again. Yes, the music stirred the feelings of the listener more. This was music that all audiences were familiar with, even if they didn't know it. It hit the emotional everyman.

She sat back from the piano, satisfied, then her shoulders drooped. How would Max feel about her tampering with his work? He had asked, but she had never shared her thoughts on adding birdsong either. She was used to people tinkering with her commercial compositions and, as a singer, there had always been constant appraisal

274

and adjustment of her technique, but she had never shared her serious compositions with anyone. What would she do if someone told her they weren't right, that they could be better, stronger? She might be OK with it, but what if the person said *this* was the way to do it? She didn't know and she didn't know Max well enough to guess his reaction.

Picking up the music and her notes, she walked back to the cabin. The sunlight was still low and its rays caught the dew on the branches. The mist on the river was disappearing and it promised to be a warm day. There wasn't a cloud to be seen.

The smell of coffee and bacon lingered in the air as she walked through the kitchen. Everything was tidy, but the aroma of coffee was still fresh. Gabe followed the scent and found Fin and Jaunty outside on the terrace. It was cool but sunny and he had wrapped a blanket around Jaunty's shoulders. Jaunty beamed when she saw Gabe.

"I've brought a cup out for you." Fin smiled at her.

"Thanks." Gabe perched on the side of the table, closed her eyes and turned her face up to the sun. Things were good. Jaunty was home and somehow she would find a way to talk to Max about the score. He didn't seem the temperamental type.

Jaunty held on to the walker and tried to pull open the desk drawer. The recent damp weather had caused it to stick and she needed two hands, which she didn't have. Her mouth moved, but the swear word she was saying didn't emerge. She was trapped in her own body,

forced to communicate in a barely legible scrawl and
with her hands and eyelids. Why hadn't she just died?
But she knew she had clung to life because her story
hadn't been finished. She needed to find everything
she'd written because she didn't remember where she
had left off and what she hadn't said. So many things
were drifting away, leaving her alone. She had left it all
too late.

"Can I help?" Fin walked through the door and
Jaunty nodded. She tugged at the drawer and then
backed up as well as she could with the walker.
Understanding immediately, he took hold of the handle
and, with one pull, released it. She hobbled over to the
bed and gathered some of the other papers and
notebooks, then she pointed at the notebook in the
drawer and Fin brought it and everything else over to
her at her desk. She could see the questions in his eyes
but couldn't respond. Instead she flipped through the
papers and tried to order them.

Afternoon sunlight filtered through the window and
the daisies on the curtains fluttered in the breeze. It was
warm, a true Indian summer, a glorious taste of what
had finished. Jaunty closed her eyes. The tide was out
and she could smell the mudflats and hear the call of a
curlew. Time was short. She picked up her pen and
wrote her last passage for Gabe.

I have lost track of where I've reached and I'm not
sure it matters any more. A priest visited while I
was in the hospital. He was a young man with

earnest eyes and he reminded me of the curate who married Alex and I.

I received the last rites, although he called them the Sacrament of the Sick. Whatever had happened, I felt more at ease, as if the knot inside me had finally loosened, although I couldn't say a word aloud. My confession is here on these pages. I stole another woman's life, her fame and her money, and no matter how I try and justify what I have done, I can't. It was wrong. I should have gone to my grandmother and she might have welcomed me. She was alone, after all. She had lost her husband, a son to the First World War and then my father to the Second. If I had gone to her, life would have been so different. Philip would have been heir to the Penrose family fortune and Polruan House, although not the title.

Polruan House has been so near yet so far. Here in Cornwall, yet a world away from Bosworgy, my retreat, my house above the water. I remember seeing my grandmother's obituary. I was tempted to leave my place of security to see her in the ground, and I wondered: if she had been a bit warmer, could I have turned to her?

Gabriella, Gabriella . . . I hope you can forgive me. I thought I was protecting us all, but with hindsight I can see everything I did was wrong. Only if you sing again will it all have been worth it, for music is your birthright and I denied you the help you should have had.

I love you.

Jaunty looked up at the ceiling made of cladding. Straight lines. Life never went in straight lines, especially not hers. Jaunty could hear Gabe's car as it moved along the track. She had gone to see Max about his opera. Gabe was singing again, singing in public. There was hope. She put the pen down and looked out on the river. A cormorant flew straight down the middle with its wings almost touching the surface. She watched until she could see it no more. She picked up her pen and a separate sheet of paper. There was one more thing she had to tell, and it was the hardest of all.

"I'm so glad I've bumped in to you." Helen Williams put her basket down on the counter and Gabe cocked her head to one side.

"It was lovely catching up with you the other day with Jenna and the kids."

"Yes, it was." Gabe frowned, wondering where this was going. She was eager to see Max, to share her thoughts now that she'd made up her mind to do it. She had only stopped in the shop to pick up a newspaper for Jaunty.

"I was only saying to JC last night how lovely it was that you were back. It's so wonderful to see the young come home."

Gabe smiled, knowing that not many could. Her job made it possible.

"And now that you're back, I thought you would be the perfect person, well musician, to help Tristan with the opening of the new library at Pengarrock. You play so beautifully and you could do the music for the opening, you see."

Gabe frowned.

"Much better to use local people rather than bring others in."

Mrs Bates walked in and joined them. This was her chance to escape. "Have Tristan call me." Gabe fled out of the store and down the lane before she could be drawn into anything else.

Suddenly, as she stood at Max's door, she changed her mind. Spinning around, she had taken the step down to the path when the door opened behind her.

"Gabe. Sorry I didn't hear you." He pointed to the headphones around his neck. "Wonderful things but they do block the world out."

Gabe smiled.

"Come in. Tell me how Jaunty's settling in."

She walked inside. "I think she's thrilled to be back home."

"I bet." Max studied her. "You look serious and you have my opera in your hands." He went to the piano.

"Um, yes." Gabe put the score down with the newspaper. "Max, I . . ." She stopped.

"Out with it. You hate it." He squinted.

"Absolutely not! I love it." She thrust her hands into her jeans pockets. "I think . . ." She trailed off, trying to find the words.

"You think what?" He smiled. "You've seen something that could be better?"

Gabe nodded.

"Excellent. I love a little collaboration." He rubbed his hands together. "Now, let me see what you've done."

After the glorious day and evening of yesterday, Gabe was surprised to be woken by howling gales. A window banging in the kitchen forced her out of bed. She pushed her hair out of her eyes and dashed through the cabin to close the culprit, and her hand and arm were soaked by the time she wrestled with the wind to secure the latch.

The storm reminded her of the night she had pulled Fin from the creek. She still wasn't sure how she had done it, but she was glad she had. How would she have managed everything recently without him? And what was it about him that transformed Jaunty? Yes, he was more than easy on the eyes, but surely that wouldn't turn Jaunty's head? There was something else, but Gabe couldn't put her finger on it, especially not now when she was so sleepy. She yawned and stuck her head through Jaunty's bedroom door to make sure all was well.

With the storm raging, Gabe listened closely for Jaunty's breathing, but she couldn't hear anything over the wind. She walked further into the room and all was stillness. No movement from Jaunty. With only the light from the sitting room coming in through the door, Gabe couldn't see much, but Jaunty was smiling. Gabe wondered what she was dreaming of. Her face looked less tired, peaceful, and Gabe's chest tightened with love. She owed so much to her.

Gabe walked up to the side of the bed, then leaned down and kissed her grandmother's cheek. It was cold. Gabe slipped to her knees then placed her hand on Jaunty's neck to try and find a pulse, but there was none. She pulled Jaunty into her arms and held her grandmother's cheek against hers, and her tears wet both their faces.

Eventually Gabe placed Jaunty gently back on the bed. What should she do now? She turned on the light. A glance at the bedside clock told her it was three in the morning. She tucked Jaunty in and went through to the kitchen, jumping when there was a knock on the door. Fin!

"I saw the light on in Jaunty's room and wondered if the storm had woken her." Rain ran off his curls and down his cheeks. Gabe just stood there looking at him, and then she began to shake.

"What's wrong?"

"She's dead."

"When?"

"I don't know." Gabe shook her head. "A window blew open and woke me and I decided to check on her." She swallowed and blinked, trying to keep the tears at bay. She focused on a butterfly flying around the ceiling light. It was a peacock. Where had that come from? Fin held open his arms and walked towards her. Enveloped in his embrace she let the tears fall again.

Fin took Gabe's hand as they walked into Jaunty's bedroom. Gabe expected to see Jaunty's eyes open, but she lay there peacefully.

"I'll ring her doctor in the morning and find out what's next." Gabe checked once more for a pulse, even though she knew it wasn't there. Her fingers caught on Jaunty's necklace and she pulled out the chain and looked at the ring which hung on it. "I've never really seen this properly, although she wore it all the time," she said, turning the gold ring over in her hand.

"It looks like a signet ring." Fin's fingers brushed her as he touched it and then pulled back quickly.

"What's wrong?" Gabe frowned.

"It's the Carrow crest."

Gabe raised an eyebrow. "Really? Carrow?" She held it out to him.

He twisted the ring in his fingers. "Carrow was my grandmother's family."

"Ah . . ." Gabe murmured thoughtfully and looked down at her grandmother.

"Interesting." He handed the ring back to her and she slipped the ring back above Jaunty's heart.

"Why?"

"Well, as far as I know it was unique to them."

"How would she have come by it? She's had it for as long as I can remember."

"Who knows?" He shrugged. "It's not important."

The flash of lightning illuminated the trees outside and a gust of wind pushed a sheet of paper off the desk. Fin retrieved it and put it back. "There's nothing we can do for the moment. Do you want a hot drink or something stronger, like Jaunty's favourite whisky?"

Gabe's lips twisted into a half smile. She took a deep breath, then said, "Make it a whisky. It would be what she would want." Gabe followed Fin out but stopped at the door, taking one last look at her grandmother. From Jaunty's smile, Gabe hoped that her grandmother had died with happy thoughts. She pulled the door closed and saw the piece of paper lift on the air again. She would deal with it later.

CHAPTER
SEVENTEEN

Gabe stood staring out of the window, watching the sky brighten. Clouds moved across the river, bouncing light in different directions. Yesterday had been long and had gone in a bit of a blur, from Dr Winslade's arrival in the morning to the undertakers removing Jaunty from the cabin. Gabe still couldn't believe that Jaunty was gone. She didn't want it to be true and all day she'd been unable to do anything she was supposed to. The handy list that the undertakers had left sat on the table. It contained helpful advice, but it didn't say how to fill the void.

Gabe rested her head against the glass. She felt it should be raining today but it was one of the most beautiful mornings she had seen.

"Stunning." Fin came up to her.

"Yes." She turned to find him staring at her. He lifted her chin and looked into her eyes. Gabe's heart stopped. She wanted him. She shouldn't have these feelings now, if ever, but he leaned down and he kissed her and she didn't move. She couldn't.

"She had a good life and she wanted you to have a good life too," he murmured, and took her hand in his.

"True." Gabe looked down at the strong hand holding hers. "I miss her, Fin."

"I'd be surprised if you didn't."

"I don't know what to do."

"There's no rush."

"True, but people are already asking about the funeral. I wish I'd asked her what she wanted." She looked up. "I don't think she or I wanted to talk about it, but it would have made things so much easier right now."

"Yes, but losing someone you love is never easy."

She nodded.

"Hello?" a woman's voice called from the kitchen.

Gabe pulled away from Fin. "Coming."

"Gabe, I am so sorry for your loss." The postmistress was standing by the back door.

"Thank you." Gabe took the post.

"Your grandmother was such a good person." The woman smiled. "She never said much but she always wanted to know the news. She'll be missed terribly."

Gabe nodded, thinking of the huge, Jaunty-shaped hole in her life.

"You'll let me know when you've sorted the funeral?"

"Of course."

"Thanks, and I'm off now, my lovely." Gabe looked at the post and then turned to the view. She couldn't do paperwork today; she needed to move, do something positive. The climbing rose was blooming again with all the sun and rain they'd had, but it had grown so wild. Today she would tackle the garden.

★   ★   ★

In the evening Gabe handed the last of the dishes to Fin, who placed them in the dresser. "Thanks for your help today," she said.

"A pleasure." He held up a hand covered with small nicks and scratches. The roses had left them both with mild injuries, but the fragrance from the bouquet on the table filled the room.

"I feel so much better for having done the garden." Gabe smiled sadly and picked up her glass of wine. "I feel Jaunty would be pleased. She loved the roses."

"Jaunty loved *you*." Fin was studying her and she couldn't make out his expression. It was if he was trying to make up his mind about something.

"I know." Gabe swallowed. She looked at the paintings on the walls. "At least I still have part of her in her paintings. I feel these are really her." She ran her finger along the bottom of a frame.

"Well, yes."

Gabe turned to Fin, frowning. "What does that mean?"

"It . . ." He stopped and looked at the paintings.

"Yes?"

"Jaunty was," he paused, "a very complex person."

Gabe pursed her mouth. "I don't think so. She was straight-forward and her painting is so honest. That's why people are so moved by her work. It's her honesty — and I'm not just saying my own feelings but those of so many art critics over the years." Gabe placed her hands on her hips and faced Fin. They had worked together so harmoniously today but right now she wondered if he was the same Fin.

"Look, I'm sorry to do this."

"To do what?"

"I'm honestly not sure she was right, but I promised her." Fin took three steps and closed the space between them, then he took her by the hand and led her into Jaunty's room to her grandmother's desk. From the drawer he pulled out several notebooks and sheets of paper. "She wanted you to have these. She was trying to put them all together the other day. For you."

Gabe looked at the papers then at Fin. "What is this?"

"Read."

Gabe shivered as she took them from him and sank on to the bed. Jaunty's perfume wafted up around her, and the fragrance wasn't comforting, it was heartbreaking. She turned towards the chest of drawers and there was Jaunty's Chanel No 5. It had always been Jaunty's one luxury.

"Do you know what's in this?" She looked up at Fin.

"I know a little a bit, that which she told me, but I haven't read any of this."

"I see." But Gabe didn't see at all. Her hands shook and she put the pile beside her on the bed.

"Shall I get you a drink?"

"Will I need one?"

"I think you might."

Gabe frowned and Fin slipped out of the room. She turned a notebook over in her hand. She had seen Jaunty with this many times in the past month but had thought nothing of it. It looked no different from the notebooks she always had with her for a quick sketch to record an idea. Opening the book, Gabe leaned back against the headboard and began reading.

Gabe's hand shook as she raised the whisky glass to her mouth and sniffed. With her legs curled under her on the sofa she watched the flames in the wood burner. Fin was in the kitchen, probably giving her space to digest what she had just read. Her grandmother was not Jaunty Blythe. Gabe looked at the paintings either side of the fire. *Honesty*. No wonder Fin had disagreed with her. Everything she'd read circled around in her thoughts. Fin came and sat on the end of the sofa and Gabe looked at him. "I don't understand."

"What part?"

Gabe laughed drily. "Most of it." She shook her head. "First question: when did you plan to show this to me?"

Shadows fell across his eyes as he turned towards the fire. "Jaunty made me promise to give you everything she'd written as soon as she died." He turned to her. "She didn't say exactly when and I will confess that I thought about not doing it."

Gabe gasped.

"You've just lost your grandmother. I didn't think you needed to lose her again so soon."

"I see, but I still don't understand."

He sighed. "Your grandmother wasn't Jaunty Blythe. She was a friend of Jaunty's."

"Yes, that part was clear." Gabe put her fingers to her mouth, trying to find what she wanted to say. "I

288

understand her not telling the world who she really was, but I don't get her not telling me or my father."

"I think she was ashamed; or at least she was for a long time." Fin reached out and put a hand on her ankle.

"It's so unfair. She lost most of her life, living as someone else" Looking at Jaunty's painting, Gabe tried to get her head around what she had just read. Her grandmother wasn't Jaunty Blythe, her great-grandmother was a famous Italian soprano and her grandfather was a German pianist. In a few hours everything had changed. Why hadn't Jaunty said any of this while she was alive?

"You looked exhausted, which isn't surprising. Look, we can solve the rest of the puzzle tomorrow as well as working on the funeral arrangements."

Gabe rolled her eyes. "But now I'm not sure what to do." She sighed. "It turns out that my grandmother was Catholic and that changes what I had thought I was doing. Maybe I need to put everything on a go-slow and talk to a priest tomorrow. I feel I should know what to do, having gone to a Catholic boarding school for years, but I guess funerals were never a big issue or one that I wanted to pay attention to." She frowned. "Because of my parents I stuck my head in the sand."

"Understandable."

Gabe stood and stretched. "I'm going to try and sleep."

"Good plan." Fin stood.

"Thank you for all your support." He really had been helpful, especially to Jaunty, who had trusted him with this information. Gabe should ask what else he knew, but she was still trying to absorb that Jaunty wasn't Jaunty. She kissed him. "I can see why Jaunty liked you."

"Did she?"

"She changed totally when she was with you." They stood so close, almost touching. "It was extraordinary."

"How so?" He ran a finger down the side of her face.

"She came alive."

"I hadn't noticed." He grinned.

"You seem to have this effect on women in this family."

"Do I?"

Gabe yawned. Fin kissed her forehead and turned her in the direction of her room.

"I'm so glad I've seen you in person." A man whose name Gabe couldn't remember came up to her in the shop. "I'm so sorry for your loss."

"Thank you."

"Jaunty was a great lady. When our house burnt down — the thatch caught — well, we weren't insured and, Jaunty, she gave us the money to rebuild. That was ten years ago now, and she didn't want anyone to know. She was so good like that." He put her hand on Gabe's arm. "Jaunty never said much to anyone but she cared."

Gabe was amazed. Then she remembered Mike Gear telling her that Jaunty had given him the seed money to buy his fishing boat. "Thank you for letting me know," she said to this man whose name she still couldn't remember. "I had no idea."

The man nodded. "She was like that. All quiet, but oh so good. We wouldn't have a roof over our heads." The man left the shop and Gabe put the milk, bread and paper on to the counter.

"Yes, Jaunty, was a wonderful lady," the woman at the till said.

Gabe smiled. "Yes, yes she was." Gabe paid and walked out, thinking Jaunty had indeed been so good and yet Gabe didn't think that Jaunty had seen that in herself. All her grandmother had seen was what she'd done to survive. It was clear Jaunty had never forgiven herself for taking Jean's identity.

"Hi, Gabe." Tamsin came up to Gabe as she was about to get into her car. "I'm so pleased I bumped into you. I'm so sorry about Jaunty. She'll be missed." Tamsin reached into the back of her car. "I planned on stopping by Bosworgy with this." Tamsin pulled a rich chocolate cake out. "I bumped into Jenna and heard that chocolate was your favourite and I thought you might need something to make you smile."

"Tamsin, that's so lovely."

"Not at all." Tamsin smiled. "You know we're here if you need us for anything."

Gabe swallowed a lump. "Thanks." She put the cake carefully in her car, thinking about what the man had said about Jaunty. At the moment she felt she hadn't known her grandmother at all. As soon as she got back to the cabin she was going to do some research on who she, Gabe, was. Was she Gabriella Blythe? Not really, despite what the birth certificate said. Was she Gabriella Carrow? If Jaunty had married Alex then that would be her name. But what if Jaunty was right and Dietrich was her grandfather? There was so much she needed to discover.

Playing with the sheets of paper that constituted her to-do list, she waited for the phone to be answered.

"St Mary's Catholic Church," a man said.

"Hi, I was wondering if I could speak to a priest."

"Speaking. How can I help?"

Gabe went through her grandmother's situation and the fact that she had had the last rites even though she couldn't speak.

"If she did that then I think maybe she would want a Catholic service, but I don't know." Gabe sank on to the stool in the kitchen. She needed to get out of the house and away from all of this. The weight of her grandmother's confession was pulling her down. If it weren't for Fin then she would totally break.

"I'm happy to help. Shall I call the vicar and see if we can organise something that will be appropriate?"

Gabe sighed. "Would you?"

"Of course."

The post lady was coming up the path. "Hello, my lover, how are you holding up?" She handed Gabe a huge pile of post.

"OK, I think. Thank you."

"Any date for the funeral yet?"

"Not yet." Gabe smiled. "Soon."

"It must be all the London people wanting to come down that's holding it up. She was so famous."

Gabe nodded her head, thinking, if you only knew, as she watched the woman walk away.

Placing the post on the table she opened her laptop and typed in Maria Lucia. This woman was her great-grandmother — if Jaunty was telling the truth. But why would she lie? Because she had lived a lie . . . Gabe dropped her head into her hands, trying to stop the circular thoughts. How could she be arranging a funeral or memorial service for someone who wasn't who they said they were? But if she didn't do something soon then people would become suspicious.

She typed in Dietrich von Hochsbrink and up popped information on his mother, who had been a renowned concert pianist. Gabe flexed her long fingers. She had not played or sung since Jaunty died. Would it have made it easier if she had known before where her talent had come from? No, that struggle would have remained the same, but knowing it now made her feel that she had let them down. Dietrich, she learned, had died during the war. But she had plenty of Von Hochsbrink relatives who survived and continued in the music world.

"Hello?" Gabe stood when she heard Max's voice.

"Hi."

"Thought you might need a hug."

Gabe nodded and Max embraced her. "So sorry about Jaunty."

"Yes."

"Is there anything I can do to help?"

Gabe shook her head slowly. "Unfortunately not."

"Well, I doubt you've had music on your mind, but I took on board what you said and I think it works so much better. I thought it might take your mind off grief — well, off Jaunty anyway, and I bet you haven't sung."

Gabe's mouth turned up at one side. "Right."

"You need to," he said seriously. "You'll feel better."

Gabe pursed her lips. "I'm not so sure, but show me what you have done."

"With the greatest of pleasure. Shall we head to your piano?"

Gabe nodded and followed him out. Maybe he was right and she did need to do something different.

Max took her through a warm-up and then he turned to his score. She could see the excitement on his face, and it was contagious. She let it fill her and sang for all she was worth. When she looked up from the music at Max he was fighting to keep control of his emotions.

"That was beautiful — and you were so right about the sea shanty. Thank you."

"Thank you for letting me be a part of it." Gabe touched his shoulder. "Max, what prompted you to write about the Lovers of Porthgwarra?"

He rubbed the side of his head. "Let's just say I lost the love of my life, who left me to make her fortune on foreign shores. But unlike these two we didn't promise to meet again after three years, no matter what."

"Oh dear. Sorry."

"At least I haven't let the tide take me, hoping that she'd be in the sea to embrace me."

Gabe put her hand over his. "Still raw?"

"I shouldn't be. She left ages ago, but the lovers' plight hit a nerve." He gave her a lopsided grin. "We weren't separated by parents who didn't think I was good enough, but by ambition." He shook his head. "Not mine but hers. I don't think I ever had enough ambition as far as she was concerned."

Gabe pictured the lovers from the story, their absolute belief in each other, their despair at being separated and both dying so that they could be together. Nancy had let the tide wash her into his arms and he died the same night in a shipwreck. She shivered.

"It's all history now, but I guess I needed to release it. Nothing like thwarted love to get the creative juices flowing."

He laughed, then gathered his music. "Would you like me to play the organ at the funeral?"

Gabe looked up. "Would you?"

"Absolutely. Anything for my star." She laughed.

After Max had gone Gabe played the piano for a while, but she couldn't get Jaunty's revelations out of her thoughts. It changed everything and, no matter how she tried, Gabe couldn't get her head around it. Looking at Jaunty's paintings around the room it was as if the artist had changed the view-point halfway through the painting and it was all upside down now. Closing the fall over the keyboard, she left the studio then stuck her head in the cabin, but there was no sign of Fin. There was a note on the counter. It read *Gone for a walk. x*

Gabe touched the x then looked out at the sun and wondered if she could catch up with him. She hurried to the gate to the main footpath and called out to Fin.

"Up here."

She went through the gate. "Where?"

"At the well."

"The well?"

"Turn left."

Gabe did. She knew he couldn't be far because his voice was so clear. She came round the bend and he called again.

"Up here."

Gabe jumped.

Fin stood on what looked like an old footpath. He took her hand. "Sorry to scare you."

Gabe put her hand to her heart.

"I thought you might not find me."

She smiled as he led her under a few low tree branches to an opening where pieces of cloth were tied in the holly trees. "What is this?" she asked. The air was cool and damp, and she could hear water trickling.

Fin pointed to a metal lid and Gabe could see water running below it.

"It's a well, or rather it was one. Judging by the trees it's considered a holy well."

"Really?" Gabe had never seen this before and yet it was so close to the house.

"I don't know for sure but . . ." He reached up and touched a piece of cloth. "I'd say that it's been visited fairly recently."

Gabe nodded and went to look at the bits of fabric. "Strange. I mean I've heard of what they call a clootie well at Madron, near Penzance — people hang bits of cloth from the trees, having dipped them in the well, and any illness they're suffering from is supposed to get better as the fabric rots. And I knew Jaunty had a well once because Dad used to mention getting the water from it when he was a kid. But he never said anything about it being a holy well."

Gabe's jumper caught on the holly when she turned.

"Careful." Fin put a hand out. "Here, let me help." He came close and disengaged the leaves from her sleeve.

"Thanks." Gabe shivered. "There's something about this place."

"Yes."

A rook cried out and Gabe jumped, slipping in the mud and falling into a ditch. "Shit!"

"Anything broken?" Fin reached down to help her up.

"My dignity."

He laughed. "Well, that can be fixed with a shower. You are absolutely covered in mud and twigs."

Gabe stood and looked down at herself. She was a total mess and her hair was full of damp leaves.

"Home now, I think." He took her hand and they walked slowly back to the cabin. Once there he kissed her nose, which seemed to be the only part of her not covered in mud.

"Go and clean yourself." He plucked a stick from her hair.

"Indeed I will." Gabe stripped off and climbed in to the shower, noting she'd skinned a knee. She watched as the filthy water swirled around the plughole, together with leaves. It would be wonderful if everything could be sorted as easily as washing away the mud. She turned the tap off and got out of the shower.

No sooner had Gabe wrapped herself in a towel than the phone rang in the kitchen. By the fourth ring it was clear that Fin wasn't there to answer it, so Gabe ran to get it. She lifted the receiver as the caller gave up and Fin walked in carrying the log basket. He took one look at her and burst out laughing.

"What's so funny?"

Fin reached out and pulled three holly leaves from her hair. "A wood nymph."

"Well, I've been called worse."

He stroked her cheek and she held her breath. "You'll catch a chill." He shut the door behind him then grabbed a towel from the cupboard and dried her hair. Blood came to the surface of her skin and it tingled as if it had been dead and was coming back to life. He looked into her eyes, then he kissed her.

Gabe lay wrapped in Fin's arms. Soft morning light fell through the window. She'd spent the whole night in his arms and had made love and been made love to slowly, gently, passionately. Without a word he understood her needs and with tender caresses taught her that she need not fear him or her desire for him. She flushed, remembering her own hunger. Once she felt safe, she had allowed herself to be loved.

298

"You OK?" He opened his eyes, still sleepy and filled with desire. She nodded, not sure she could speak. He ran a finger from her ear down to her collarbone then traced the hollow.

"Are you going to speak to me?"

She nodded, trying to believe it was real. She had made love and it had been wonderful. She didn't break. In fact, she felt exactly the opposite — she was whole again. "Thank you." She kissed him quickly, pulling the sheet up to her chin. He wiggled closer, closing his eyes and putting his head against her cheek.

There was a knock on the door and Gabe lunged to go and answer it, wondering who would be calling at this hour. She tried to pull the sheet with her but Fin had rolled on to his back and trapped it beneath him so she made a dash for her robe and then went out to the door.

"Hello!" She sounded as if she'd run a marathon and not a few feet. Mrs Bates thrust a pile of newspapers at her and Gabe blinked.

"Gabe. I'm so sorry. I thought you'd want the papers and might not have time to collect them with everything you have to do at the moment. Your grandmother was a wonderful woman. So good to so many, you know. She didn't want people to know that she was a famous artist, so we never spoke of it, but we all knew." Mrs Bates looked around the kitchen. "She lived so simply and you were never spoiled."

"Thank you, Mrs Bates." Gabe tied the belt tightly around her waist and put the papers on the counter.

She hadn't even had a cup of coffee and her world had spun round and then some.

"Have you organised the funeral yet?"

Gabe pushed her hair back. "Working on it. I'll post a notice in the shop so that everyone will know."

"Thank you, dear. Take care of yourself." Mrs Bates turned as she reached the steps. "Call me if you need anything. And, one more thing: my nephew's just started working as a reporter at the local paper and he wondered if you'd let him cover the funeral? I said I'd ask you."

Gabe blinked. She heard Fin moving in the bedroom. "Of course, that would be fine."

"That's lovely. He's just starting there and, well, she was ours."

Gabe closed the door as Fin walked out of the bedroom without a stitch on, and Gabe wanted to giggle. If Mrs Bates had seen him like that the village would be alight with gossip.

"All OK?" Fin walked up to her and took her face in his hands. He kissed her slowly.

"Fine." Gabe smiled and glanced down. "I'm going to get dressed in case any more unexpected visitors appear." She held his hand to her face and then dashed into her room. The memory of last night made her feel light-headed.

In the kitchen she heard the kettle click. "I'll make some breakfast," Fin called.

"Be there in a minute." Gabe scooped up her mud-covered clothes and dropped them in the washing machine before she joined him at the table. He must have gone to the studio as he was fully dressed, so there was no chance of scandalising Mrs Bates or anyone else. Well, possibly just herself.

Breakfast was on the table, waiting along with the papers. Fin looked up over the rim of his coffee cup and smiled. Gabe's stomach dropped. She didn't want breakfast; she wanted to take Fin by the hand straight back to her room. Instead she took a deep breath and sat down.

Gabe buttered a piece of toast and began looking through the papers, trying to focus on the news and not the man opposite her. There was nothing that held her attention and she had just finished her toast when she dropped the paper. Her hand shook when she saw an obituary for Jaunty. "I can't believe they have the obit in the paper already." Gabe put *The Times* down.

Fin looked up from the *Independent*. "Jaunty was famous, so it doesn't surprise me."

"But who notified them of her death?" Gabe picked at her breakfast.

"Good question, but the word spread quickly in the village so maybe the grapevine did the job."

"I suppose it's one less thing to do." Gabe shivered. She left the table and sank on to the sofa with the *Guardian*. She flipped through it until she came to the right section.

A large photo of Jaunty taken twenty years ago filled a quarter of the page. It had been taken at the request of the gallery and in it her hair was a short crop and she was turned away from the camera, staring out at the river, wearing her old sailing smock. It gave a sense of

301

her but didn't show what she actually looked like, and now Gabe knew why. She scanned the words.

Jean Blythe, known as Jaunty, died at her home in Cornwall on 9th October. Little is known about this reclusive artist, born just after the First World War. Blythe was the only child of Oliver and Mary Blythe and her work burst on the art scene when the London Gallery in Belgravia showed her work.

Gabe looked up. These, of course, were all lies. Except for the facts at the end.

Blythe had one child, Philip, who was killed in an oilrig explosion in the North Sea in 1996. She is survived by her granddaughter, Gabriella Blythe.

This was all wrong. Jaunty wasn't Jaunty Blythe, but Jeannette Penrose, also an artist, but of evocative, moody seascapes, not the famous paintings of Paris. Jaunty had lived the lie until the very end and then left Gabe with it.

She set off from the cabin and came out on the public footpath that led to the head of the creek. Leaves covered the ground in a layered slippery carpet. The sun played hide-and-seek with the clouds, creating ever-changing shadows as light fell through the gaps in the branches.

Gabe bent down to look at a group of mushrooms sprouting in the dense leaf mould at the base of an oak.

She was never good at mushroom recognition so she left them untouched and walked onto a fallen tree that rested on the riverbed. The water was slowly making its way back into the creek and a pair of swans swam in the channel. Gabe sat perfectly still so as not to disturb them. They made a perfect couple, a pair for life.

Jaunty must have felt that way about Alex — or was it that she couldn't risk allowing anyone else in? How could you keep the secrets she held so close from a lover? You couldn't, so Jaunty hadn't had another. Of course Gabe didn't question Jaunty's love for Alex; the ring over her heart spoke louder than any words could.

Gabe jumped up. She hadn't taken the necklace off Jaunty! The swans batted their wings in protest at her sudden movements and as quickly as she could Gabe ran back to the cabin. Jaunty was going to be cremated when Gabe had finally resolved the funeral and the chain and the ring it held was something of Jeanette's. It would be a shame to destroy that one connection to her past.

She stopped before she entered the cabin. The ring. It was a signet ring with the Carrow crest. What was it that Fin said when he saw the ring? He said his grandmother was a Carrow. Did that mean Alex was related to Fin? Had Jaunty known that? Guessed that? Is that why she had invited him to stay? Did Fin know? If he did, why hadn't he said anything to her? As she entered the cabin she saw Fin coming out of Jaunty's room. Gabe frowned.

"There is something you should see." Fin walked up to her.

Gabe frowned. "Now?"

"Yes."

Gabe joined him at the door. He reached for her hand and her breath caught. She wasn't sure she was ever going to become used to his touch.

In the studio, the bed was pushed aside and the back wall had been opened up. Gabe stood with her mouth gaping. How had she never seen this door?

"Jaunty knew her days were coming to an end." Fin began pulling out canvas after canvas, followed by portfolios filled with heavy watercolour paper. "She showed me these paintings."

Gabe tried to take in the completely different style of work, especially the portrait of her father as a young boy.

"When did she show you these?" Gabe looked at him. Why had Jaunty trusted him and not her?

"On her birthday." He pulled out a portrait of Gabe and she gasped.

He smiled at her. "Stunning, both the subject and the painting."

"When did she paint that?" Gabe stared at the painting.

He squinted while looking at the back of it. "Six years ago. There is a whole series of you, from about two years old until she painted this last one a year ago." He held up another canvas. The contrast was striking. All the softness had gone from Gabe's face and angles had appeared. Her hair, which in the previous painting hung like a burnished halo around her face, was pulled back tight. Hard, closed, totally withdrawn. She turned away and let her hair fall across her face.

Fin reached out and pulled her into his arms. "You don't look like that any more."

"How do I look?"

"Beautiful, fragile, perfect."

"When were your eyes last tested?" Gabe laughed. "So what do I do with all of these?" Gabe swept her hand towards the many portraits, traditional landscapes and more experimental works.

"Keep the ones you want and sell the rest."

"I can't sell any more of Jaunty's paintings." She frowned. "Knowing what I do it would be very wrong." She closed her eyes. "Even all the obituaries are wrong. Oh, why did she have to tell me?"

CHAPTER
EIGHTEEN

"I know this isn't ideal timing but I'll be back in a day once I sort out things." Fin held Gabe tight.

"It's fine." She kissed him and pulled away. "The train will be here in a minute. You'd better get on to the platform."

"I'll call you when I'm there." He held her hand.

"OK."

Fin released her hand and went through the barrier and Gabe walked back to the car. This didn't feel right, Fin going away. Of course she knew that he must have a life somewhere else, but for the past weeks he hadn't. He had been a part of Bosworgy. He'd mentioned something about verifying a painting and his old business, the one that his ex now ran.

The train pulled out of the station and she could see him waving from a carriage window. Her heart beat just that little bit faster. She was falling for him, had been for ages, and this was a good thing. Her therapist had said she needed to learn to trust again, that all men weren't rapists, but for the past few years she had only trusted Jaunty. Gabe stopped abruptly. She had trusted Jaunty but Jaunty had lied and lied and lied to her.

Driving away from the station, Gabe turned on the radio, hoping music would fill the void that had opened up within her. Verdi's *Requiem* lifted her in a strange way and she decided to visit the undertakers to collect the necklace and ring. She wondered if they would allow her to view her grandmother's body. The need to see her was almost overwhelming.

"Hello, Miss Blythe." The old man stood up from behind his desk.

"Hello, Mr Best. Sorry to disturb you but I've come to collect my grandmother's necklace and the ring that was on it."

"Of course, my dear. Have a seat and I'll go and get it."

Gabe sat and looked at the old photos on the walls. Somehow, knowing this family had been taking care of death for years seemed comforting. A few deep breaths, then Gabe lowered her shoulders, forcing the tension to leave. Fin was only going to be away for a day or two at most. She could survive without him, even if she didn't want to.

Looking at all the bereavement pamphlets, it was clear there was one for most situations, but not one for someone who was actually someone else. They still hadn't set a date for the funeral, but the priest from Helston had been a star. It would all work out and Jaunty would be buried with her secret, and from the church where she had hoped to marry Alex for the second time.

No matter how many times she wrestled with the idea, Gabe kept coming back to letting Jaunty's secret

just be that. Revealing it wouldn't help anyone. Gabe
didn't need the world to know that Maria Lucia was
her great-grandmother and that the real Jaunty, Jean
Blythe, was dead and had been since the awful attack
on the *Lancastria*. Gabe's searches had revealed that
she had no family so no one had been deprived of her
money or her fame.

Her grandmother's family no longer existed. With
the death of her great-grandfather and no male heir, the
title had lapsed and with no one to inherit what was an
entailed estate, the house on the Lynher had gone to
the Crown. Who knew what had become of any family
heirlooms? Maybe the Italian side of the family had
benefitted, as Maria Lucia would have inherited
whatever her husband had left. It was all neatly tied up,
so why had Jaunty disturbed the past?

Gabe jumped at the sound of a slammed door and
some shouting.

"Sorry about that. Here's your necklace." He smiled
at her.

Gabe looked up from the envelope in her hands.
"Can I see my grandmother?"

"Of course. Follow me." They walked to the back
room that had been made to look like a chapel of rest
and he stood by the door. "Just come by the office
when you leave or if you need anything."

Gabe adjusted the blue scarf around her grandmother's
neck. She looked peaceful and pale, but her hair was far
too tidy and Gabe messed it up a bit. A lump too large
to swallow blocked her throat. Jaunty's hands were

folded together and looked so beautiful, despite the knuckles enlarged with arthritis and the liver spots.

"Why, Jaunty?" Gabe fiddled with the scarf again, still not happy with the presentation. "Why not tell me when you were alive and I could ask all the questions that are in my head? We could have listened to your mother together and I could have appreciated it all the more, knowing the connection with you and with me. Listening to Maria Lucia, all I feel is a hole in the space between where you should have been and the sound. This link would have brought us closer together."

There was a cough behind her. "I'm sorry to disturb you but I've had an urgent call to visit with a client and I must go."

Gabe nodded and took one last look at her grandmother before she followed the man out of the little room.

Gabe walked into the cabin and the first place she glanced was at Jaunty's chair. A blanket lay over the back of it but otherwise it was empty and the house was too quiet. Even the wind and the birds made no sound. Gabe stopped walking, wanting to hear the water hit the quay or the wind whistle through the pines, but no, there was nothing.

The door to Jaunty's room was closed. She had shut it days ago and had not gone in there since. Gabe paused outside with her hand on the handle. Although she knew Jaunty wasn't in there having a rest, part of her still believed she was. How she could think this when she had just seen her lying in a simple pine coffin,

Gabe didn't know, but the mind was a funny thing. For years she had blamed herself for being raped, knew it had to have been her fault. Despite what the therapist had said, it was there, underlining every thought and every action. But now her vision was clearing.

Opening the door sent a wave of Jaunty's fragrance swirling around her. After all these days, the scent still lingered. She walked to the dresser and made sure the stopper was on the bottle, then trailed her fingers across the surface until she reached a black-and-white picture of her father in a silver frame. He must have been about eighteen when it was taken. Thick dark hair fell across his forehead and a slight smile lit his face. Why hadn't Jaunty told him? Or maybe she had. He looked so like Jaunty with his dark hair and blue eyes.

Gabe had always thought she looked like her mother but Jaunty said that she had her grandfather's eyes. She looked in the mirror and her tawny eyes stared back. Tiger eyes, Jaunty had called them. Did real tigers ever show fear? Because that was what Gabe saw in them right now. She turned away. She wasn't ready to sort this room. It was still too soon. If Gabe closed her eyes she could imagine her grandmother was still lying in bed, but it was just a dream. Jaunty was lying in the undertakers.

Leaving the bedroom, Gabe sat down at her computer and looked her grandmother up. There was one photo of the early Paris paintings, but no picture of Jaunty. She googled images and some of Jaunty's work appeared, plus the picture used in the obituary. Only after going through several pages did Gabe find a grainy photo of what must be the real Jaunty, taken in Paris in 1938. The hair was short and dark and she wore trousers and a man's shirt, but the quality was so bad that it could be her grandmother. The secret was safe.

Gabe looked away from the screen, wanting to share her concerns with Fin, but he wasn't here. She mustn't rely on him, but she had been. As Jaunty had. Her grandmother had trusted him but Gabe's first instincts had been the opposite. He was a stranger and he brought change. But the change he brought had made Jaunty smile and he had helped Gabe begin to heal when she had thought she never could, never would. And it had happened so fast. Looking out across the creek to Merthen Wood, she noticed how the leaves had changed colour. The hillside had been green a month ago, but now it was russet. The gentle hum of the farmer's combine harvester competed with the call of the birds patrolling the mudflats. She rubbed her temples. She needed to do something, so she ran to the studio.

A sea fog had rolled in in the past two hours while Gabe had photographed and catalogued twenty paintings. Looking out of the studio window she couldn't even see the north shore. Turning, she looked at the cupboards behind the bed, then her phone rang and she jumped. The wind must be blowing in the right direction. "Hello?"

"Hi, Gabe."

Her breath caught just listening to Fin's voice. "How are you?"

"Missing you. Missing Cornwall."

"Come back."

"I'd be on the next train but things are looking a bit messier here than I'd thought. Do you have the funeral date yet?"

Gabe sighed. "No. Hopefully tomorrow."

"Let me know as soon as you do and I'll be as quick as I can."

Gabe frowned as she put the phone down. She missed him. She knew he had no reason to come back other than for the few things he'd left behind, that there was no obligation. He had only been in her life a few weeks, after all. She wanted him back for so many reasons, but right now it was because he knew the secret and she could talk to him about it. It just kept growing bigger inside her all of the time. How had Jaunty held on to it for so long? What had keeping it done to her?

Gabe picked up the camera and snapped a picture of a stormy sea in grey with hints of red beneath. It was like pain was poking through. Noting it down, Gabe moved on. That painting disturbed her. She turned to the door behind the bed. What was she going to do about these paintings? How could she have them valued for probate? They were so different from the rest of Jaunty's work that someone would smell a rat.

Gabe turned the kettle on and sank on to the chair. What should she do? She wasn't trying to cheat the taxman, but if she brought these pictures into a gallery for appraisal someone would question them. She knew they would. Many of them were paintings of family and of course Gabe would never part with them. In fact, she wouldn't want to sell any of the paintings that were here, except maybe the last one. That hurt too much. It was a reflection of her or how she had been, grey on the surface with flashes of pain coming through.

Now she was beginning to see more clearly, but it had taken years.

Gabe stood beside the organ at the back of St Anthony's church. Max was playing the opening of Schubert's "Ave Maria". This she would sing for Jaunty. She had repeatedly listened to her great-grandmother's rendition and now, for Jaunty, she would sing her own. Max looked up and Gabe began. They were alone in the candlelit church. Outside the dusk had fallen and the church smelled of the many flowers that adorned the altar and each pillar. The women of the village had offered their help and Gabe had accepted. Each one had a story to relate to Gabe of some small kindness her grandmother had done. It was clear now that even though her grandmother had been a recluse, over the years she had become a part of the community and they held her close. Jaunty belonged to them as much as she did to Gabe. She had come to them as a stranger, a war widow with a young child, and they had asked no questions. Gabe supposed there were so many women widowed after the war that this didn't seem unusual.

She scanned the music. She knew this well, although she hadn't sung it in years. During her student days, she had kept money coming in by singing anywhere and everywhere, and during the Christmas season she must have sung this a hundred or more times.

The sound of clapping snapped Gabe back to here and now. A Catholic priest stood in the doorway. "That was magnificent."

"She's brilliant, isn't she?" Max stood.

"I've just come from talking with the vicar and everything seems to be in place for tomorrow's funeral mass."

Father Tim looked about the ancient church. "I remember visiting here as a child when we came on holiday. I always wondered what it was like in candlelight."

"It's better when there are more lit." Gabe realised that she recognised him. He christened Toby. He nodded as he walked up to the altar. Over the years Gabe had taken the beauty of this church and its setting for granted. How it must have hurt Jaunty to visit here over the years, knowing that this was where Alex had wanted to marry her for the second time. Yet somehow it felt right that this was the church for the funeral. It was so close to the water and being close to water was so important to Jaunty.

"Shall we run through 'Amazing Grace'?" Max asked.

Gabe wrinkled her nose. It had been one of Jaunty's favourites so she had included it, but she wanted the congregation to sing it, not for her to sing a solo.

314

"I know you don't want to do this, so maybe just sing the first verse alone and then everyone can join in."

Gabe sighed. "OK, although I don't know why I'm listening to you."

"Simple: because I am a genius." Max grinned.

Gabe couldn't really argue with that.

Amazing grace, how sweet the sound
That saved a wretch like me.
I once was lost, but now am found,
Was blind, but now I see.

CHAPTER
NINETEEN

The lights were on in the cabin as Gabe walked down the path, and her breath caught in her throat. It could only mean one thing — Fin had returned. The smell of roasting lamb and cinnamon wafted out of the kitchen.

"Hi." Gabe stood in the doorway. Fin was at the stove with a wooden spoon in his hand. A smile spread across his face and his eyes lit up. Gabe couldn't move.

"Hello, beautiful." He placed the spoon in the pot and walked towards her with his arms open. Gabe dropped the sheet music in her hands on the counter and embraced him. This is what she wanted, what she had longed for.

"I've missed you." Gabe's head rested against his chest and the steady rhythm of his heart played to her. Home. This was home. She looked up. His eyes were still smiling at her and all the defences she had built seemed so stupid now.

His mouth met hers. Gabe pulled him closer as her hands caressed his back through his shirt. Need swamped her.

The phone rang.

He sighed. "I think you should answer it and I should tend to dinner before it burns."

Gabe nodded and stumbled on wobbly legs to the phone to pick up the handset. "Hello?"

"Hi, Gabe, it's Hannah."

Gabe grinned. "Hi."

"I'm just calling to check on you."

She was touched by Hannah's concern. She didn't think she'd have been so sensitive to others at seventeen. "Thank you."

"I'll be there on Friday. I've taken the day off school. I want to be there for you."

Gabe blinked. "You don't need to do that."

"Yes, I do. You were there for me."

"Thank you."

"I'll be there early to help with anything. See you then. Bye."

Gabe put the phone down. Friday. It would be the end. There would be a funeral mass, then Jaunty would be cremated. Only the loose threads of probate would remain to be tied up. A life finished and somehow Gabe must move forward. She brushed her hand against her eyes.

Fin reached out and touched her. "OK?"

She jumped. When had he appeared in front of her? "Yes, that was Hannah. She'll be at the service."

"Good. Dinner's ready." He held out his hand and Gabe took it. Reassurance and excitement mixed in the clasp.

"How was London?"

Fin glanced at her, then looked away. "Fine." He walked to the kitchen. Gabe studied his back. She might be imagining things but his shoulders looked rigid. Something was troubling him. He came back to the table with a smile on his face that didn't reach his eyes.

"Sure?"

"Well, not really." He sighed. "It's complicated, but a painting that sold through my old business may be a fraud and it's becoming messy." He sat down and reached for the wine.

"Doesn't sound good."

"Not good on many fronts but mainly because I have to deal with Patricia."

Gabe touched his hand as it worried the edge of the table.

He looked up. His eyes were dark and thoughtful. "I wasn't in London the whole time. I went to visit my mother to see if she had heard my grandmother mention anything about Jaunty or Jeanette as she really was."

Gabe straightened in her chair. Had he told his mother Jaunty's secret? "And?"

"No, she didn't but I went through some of my grandmother's papers and found some letters exchanged between them."

"Yes?"

"Nothing exciting, I'm afraid, but Jaunty — Jeanette — did spend time with them as she mentioned."

"Was there anything from your uncle?"

"No paperwork." Fin paused and poured the wine. "I have a painting, though." He looked at her briefly, then served the lamb tagine.

"A painting?"

318

He nodded.

"Your great-uncle was a painter too?"

"No. When my grandmother died she, among other things, left me a painting that belonged to Alex. She'd known how important it was to him and I'd always reminded her of him."

Fin stood and collected a briefcase Gabe hadn't noticed by the wall. He pulled out a clear protective sleeve and handed it to Gabe. It held an unframed watercolour on heavy paper.

"Oh." Blood drained from her and she felt a chill. It was Jaunty's work without a doubt. She turned it over and there, in Jaunty's writing, was her declaration of love — but the signature was different. It read Jeanette. If there had been any lingering doubts in her mind, they were gone.

Morning light slipped in through a gap in the curtains. Gabe snuggled closer to Fin. She had slept so soundly, the best she had in ages. This must be what contentment felt like. It was magic. Fin's chest rose and fell with his breathing. She had missed this while he was away. Could it really only have been a month since he had turned up on Bosworgy's quay? The light caught his morning stubble and her fingers itched to touch his cheeks, every part of him, but she didn't want to wake him just yet. For the moment she enjoyed studying his eyelashes resting on his cheek. She swallowed. Her glance strayed to his mouth, which smiled slightly. How could she ever have thought him a stranger or a threat? Jaunty had been right to invite him into their lives. Had

Jaunty known that Gabe would fall for him? Or had Jaunty just enjoyed the rekindling of her memories of Alex.

After tomorrow was over Gabe would talk to a lawyer about Jaunty's revelations and see how she should proceed with what she knew, and also how to handle the body of work that wasn't Jaunty but Jeanette. Fin murmured in his sleep and Gabe tried to listen, wondering what he was dreaming of.

He moved and his arms pulled her closer to him and he nuzzled her ear.

"Morning."

Chills went done her spine. "It's good to have you back."

"Hmmm." He planted light kisses down her neck and Gabe closed her eyes. "I missed you."

"So you said last night."

He trailed a finger across her breast. "You don't know how much."

"Show me." Gabe ran a hand over his hip.

"With pleasure," he whispered as he rolled over.

They set off from the cabin hand in hand. The sun had set but the sky was still light and tinged with pink as they walked along the track, hopping over puddles and laughing. Her head was spinning from all the final arrangements for tomorrow; hymns, orders of service, the readings, the priest, the vicar, the undertakers, the reception in the village hall afterwards. She had jumped at Fin's suggestion of dinner down at the pub. She was dreading tomorrow and the final goodbye, yet longing for it to be all over. The urge to begin again was strong. She stole a glance at Fin. She knew he was a huge part of that desire. Desire. She smiled, remembering this morning before the phone had begun ringing and all the world seemed to want to talk to them both. Fin had spent the best part of the day pacing by the car where he had the best phone reception. Now, he was looking out over the fields to Falmouth Bay. His expression was thoughtful, almost sad. Three jackdaws sat on the telephone wire watching them as she and Fin moved along. She shivered.

"OK?" He turned to her with a lopsided smile.

She nodded and kissed his cheek. He wrapped his arm around her and pulled her to his side as they turned down the lane to Penarvon Cove. It was darker under the cover of the trees and Gabe squinted until she adjusted to the lower light. She touched the torch in her jacket pocket. It wasn't needed yet.

Fin's phone rang and as he took the call he stepped away from her. She assumed it was the painting crisis. She half listened to his curt greeting and talk of a painting before he lost signal. She knew so little about his life, but then that was something she could look forward to learning about.

Just as they arrived at the Shipwrights, Fin's phone rang again. Gabe left him standing outside and stood inside the outer door out of the light rain that had begun to fall.

"Frenchman's Creek. It's an unusual and unique early painting." Fin's voice was drifting away. "There is a long story."

He was going to sell Jaunty's painting! Gabe froze and listened carefully to what else she could hear. Fin's motives were now clear: money.

Mist hung over the creek. The sky was a pale blue above it so it should clear by eleven. Gabe stood by the window and adjusted her dress. She could do this. Fin's motives for coming here in the first place didn't matter. She'd never asked him but maybe he'd wanted to find the location of the painting, and he had. It was a bonus for him that he discovered the artist too. He was clever and quickly put things together — it was his work — and Jaunty had known what he did and she hadn't worried. So there was no reason for Gabe to feel so angry. It didn't matter now. She was being ridiculous.

Wiping her palms on a teatowel, she tried to shake the feeling that Jaunty's story and the painting could change Fin's fortunes. It could instantly rebuild his career after his ex-wife had stripped it from him, because Jaunty's story would put him on the front page and that early painting would make him a mint. He could begin again if that was what he wanted.

Gabe swallowed. She would not think about it today. Today was about Jaunty, the Jaunty this community knew. It was about saying farewell. Today Gabe would sing for Jaunty one last time, then she must begin to work again to pay the bills. Life had to continue and Fin would leave after today, that was inevitable. It was OK. And she was too.

"Do you want anything to eat?" Fin walked into the cabin.

322

"No, thanks." Instead of falling into his arms last night, Gabe had crawled into bed alone. She had been quiet all through their meal and Fin had expressed concern, but Gabe had said it was worries about the funeral. She wanted to scream that he'd betrayed her and Jaunty. But she hadn't. He was human. He needed money and Jaunty's painting would get some for him. She would call the solicitor first thing on Monday and discuss how to go about telling the truth to the world.

But right now just hearing his voice sent shivers of memory across her skin. Last night, when she had heard the door close behind him, she'd let the tears fall. But it was fine. He had helped her to break down the walls, and though she was now open, exposed and very cold, it really was fine. Because she was fully alive again.

"It will be a long morning on an empty stomach." He reached a hand towards her and she pulled back.

"True, but I can't face food." She turned. He was so close and the scent of his aftershave, the freshness of citrus, hung in the space that separated them.

"Shall we leave?" she asked.

"There's still time." His hands clenched and unclenched.

Gabe shook her head. There wasn't time. Their time had finished and she needed to get through today and get beyond him. The next phase of her life needed to begin. Jaunty had survived and so could she.

She looked up into his eyes and that was a mistake. His concern showed he cared and she didn't want to think about that. It was easier if she thought him mercenary. She stepped aside and grabbed her coat and bag. The sooner she began, the sooner she could rebuild.

Gabe drove in silence through the lanes towards St Anthony's. The mist had cleared over Falmouth Bay and it was a perfect October day. She took the turning above the graveyard. At a later point she would have Jaunty's ashes interred with her parents in Manaccan graveyard, although she really wanted to spread them across the water near the Isles of Scilly so that Jaunty could be one with the sea and with her Alex. Gabe turned the car into a space between boats laid up for the winter. She hadn't said a word to Fin on the whole journey. She would deal with him after today was over. Now she scurried down to the church, not waiting for him to catch up with her. As she turned the corner, she saw the sailing boats beached for the winter. What had become of Fin's boat, *Jezebel*, that Jaunty had sailed with Alex? Gabe was sure it was the same boat, remembering how Jaunty had reacted, the emotion that had been in her voice when she'd said the name. Fin hadn't mentioned it. She shook her head. She had many more important things to think about.

As she slipped in to the porch she saw a flash of light and heard the sound of a digital camera click, but when she turned she only saw Fin behind her. She must be imagining things. Or maybe it was Mrs Bates's nephew from the local paper. Gabe hadn't really thought about it when she'd said yes, but she supposed Jaunty was something of a local celebrity.

Hannah was straightening the piles of the order of service when Gabe entered the church. She looked lovely in a navy dress, her blonde hair sleek and shining. She rushed over to hug Gabe.

"You OK?"

Gabe nodded, noting that Max was already sitting at the organ. "Morning," he said.

"Hi."

"Shall we have a quick run through? Father Tim is already here. He's chatting with the vicar in the vestry."

Gabe moved to the side of the organ. The acid in her empty stomach roiled. She didn't have to do this, just the music alone would be beautiful. Out of the corner of her eye she saw Mrs Bates topping up the water in the flower arrangements, and she had helpfully organised for tea and coffee to be served in the village hall after the service as well. Gabe would stop in there briefly before going to the crematorium in Truro. The undertaker had told her there was no need for her to go, but Gabe felt she had to be with Jaunty on this last trip. It was her final journey and Gabe didn't want her to do it with only strangers for company.

"Let's run through the Schubert once more." Max gave her hand a squeeze.

Gabe nodded. The opening notes of the music began and she sang despite hearing the heavy wooden door open close behind her. When she had finished, a tap on her shoulder made her shake.

"Sorry to trouble you, miss. We're all set. Your grandmother is here."

Gabe swung round even though she knew Jaunty wasn't *here* any more.

"The coffin is outside."

"Thank you. Do you need anything else from me?"

"No." He shook his head. "You have a beautiful voice." The man coloured as he said the words and Gabe smiled. The Cornish loved their singing.

"Thank you."

"You take a seat in the front pew when you're ready." He nodded and backed out of the church.

Gabe turned to Max. "I don't need to practise 'Amazing Grace'."

"Agreed." He smiled and Gabe, fiddling with the neckline of her dress, walked to the front pew. She was stunned to see the church was full. Most of the faces she knew, including the new owner of the gallery. He was already pressing her about a retrospective of Jaunty's work. If he only knew, he wouldn't be asking, she thought. Hannah was handing out the order of service to everyone and Gabe wondered if she'd had enough printed. On the cover was a photograph of Jaunty in her usual pose, looking into the distance. Always looking for something that was out of reach, and finally Gabe knew what that was. No wonder it had absorbed her so.

The level of discreet coughs and whispers grew. Gabe focused on the paper in her hand. Everything was organised. All she had to do was sing twice. She wasn't speaking, only the priest would be saying a few words. The lily in the centre of the main bouquet on the altar calmed her with its scent and simplicity. Jaunty would have approved of the flowers. The lilies came from the florist but many of the other flowers were from local gardens.

The organ began with the opening of "Guide me, O Thou Great Jehovah" as they brought the coffin in. Gabe turned and was stunned to feel tears prick the back of her eyes. She thought she had finished with them, but obviously not. Fin was one of the pallbearers and she recognised Mark Triggs and Mike Gear. Tamsin Polcrebar's husband, Anthony, the local builder, and Tristan Trevillion and one of Anthony's sons were also helping. Jaunty certainly didn't require six men to carry her, but Gabe thought she might find it a bit amusing. Mrs Bates, in the pew behind, belted out the words to the second verse in a completely different key to everyone else, so for the final verse Gabe went to full volume and the church dropped to total silence as she held the last note. It wasn't quite the effect she had wanted, but at least it had drowned Mrs Bates out.

Hannah squeezed into the pew to her left while Fin sat next to her on her right. Father Tim began and before she knew it Gabe was walking to the back of the church. All eyes were on her and she tried not to stumble when she saw the size of the crowd. The rear of the church was standing room only. They made space for her as she approached Max.

Everything inside her froze. It wasn't supposed to be like this. This was a small local funeral, not a memorial service for a celebrity, but the door was open and

327

people were standing outside, trying to listen, so it made it feel that way. Max made eye contact. His expression said it all, then he put on his best conductor face as if he knew that something inside her would respond because she couldn't let Jaunty down, couldn't let Maria Lucia, her great-grandmother down. Gabe blocked out the crowd and focused on the beauty of the music, let it take her over. As the last note finished the church was totally silent and Max placed his hand on her arm. Gabe didn't dare look at him because she knew she would crack. Right now it was all too much.

The priest delivered an appropriate homily, mentioning Jaunty's dedication to family and to work. He spoke of her lasting legacy to the art world and blissfully he kept it brief. Gabe dreaded the next bit, but without leaving the pew she began: *Amazing Grace, how great though art . . .*

The priest began the final blessing and Fin slipped out of the pew. Gabe felt naked without him beside her. How was she going to walk out of this church alone? Fin, with the others, took Jaunty's coffin out of the church and Hannah took Gabe's hand.

"I have plenty of experience with funerals unfortunately," Hannah whispered in her ear. "My father's and a special friend's."

The priest announced that there would be a small reception in Manaccan village hall, and Hannah gave her hand a squeeze as they walked down the aisle with the crowd filing out behind them. The beautiful day had disappeared in to a heavy shower and Fin threw his coat over Gabe's shoulders and opened the back seat of the limo and helped her in. He was going to follow in Gabe's car.

As the black car reversed out, a few people chatted in the rain and Gabe noticed the newspaper covering a little girl's head. The headline read: "Acclaimed Artist Jaunty Blythe Is A Fraud".

CHAPTER
TWENTY

Gabe was going to be sick. How had this happened? Fin. It had to be Fin! She pressed the button and the window came down, then she gulped in air as they drove up the hill to Manaccan. The car slowed in front of the hall but Gabe shook her head. She couldn't go in and face everyone. Tamsin ran down to the car and hopped in.

"Take us straight to my house, John," she said to the driver.

Tamsin turned to Gabe and took her hand. "I've seen the paper, and there's been a bloke going round the village asking questions, so I'm taking you to ours and then we'll sort it out."

At Tamsin's house Gabe was bustled into the kitchen and despite the heat from the Aga she found it cold. She pulled Fin's coat tighter around her, then threw it off. The only way the journalists could have known would be through him. He had betrayed her, betrayed Jaunty.

"Brandy, I think." Tamsin disappeared and Gabe saw the kitchen table covered with all the papers. It was only in one but it was on the front page. The story followed the lines of "privileged woman steals East End girl's glory".

Gabe sank into a chair. That wasn't what happened! How could Fin have done this? Was he that desperate for money?

"Now, just heard from Anthony and they're all on their way back here." Tamsin sat down and pushed a glass towards Gabe. "Mrs Bates is in floods of tears. She fears it's all her fault for wanting her Timothy to cover the funeral for the paper." Tamsin shook her head. "Somehow I don't see Tim as being the cause, but I could be wrong."

Gabe shook her head. "I should have done something."

"You knew?"

"Only just." Gabe took a sip of the brandy. "Jaunty wrote a confession of sorts for me."

"Ah."

"And well, I was still trying to figure out what to do." A tear slipped down Gabe's cheek. "It all spiralled ahead, beginning with the obituaries hitting the papers when I hadn't even called them."

"Well, you know how news spreads here. It could have reached them in any number of ways and once they heard it would be easy enough to confirm." Tamsin made herself a cup of tea. "In fact, thinking about it, I saw something on Facebook. Nothing bad, just someone noting how sad they were that she had died."

Gabe nodded.

"She was so good, frankly, I don't see what all the fuss is about. There can't be any other news at the moment. It would be jolly convenient if some minister was caught shagging someone. Not to worry, Gabe, we'll get it sorted. Now finish that drink and get some colour back into your cheeks."

Gabe wore a big woolly jumper of Tamsin's and was surrounded by what felt like half the village. Tamsin's son Fred had been sent to check the cabin and make sure that it and the studio were secure. He found a stranger with several cameras loitering on the track to the cabin. He'd asked if he was lost and told him that he'd get some great wildlife shots but not much else.

Everyone moved around and discussed how to handle the crisis. Fin stood on the outskirts. He wasn't speaking, just listening, as she was. People Gabe had known but not known well all her life were closing round her to protect her. She was theirs and so was Jaunty.

"It's clear we have to get the full and correct story out." Tristan spoke. "I'm afraid it will have to be Gabe presenting it." He looked at her and Gabe didn't know what to do.

"I could do it." Fin stepped forward. "I'm an art historian. If I speak then they will listen."

"They will still want to hear Gabe's thoughts. Like, did she know and everything." Tamsin rubbed Gabe's shoulders. Gabe was shaking. How could Fin stand there as if he was innocent? The world would still be in ignorance if he had kept his mouth shut. But he hadn't.

"Hey, they have linked to a video of Gabe singing!" Anthony looked up from the computer screen and everyone except Gabe and Fin huddled around Anthony, watching. Gabe froze. Without looking at the screen she recognised it. It was the final performance of the competition.

As the last note faded Gabe's glance met Fin's. She knew and he knew.

"Wow, we knew you could sing, Gabe, but that was fabulous." Anthony's voice came from the centre of the group.

Gabe grabbed the back of the chair in front of her. She couldn't breathe. The room started disappearing and then . . . nothing.

Air blew across Gabe's face and she heard voices around her, but opening her eyes was a problem. Maybe if she didn't the world would go away. She should have let herself drown the night she rescued Fin. His life jacket would have saved him without her help. This was his fault.

Save a stranger from the sea, and he'll turn your enemy.

"Gabe!" Hannah's voice called. It sounded as if it came from across the room, but Gabe knew someone was holding her hand, and it wasn't Fin. Her pulse wasn't racing and she knew that her body would respond to his traitor's touch. The noise of the voices all talking at once almost drowned out the quiet singing that Hannah began. She sang the hymn that Gabe had sung the night she saved Fin.

Refuge in grief, Star of the sea,
Pray for the mourner, pray for me.

Hannah's voice was so sincere that Gabe opened her eyes.

"You're with us again." Hannah smiled.

"I think Gabe needs to rest." Tamsin came over and took Gabe's hand. "You'll stay here tonight so we can look after you."

There was no option, Gabe could tell, and before she knew it she was tucked in Tamsin's guest room.

"Take these sleeping pills. You get a good night's rest and everything will look better in the morning."

Gabe swallowed them but didn't see how things would improve with her grandmother's deception splashed across the papers.

Gabe clawed her way out of a terrible dream. Forcing her eyes open, she didn't know where she was. Weight pressed down on her chest, and gasping for air she tried to scream but no sound came out. Her limbs were heavy and she felt drugged — and that's when she remembered where she was and what had happened. Sleeping tablets.

The sun was high in the sky; she must have slept for more than twelve hours. There was a tap on the door and Tamsin popped her head round it. "Hi." She brought in a tray with tea and toast and Gabe struggled to push up into a sitting position. Nothing was working properly and her mouth was painfully dry.

"You've been asleep for ever. You must have needed it."

Gabe nodded, not trusting her voice. Tamsin handed her a mug of tea.

"Things are much better now, much calmer," Tamsin said, walking to the door. "I'll leave you to drink your tea and eat in peace. I got Fred to bring some of your clothes from the cabin." Tamsin frowned. "Not what you or I would have chosen to go together but they'll have to do. I put them in the bathroom on the towel rail."

"Thanks," Gabe croaked.

"No problem. Come down when you're ready."

Gabe sipped her tea, thinking that might mean never leaving the safety of this pretty room.

Fin was the first person Gabe saw as she walked into Tamsin's kitchen. She stopped. Didn't these kind people know that he was the cause of the problem?

"Good afternoon," Anthony greeted her from where he stood by the window.

"Yes, you could say I overslept."

"Not to worry about it." Tamsin pulled a cake out of the Aga and the aroma of warm chocolate and almonds filled the air.

"All's cool here at crisis central." Fred looked up from the computer on the table. "While you were sleeping Fin's handled the press and has so far, by my count, given ten interviews to the media. He's a real pro."

"Oh my God." Gabe clutched the doorframe. She should have been up hours ago. She couldn't believe they'd let Fin speak for her or for Jaunty. She wasn't sure it could get any worse.

"You look like you've seen a ghost." Anthony handed her a cup of coffee. "Do you need some fresh air?"

Gabe nodded and stumbled out the back door. This wasn't happening to her. If she had put her foot down and sent Fin on his way immediately none of this would have happened. Why hadn't she questioned his reasons for being here? Alarm bells should have rung loud and clear when he said he was an art historian. She was such a fool. She hadn't followed her instincts until they had been blinded by his charm, and by then her hormones had kicked into overdrive. She had slept with him, not once, but countless times. She flushed and walked further into the garden towards a summerhouse where she stood and let the tears run down her cheeks. She would allow herself these few moments of self-pity and then she had to find Jaunty's determination and take control of the situation. She blew her nose.

"Gabe." Fin was beside her.

"You!" She stepped away.

"I know you hate me, but believe me, I'm on your side."

"You're joking, right?"

"No." He walked closer and Gabe couldn't back away any further.

"Look, I know you won't believe me but I wanted to make sure you, and only you, saw this." He handed her a folded sheet of paper.

"What's this? Your apology for ruining Jaunty's reputation." He didn't say anything and Gabe opened it. Jaunty's handwriting looked so shaky.

My dearest girl. As always I have left the hardest bit to the very last. This is the part that has tormented me the most. Even now, having made my confession, this is the one thing I cannot forgive myself for. That in itself is a sin. Pride. I always had far too much of that.

But I delay.

On the night that Alex and I fled France I was to meet Dietrich. I had told Alex this but he said there was no time and I was buoyant as we left the priest. I was finally married to my love. We went through the wood to the meeting point. Alex told me to wait while he went and sent the signals. I stood shivering by a tree, planning for our future.

Dietrich must have been worried when I hadn't turned up at our appointed time because he came looking for me and found me alone. His face was full of relief and love. But, of course, within moments, he wanted to know why I was hiding in the woods near a dirt track.

We argued and eventually the truth came out of me. He begged me not to go and I refused. I knew, above all, he mustn't see Alex. Alex couldn't be compromised. I began to run away from the road and Dietrich followed, declaring his love. He wouldn't listen and I heard Alex's signal in the distance. Then I saw Alex's light. He was searching for me. He must have heard the arguing.

I pulled out the small pistol Alex had given me earlier and I threatened Dietrich, but he wouldn't listen. He wouldn't leave. Alex came up to us and it was too late. Dietrich should have gone when I asked. It all would have worked out. Alex stood there. He was compromised, the whole operation was. I had to choose, Alex and my country or Dietrich my friend and lover.

I shot Dietrich as he was saying, yet again, that he loved me more than life. He fell to the ground. Alex took my hand, then I ran, looking back only once. Dietrich hadn't moved. I'd killed him.

Gabe's hand shook. Jaunty's writing was almost illegible and the *m* on the end slid off the page. "Where did you find this?"

"When I checked the cabin I found a window open in Jaunty's room. The wind had caused an unholy mess and as I picked up the last papers I saw this one poking out from under the side of the bed."

"Have you read it?"

He nodded.

"Have you told anyone?" Gabe looked at him, hating that part of her wanted to be in his arms.

"No, nor would I."

"I'm afraid I find that hard to believe." Gabe took a deep breath.

"Gabe!" Tamsin called from the kitchen.

"Gabe, wait." The look in Fin's eyes pleaded with her.

She turned away from him. Gabe folded the letter and put it in to her pocket. "Coming." She didn't know what to think or feel at this moment, but she knew the last thing she wanted to do was talk to Fin. These good people had no idea what they had done by relying on him. Unfortunately Gabe knew all too well.

338

The newspapers were spread out over the table. Being the weekend all of them had found space to run the story in more detail. They had unearthed photos of Jaunty as a child with her parents and Gabe was thrilled to see them, but at the same time she was horrified that the world was viewing them at the same time as she did. Jaunty wouldn't have wanted this.

Among the pictures were statements saying that Gabriella, Jeanette's granddaughter, was unable to comment at this time, that this was all news to her. She hadn't known about her grandmother's other life, that she hadn't withheld anything, but was in the process of investigating the story. It mentioned that she was in mourning and wished her privacy to be respected. But of course it wasn't. The papers had left no stone unturned from Gabe's past and it appeared that many of her old colleagues were happy to chime in, probably for the name-check that they would receive.

She put her head in her hands. How was she going to fix this? Was there even a way she could? Every one of the articles had taken against Jaunty. None of them looked at what her situation had been or what she had done in the war. Gabe wondered if her service had ever been noted or would it be under Jean's name? But of course it hadn't been Jean. She had been on the *Lancastria*.

There were inset articles giving the terrible statistics and background on the tragedy of the ship, even a picture of the ship's manifest listing Jeanette Penrose. It made for depressing reading. One of the papers harped on about her privileged upbringing and showed photos of Polruan House and the Lake Garda villa where they had summered. It was all wrong.

"We're so sorry about all of this." Tamsin sat next to her and put her hand on her shoulder.

"You've been so kind."

"Nonsense. It's the only way that humans should behave. Now, I think that it is far too late for us to do anything today and that Gabe should stay here again tonight, and we shouldn't talk about any of this until tomorrow morning when we are all rested and can make sensible plans."

She looked round the room and every head nodded in agreement.

Anthony walked through the door with the Sunday papers, and Gabe wasn't sure if she could bear to read any more. She was drained by Jaunty's final revelation, and if she thought about it too much it would finish off what sanity she still had left.

"That's better." Anthony handed her the paper he'd taken to read. It was open at a page with an article written by an Alexander Falk, an art historian, said the byline. In it he took Jaunty's side and explained how Jeanette had become Jean and the assumptions people had made. It was all very calm and reasoned. The next article was by Sam Marks, a well-known art critic. Gabe put the paper down. Wasn't that the name of the man she'd met with Fin?

Gabe scanned it and saw that he argued that it didn't matter that one artist had painted one set of work and the other painted another. Both were war artists. Both had studied with the same painter, Pierre François. Jeanette's unique vision had developed in a manner that was equal to the works of Jean, and the weaving of their stories made it all the more intriguing, as had Jeanette's divergence from her initial strengths as a portrait painter. There was a photograph of one of Jaunty's paintings that she had hidden, a portrait of Gabe's father. He then went on to contrast the styles, highlighting how the need to be unidentifiable had pushed Jeanette's art to greater heights. Her portraiture, from what he had seen, was excellent, but not to the level of her near abstract seascapes.

Gabe knew she had Fin to thank, if that was the right word for this. He must have photographed the portrait and given it to Sam. But where was Fin now? He certainly wasn't in Tamsin's house.

"Where's Fin?"

"Ah, he's a star. He's our man in London and he's doing a stellar job." Tamsin smiled and handed Gabe a biscuit. As Gabe bit into the still warm ginger snap she wasn't so sure about that.

CHAPTER
TWENTY-ONE

It was two more days later before they allowed Gabe to go home. In that time the press had begun to turn around. More articles appeared in the form of editorials with large quotes from Alexander Falk. She had heard nothing from Fin, but he was obviously liaising with the little committee that had formed to look after her and Jaunty's name. Gabe was so touched by their support.

"Are you sure you don't want me to come with you?" Tamsin put her hand on Gabe's.

"I'm fine. This is my home."

"Well, Anthony tells me that all is OK there."

"Thanks." Gabe took a breath. "Thanks for everything."

"Ah, it was nothing. It's not right what they've done, but we'll see it's sorted."

"I don't know what to say. You don't have to do this."

"Ah, but we do. Jaunty was our reclusive artist — she came here to be safe."

Gabe nodded. That was true.

"Well, thank you again." Gabe stepped out of Tamsin's car and took a deep breath. Eucalyptus and pine. She turned and waved at Tamsin, then walked down the path to the steps. On the top one she stopped to look at the view. In front of her the pines were still half covered in a morning mist and the river was only just visible. Slowly she walked down the steps. A spider had spun a web across the terrace like yellow crime-scene tape. Drops of dew shimmered in the breeze, reflecting the golden morning light.

No crime had taken place here. Only a life lived as best as it could be. Gabe swallowed and unlocked the kitchen door. There would be no Jaunty and no Fin. From here on she was truly alone, which is exactly what she had hoped for a few weeks ago. But now everything had changed, especially her.

Her phone beeped. She had a voice message. Dropping her bag on the bench, she walked down the stone steps to the creek. She watched an egret fly across the water and land on a bare branch on the opposite shore.

"Hi, Gabe. I know you don't want to speak to me, but I need to talk to you about so much and I've had a request from *Spotlight on Art* to be interviewed about Jaunty. What do you want me to do? Please call."

Just listening to his voice and her legs were wobbling. How had she been so foolish? Well, that didn't matter now. She had to deal with *this*. She dialled his number and clenched her free hand. She had no idea what she would say. His voicemail was garbled and Gabe cursed the lack of decent signal.

"It's Gabe. Go ahead and give the interview. The damage is done."

The line went dead. There was no need to ring him back because she had nothing else to say and she had many other things that she needed to think about and do. Fin could do what he liked. Jaunty's reputation was in pieces and Gabe had to sort out probate as well as telling the gallery that she didn't want a retrospective of Jaunty's work. They had rung her and insisted that there would be more interest now than ever before, but that was the last thing she wanted, and Jaunty had avoided all that interest during her lifetime. Why would she desire it in death?

Shutting off her phone, she smiled when she saw the flowers on the dining table. That would have been Tamsin. She touched the roses and then knew what she needed to do. Locking the cabin in case there were still people about, she walked to the studio. The mist had gone and the north shore was glowing in the sunlight. The river appeared still through the trees.

Unlocking the studio, Gabe turned to the bed. It was made and there were no signs of Fin's occupation. Even the lemony scent of his aftershave had gone, replaced with the usual musty, closed-up smell. She left the door open and flipped through her music until she came to Grieg's Piano Concerto No I in A minor. Placing the music on the piano she sat and, taking a deep breath, she played, letting the music speak her feelings.

By the time she'd finished a sea fog had rolled in. She looked out of the window and she couldn't even see the river, let alone the other side. She closed the piano and locked the studio, then practically felt her way along the path. The mist was so dense she nearly walked into the cabin itself. She went in then locked the door behind her.

She needed to tackle Jaunty's room. Nothing had been done in there since her grandmother had died.

Gabe hesitated at the door. Someone had closed the curtains and the room looked wrong that way. She opened them but that didn't help the closed-in feeling. She could see nothing but the opaque fog moving past.

Almost at the laundry room, Gabe dropped Jaunty's sheets when there was a tap on the door behind her. The undertaker stood in a black suit at the door.

She let him in. "Hi."

"Miss Blythe, I'm so sorry for all the trouble."

Gabe nodded. No one was more sorry than she was.

"I'd heard from the crematorium that you hadn't been in so I thought it was best if I collected your grandmother and brought her to you." He held out a shopping bag.

Gabe swallowed. She'd forgotten about Jaunty's ashes in all the scandal.

"Thank you so much." She took the bag and was surprised at the weight. "It was very kind of you."

"Happy to help." He looked round. "A bit lonely here, isn't it?"

Gabe looked out to the river. It was still shrouded in low cloud and fog. "It's normally not this bad." She forced a smile on to her face.

"That's good then. Hope there are no strangers lurking about."

Gabe coughed. "Me too." But she was missing the stranger — even though he'd betrayed them. She watched the man walk up the steps and then she scurried back into the cabin and locked the door. She hoped the weather would improve soon. She needed some bright, clear days to lift her mood.

Inside the bag was an urn of sorts, but it looked more like an overgrown coffee canister. Gabe placed it on the dining table. What was she going to do with it? Father Tim had said that Jaunty must be buried in consecrated ground, so she could put her with her parents in Manaccan graveyard, but that was far from Jaunty's beloved river. Gabe touched the urn.

"Well, Jaunty, I don't know what to do, so you will have to stay with me a bit longer." Gabe looked around. "In fact, it will be good to have someone besides myself to talk to." She welled up but blinked the tears away. That wasn't going to get anything done. She picked up the sheets and put the laundry on.

The phone rang and Gabe glared at it. She did *not* want to speak to anyone. She had been reading a client brief and was struggling to think of anything other than blah blah blah. How could she create music about loo cleaner? It was essential to have work, but that was the only good thing she could think of at the moment. Her mind was everywhere it shouldn't be: composing her Sonata of the Tides, singing Nancy in *The Lovers* and, worst of all, longing for Fin.

The phone finally stopped ringing. Gabe stood. Maybe if she worked on her own composition it would expel one of her irritants. Locking the cabin door behind her, she could smell a bonfire drifting over from the north shore. Gabe stopped and listened to the wind in the trees. Today she could feel winter coming. She shivered and hurried to the studio. Despite the air freshener she had put in here the other day the musty scent lingered.

All around her piano were things waiting to be dealt with. Soon she would have to have someone come and evaluate all these works. But right now she was going to do something for herself. Putting her sonata on the piano, she sat down and began to play, stopping and starting as another variation came to mind. Finally she was happy with the first movement. She played it and then stopped, sniffing the air. Pizza. She turned. Max stood in the doorway holding two boxes.

"You didn't answer my call so I brought you a margarita."

Gabe laughed. "Ah, sorry, I didn't know it was you."

"So it's not just *my* calls that you're avoiding?" He came over to the piano.

Gabe stood and blocked the view of her work. "No, the world. But a man bringing dinner is most welcome."

"Pleased to hear it." He smiled. "But before we go, what was that piece you were playing. I've not heard it before."

"Nothing."

"That wasn't nothing. It was glorious. The sea and the tide somehow."

Gabe turned to him. "Really?"

"Yes, definitely. That's your work, isn't it?"

Gabe nodded as she locked the studio behind them. Pine needles dropped on her head as she followed Max, feeling lifted by his comments. But she mustn't build her hopes, and right now she needed to think of something wonderful about loo cleaner. Loo cleaner paid the bills. Random sonatas pleased the soul but did nothing else.

"How are you?" Max asked as he popped the pizzas in the oven to reheat.

"Fine." Gabe left to go and lay the table.

"I don't believe you, but I won't push." Max watched her from the kitchen doorway.

"You've dealt with enough divas then, have you?" Gabe looked up at him.

"You could say that." He handed her a glass of wine.

"Why do I get the sense that you are trying to soften me up?"

"Wouldn't know." He looked innocently at the ceiling and Gabe laughed.

"Hannah sends her love," he said.

"How's she doing?" Gabe took a sip of wine.

"Good." Max fixed her with his stare. "Enough about everyone else. You?"

"I told you, I'm fine."

"Really? No one has heard from you or seen you in a week."

Gabe bent to the wood burner and began to light the fire. "The post mistress knew I was alive."

"Gabe, that's not good enough. People care."

She knelt down. "OK, I think I was doing fine with Jaunty's death and revelation, but I'm afraid that the digging up of the past has more than unsettled me." She stood and followed Max into the kitchen.

"That I can understand." Max took the pizzas out of the oven and placed them on the table. "Do you want to talk about it?"

348

Gabe fixed him with a stare. "No."

"Sure?" He topped up her wine glass, then said quietly, "It was Victor Justin, wasn't it?"

Gabe's head swung up, which was a mistake. The room swayed a bit with the blood rush. She reached for the table to steady herself.

"You know he's in custody, don't you?"

"No!" Gabe ran her hand around her neck.

"With all that came out recently about that . . ." Max paused ". . . that generation, for lack of a better word, of men, a few of his victims have come forward."

Gabe closed her eyes. He was in jail. He was in jail. What did that mean? She swallowed and opened her eyes. "Thank you for telling me."

"What happened was wrong." Max reached across the table and took her hand in his. "That's totally inadequate. It was more than wrong it was criminal and beyond."

Gabe nodded, thinking of the lost years, the guilt, the self-hate. "Thanks."

Max held out the chair for her to sit, and innocently added, "Fin has been asking about you."

Gabe turned away. She wasn't going down this route.

"What happened between you?"

"Not a subject for discussion." She stood and walked past Max to the kitchen. No amount of wine, pizza or kindness was going to make her talk about Fin.

On Jaunty's desk were the notebooks and the loose sheets of paper that her grandmother had written. Gabe wanted to sit and read them again, but before she did that she needed to reconnect with the rest of the world.

She had lost time in the black hole of Jaunty's death, and although Gabe had seen the papers she'd only read what had related to her grandmother. A nuclear bomb could have been detonated or a cure for cancer found and she would have no idea.

So she poured herself a glass of wine and powered up her computer to read the headlines. Then she debated checking to see what else had been written about Jaunty. She did and she didn't want to know. However, she sort of needed to know what was likely to happen, so she typed in Jaunty's name and the first link up was a video clip.

Art expert Alexander Falk talks about the recent upset that has rocked the art world.

Gabe looked at the name and recognised it as the man who'd written the balanced article in the Sunday paper. As the opening credits rolled Gabe realised that it was the programme that Fin had called about. He must have declined to be interviewed.

The voice of the host recapped Jaunty's story and pictures flashed past of Jaunty's work and suddenly, shockingly, Fin was on her screen.

"We have art historian Alexander Falk with us today in the studio to discuss the recently deceased local artist known as Jaunty Blythe." The newsreader turned to Fin. "So you met the artist just before her death?"

"Yes, just over a month ago." He wore a dark suit with a white shirt open at the neck.

Gabe swallowed. Alexander was Fin?

"And what can you tell us about her and what many are calling her fraud?"

Fin sat forward and looked directly at the woman. "First, that isn't correct and I'll come back to that point. Jeanette Penrose did what she needed to do to survive. She'd been trapped in occupied France, having selflessly given her passage to England to Jean Blythe. What Jeanette did was an act of kindness and bravery, which people seem to have forgotten with this whole ruckus about fraud." He looked directly at the camera. He'd had his hair cut and it was combed into place. "This left her stranded in France."

Gabe realised what had bothered her about him. Now that he was tidy and in a suit she recognised him. She'd seen him on television a while ago discussing Renaissance art.

"And what do you know about this period of her life?"

The camera moved to a close-up of Fin's face and his eyes seemed to be looking directly at Gabe.

"Jeanette managed to buy French identity papers and find herself a job in Brittany. Because of her background she was fluent in German as well as French and soon realised that some of the things she overheard could be useful and she took the enormous risk of seeking out the resistance."

Gabe held her breath as she listened. Was he going to reveal Jaunty's relationship with Dietrich? That would complete the betrayal.

"So she was a spy?"

"Yes. For two years she passed on information to the allies."

"Then what happened?"

"She fell pregnant and it was imperative that she return to England. On her return, the boat carrying her was hit just off the coast of Cornwall and everyone but her had drowned. Back in England she discovered that both her parents were dead and she had no one to turn to because she had spent very little time in England and everyone believed she had died on the *Lancastria*."

"But it was Jean Blythe who died?"

"Yes. Look, Jeanette Penrose had little choice but to take on her friend's identity and we can't judge her by today's morals. She was single mother with a child to support. Society was not as forgiving then."

Gabe stood up and wanted to walk away from the computer but she couldn't stop watching.

"She borrowed enough of Jean's money from the sale of her work to buy a car and the cabin. What the fuss is about is that she then painted using the letter J to sign her paintings and people bought them believing that they were buying Jean Blythe. And I'm afraid the fault for that lies with the gallery and not the artist."

"You don't agree that she was the one who led them to do that?"

"Yes and no. She did what she needed to to survive, but her own art is so radically different that the buyers should have known. *Caveat emptor.*"

The newsreader nodded. "Buyer beware."

"However, there is no question that Jeanette's seascapes are worthy of fame in their own right. She developed her style without outside influence."

"So you feel it is a fuss about nothing?"

"Exactly. You have two painters with unique styles. Both worthy of all the accolades they have received."

"One last question: what of her granddaughter, Gabriella Blythe? How is she coping with all this information about her grandmother and her own roots?"

Gabe's mouth went dry.

"It's not my place to say. Gabriella has been overwhelmed by her grandmother's death and by the revelations. I believe very strongly that she should be left in peace to grieve and rebuild her life."

The camera left his face as the newsreader thanked him for taking the time to speak with them.

Gabe closed the window on her computer and googled Alexander Falk. This explained why she had found nothing for him under Fin Alexander. However, under his real name there was plenty of information, from his impressive academic credentials to his divorce. His ex-wife Patricia was stunning, possibly the sexiest woman Gabe had ever seen, and they'd made a striking couple. At least he hadn't lied about the divorce — the tabloids had had a field day with it.

Fin was more than qualified to speak about Jaunty's work, and the man in the hospital was the arts editor for The Times. But why had Fin done this? It was clear from reading everything on the web about him that he didn't need a big scoop to kick-start his career. Just two years ago he'd done a major television series on the war artists. That was why Jenna must have thought he was familiar. Gabe took one last look at his picture on the screen and closed the laptop. Nothing made sense. Why hadn't he told them his real name when he arrived? There was no need for secrecy. Gabe didn't understand anything any more, most of all her feelings for this man.

It was midday and the phone rang, probably for the fifth time. Gabe frowned. She would have to begin answering it again sometime. It might as well be now. "Hello."

"Gabe." Fin's voice ran through her.

She leant against the counter. "Yes."

"You haven't been answering the phone."

"No."

"Is the press still hounding you?"

"Don't know."

He laughed and she had to force herself to breathe. "Are you OK?"

"Fine." She was so far from fine but she couldn't say that.

"Liar."

Gabe swallowed. He was the reason her life was upside down. "Thank you for all the fire-fighting on Jaunty's reputation."

"It's not finished."

"The interest should die down now." Gabe played with Jaunty's necklace.

"True." He paused. "I'm worried about you."

"I'm fine. Thanks for checking on me." Gabe could hear French being spoken in the background. At least Fin wasn't going to spring on her that he was standing at the top of the lane and wanted to see her.

"Gabe, there are things I need to say."

"Don't worry, Fin. All is forgiven. Take care." Gabe hung up before she said any more. She wanted to hate him, but she didn't. Even after all he'd done she loved him. She would have been so much better off right now if she hadn't let him in to her life. That cast-iron bubble she had constructed around herself would have been perfect for now and for always, but it was gone.

CHAPTER
TWENTY-TWO

Gabe squelched through the mud on the path. The leaves were mostly gone from the trees. It seemed to have happened overnight and the twisted shapes of the branches filled the space above her. Gabe pulled her coat tighter about herself.

The tide was out and only a small channel of water remained. Gabe climbed down the bank to the decaying iron carcass of the boat near the quay. She walked closer and inspected the rusting hull. It had been here for as long as she could remember but she had never identified with it before. There were huge holes and the top was lost all together. It would never set sail again. Gabe touched the barnacle-covered wreck then walked on past it to the quay.

The mud was soft and she trod carefully. The last time she had made this walk Jaunty was still alive, and later that evening Fin had sailed into their lives. Gabe stopped. Everything had changed. Jaunty was gone, her reputation in tatters. Gabe looked up to the cabin. It was almost invisible, which was what Gabe was trying to achieve. Yet part of her longed to reconnect. She wanted to go to Italy and find her relatives, and to Germany as well, although she didn't know how to begin to approach the von Hochsbrinks. They, of course, probably didn't know that Jaunty and Dietrich had found each other during the war, and they certainly didn't know the awful end. Were her eyes so like his that they would know upon seeing her, or was it only Jaunty's guilt that made the connection? Was there a way that she could verify the link without betraying Jaunty further? She shook her head. How could she want to be so alone yet desire to become a part of something?

It was another big spring tide and the creek was a vast mudflat. Curlews walked the far shore and their cries ripped through her as she counted the lobster pots sitting on the riverbed. One curlew called and then another replied. Overhead the cloud level was descending. She could see the rain falling on Merthen Wood. It would be here before long, but under the overhang of the pine trees she felt cocooned. The wind blew from the east against the tide's journey out to sea and the river was deserted. She hadn't even heard the fishing boats heading out this morning, although she knew they must have. Nights had been spent striving for sleep, only to be denied until the early hours. Waking late she would plough through her days doing what was required and avoiding the world.

She had to pull herself up and move on. This half life wasn't worth living. First, she would join with the other victims of Victor Justin and fight for justice. If they could be strong, so could she. Then she would go away, go and find her European roots. A curlew called again and this time no other bird answered.

★ ★ ★

Flights were booked. She would fly out in a few days' time. She had finished everything in her inbox and given evidence via a video link, finding the support of the other victims healing although painful too. Now all that was left was to clear out Jaunty's room. She had put this off, but she wouldn't want to face the task when she returned. Both Hannah and Tamsin had offered to help, but this was the second last step and she needed to do it herself. Her grandmother's ashes still sat in the urn in the centre of the dining table, not yet interred in the graveyard; the words of Max's libretto floated in her head every time she thought about doing it.

> I am thine,
> Thou art mine,
> Beyond control;
>
> In the wave,
> Be the grave
> Of heart and soul

With bin bags in hand, Gabe turned from the urn to the bedroom. She opened the door and sunlight poured in the far windows on to the desk. Gabe began with the cupboards. There wasn't much. In the chest of drawers she found little except the notebook that had been tucked away. Opening, Gabe was stunned to find it was filled with sketches of Gabe. Her whole life was captured in pencil and watercolour. Gabe swallowed hard, looking at her small chubby fist on one page, her dressed as an angel for Christmas on another. It was something to cherish. She stroked the cover then turned to the end to see what was the last sketch her grandmother had made. Her breath caught. It was of her and Fin. Their heads close together. The expression captured spoke of hunger, need . . . love. How had her grandmother seen so much? With unsteady hands Gabe placed it down on the desk and sighed. That was Jaunty's final wish for Gabe and it was a lovely memory, but it was time to move forward.

Jaunty had almost lived the life of a nun with a habit of smocks, trousers and plimsolls. Gabe doubted even a charity shop would find much use for any of these. She placed the bag on the unmade bed and the mattress dipped, and Gabe ran her hand over it. Turning, she swiftly pulled one set of the "uniform" out of the bag. She had to have something to keep and she couldn't hold on to the mattress. She laughed as she considered moving in here and creating a matching dent on the other side. But she didn't want to be found here alone, dead in the bed. It would more than likely happen, but she wouldn't dwell on it.

On top of the bureau were just three things, the picture of her father, a picture of Gabe and the perfume. Gabe turned to the desk. Jaunty's confession was sitting on top. How different would things have been if Jaunty had just been Jaunty? Maybe Fin would still be here.

No, he might not have come in the first place. His uncle's boat and painting wouldn't have led him here. Despite the pain she was glad he had come into their lives. He had given Jaunty a zest to her final days. And well, she could say the same, but they weren't her final days.

Gabe rowed through the soft rain down the creek. The north wind was biting and she couldn't face a swim, but the water called to her. The silence of the creek at high tide always affected her. When the tide was out the river birds filled it, chatting to each other, but when the creek was full the only sound was the wind in the trees and her oars disturbing the water. She was alone. No walkers ventured on the paths today in such desolate November weather. The trees seemed to hunch lower to the water's edge, seeking protection from the bitter north wind.

She rowed onward. Tomorrow she began her trip with a drive past Polruan House, the first stop on the journey to find out who she really was. All her life she had been Gabriella Blythe, daughter of Philip and granddaughter to famous artist Jaunty Blythe. Now she knew she was still Gabriella, daughter and granddaughter, but not Blythe at all. This wasn't a case of reinventing herself but of connecting with parts of herself she had never known.

Turning the boat around, she slowly rowed back. Before she left there was another thing she needed to do. Her dismissive *take care* to Fin days ago was supposed to be final, but she owed him an apology. She didn't know what had been said between Jaunty and Fin, and her grandmother's belief in him haunted Gabe. She had to let go and move on; only by saying sorry would she be able to do that.

She reached the quay and secured the rowing boat, checking the ropes. Mike was going to come by while she was away and take it out of the water for the winter. Standing on the quay watching the mizzle lift a bit, she saw the last of the afternoon sun bounce off the river. This was where she had met him, and that warm September evening seemed such a long time ago. Gabe sighed, knowing she couldn't put off this call any longer.

Leaving the quay, she walked back to the cabin. She was soaked. The moisture had worked its way through her sweater to her skin and a chill settled on her. She raced down the last few steps to the cabin, but by the time she was inside her teeth were chattering. She shed the sweater and warmed herself by the fire. It had been stupid to go rowing in this weather, but she'd needed to think. Now she must make the phone call, then she would be free to move on.

She punched in the number before she changed her mind. She jumped when it went straight to his voicemail.

"This is Alexander Falk. I am sorry, I am unable to take your call. Please leave a message."

Gabe bit her lip but then said, "Hi, Fin. I mean, Alexander. It's Gabe." She took a deep breath. "I'm calling to apologise. I . . ." She stopped because the shivering had started again. "I am so sorry for the way I behaved towards you, it wasn't very grown up," she said, her teeth chattering. "Thank you for all the help with the aftermath of the news about Jaunty." Gabe

361

paused. There was more she wanted to say but didn't know where to begin.

"Thank you."

Gabe dropped the phone and spun round. Fin stood in the doorway, water drops resting on his curls. She couldn't breathe. He was here.

With two strides he was beside her. He pushed the hair out of her face. "You're soaked and you're freezing." He looked into her eyes. "Have you been swimming in this weather?"

She shook her head. All she could think was that he was here.

"You need a shower."

She nodded. He took her hand and led her into the bathroom, turned on the shower and helped her undress before he placed her under the stream of water. Warmth spread through her but stopped when he backed out of the room. It said so much. Gabe swiftly washed her hair and finished. When she was dressed, she came out to find Fin adding another log to the fire.

"Hi." Gabe watched him from a distance. Why had he come?

He looked up at her. "Hello."

The sofa stood between them but Gabe knew the divide between them contained bigger obstacles. She couldn't move.

He glanced at her ticket and passport on the coffee table. "Milan."

She nodded.

"La Scala?" He stood.

She laughed. "I haven't booked tickets yet."

"Do your relatives know you are coming?"

"Yes. But I don't know how much was understood." Gabe took two steps into the room and put her hands on the back of the sofa. "My Italian isn't bad, but I haven't used it in a while."

"So you may have told them that you are a psychotic killer."

"Something like that." She bit her lip. "Fin, I'm so sorry."

"So you said." He put his hands into his pockets.

"It was all too much and only the two of us knew the truth."

He nodded.

Gabe closed her eyes for a moment. Why? Why had he done it? "Fin, I need to know why you did it?" She swallowed. "I need to understand." She looked up at him. "I've been wondering, did Jaunty ask you to?"

"Yes."

Gabe looked at her clasped hands, waiting.

"I didn't want to." Fin shook his head. "She made me promise. I thought you should be consulted but she said no." He took a step closer. "I wanted to tell you but that was another promise she extracted from me. I wish I could take the pain away that I've caused."

Gabe tried to digest this. Even though it was what she had begun to suspect, it still hurt. She frowned. "Why did you lie about your name?"

"I didn't."

"You are not Fin Alexander." She frowned.

He laughed. "Well, I am Alexander Finbar Carrow Falk."

She stared at him. "That's not Fin Alexander."

"My mother wanted to call me Finbar after her father."

"And?"

He took a step closer to her. "But my father said no. He liked Fin but not Finbar. So they took the family name of Alexander and gave me Finbar as my second."

"That still doesn't tell me what I want to know." She played with the ring on Jaunty's necklace that hung round her neck now.

"No. All my family and friends call me Fin and have done all my life. I only use Alexander professionally." He paused. "When I received Alex's things, and in particular the painting, something clicked and I thought I knew the location of the painting." He looked out of the window. "When I had researched the programme on the war painters a few years ago I had tried to interview Jaunty. I had put the request through the gallery. They had forwarded her reply to me. It was post-marked Helston." He ran his fingers across the back of the sofa. Gabe followed their path, remembering the feel of them on her body. "I own several of Jaunty's paintings and I knew she painted in this area; I had a hunch and I had time on my hands."

"So you came here to out her?" Gabe stepped back.

"No! I came to solve a puzzle." He ran his hand through his hair, making a mess of his curls. "As soon as I met Jaunty I knew she was the reclusive painter before she said her name. I wanted her to be at ease with me. And I thought she'd recognise me so I used two of my names to put her off." He laughed. "I didn't know that she would have no idea who I was because she didn't even have a television."

"But she opened up to you."

"Yes, but not to Alexander Falk, art historian. She saw Alex in me and she knew *Jezebel*, of course she did."

Gabe swallowed.

He took a step towards her. "I just wanted to solve the question in my mind: how did Alex come by a painting that seemed so close to Jaunty's work but was signed by someone else."

"Intellectual pride."

He gave a dry laugh. "Partially, but more something to take me away from feeling sorry for myself."

Gabe put her hand out but then took it back to her side. Touching him would be a mistake. "Having kept the secret so long I don't know why she wanted the world to know now." Gabe shifted from foot to foot, looking down. "I still don't understand that."

"I did, which is why she asked me to do it, to give the story to a reputable newspaper. And so I gave it to a friend, with strict instructions that it wasn't to go out until I told him to use it. Unfortunately it didn't happen the way it was supposed to." He sighed. "Someone in the newsroom needed a story fast when another fell through and my friend was on leave because his first child was being born. He wasn't consulted and the story was rewritten to make better headlines."

"OK, that explains the terrible timing. There was so much drama."

"I'm sorry about that. It was not the way I planned it."

Gabe took a deep breath, then looked at Fin. Her whole body tightened. "Thank you for not talking about Dietrich."

"There are some things they don't need to know, but you did."

Gabe frowned. "Thank you."

He stepped round the coffee table and moved closer to Gabe. She held her breath. "Fin," she whispered.

"Yes?" He stopped inches away from her.

"Why are you here?"

"I needed to see you." His eyes were so intent.

"Oh." Gabe couldn't look away and his mouth hovered just above hers. "Anything else?"

"I missed you." His lips touched hers on the corner of her mouth. "I haven't been able to think of anything but you." He kissed her lightly, still holding himself apart from her. "I needed to know if you might feel the same."

Gabe took his hand in hers and pulled him to her, closing the gap between them. "Yes, I do."

Epilogue

There wasn't a cloud to be seen in the July sky. *Jezebel* rocked on the gentle swell with Fin at the tiller. Gabe stood and kissed Fin, her engagement ring glittering in the sunlight as she held the small jar. Most of Jaunty's ashes were buried in the grave with Gabe's parents, but she hadn't been able to let go of the feeling that her grandmother belonged at sea with Alex.

"This looks like a good spot." As Fin pressed the CD player she could see Alex's ring on his finger and she knew Jaunty would approve. The opening notes of the aria she would be performing at tomorrow's premiere of *The Lovers* travelled across the boat. Gabe began singing and as she came to the words

I am thine,
Thou art mine,
Beyond control;

In the wave,
Be the grave
Of heart and soul

Fin's hand joined hers and they spread the last of Jaunty's ashes across the water.

Acknowledgements

As with every book there are many people who help make it happen. Without the expertise of Adam Temple-Smith I would have no idea about the life of an opera singer, let alone the life of a student in training. He has patiently answered my endless questions on arias and breathing. Caroline Macworth-Praed and Jacky Kellet have provided me with technical advice when I would have chosen the wrong music or used the wrong vocabulary.

Clare Mackintosh and Dr Kate Gearing saved me with their professional knowledge. I am indebted to the wonderful Myra Fraser for sharing her memories of coming to Helford as a young mother in the early years after the war. I'd also like to thank my German editor Almuth Andreae for her helpful insights, and my sister-in-law, Deborah Barton, for advice on colours.

Without Brigid Coady I would go insane. She listens, reads and cajoles me through the writing process. As in the past the lovely Julia Hayward fights her way through my dyslexic typos and provides vital feedback. A huge shout of thanks goes to Sarah Callejo whose laser-sharp insights and encouraging words buoyed me up when I needed it most. The Romantic Novelist Association continues to provide me with support and friendship.

Thank you to Jasper Falk for his generous bid in the silent charity auction for Icknield School, a school for children with severe learning disabilities, to have a character named after a person of his choice.

A special note of thanks to Andrew Fenwick for his proof-reading and for putting his A★ in A level History to good use.

I want to thank my agent Carole Blake, who is wise, patient and makes the best gin and tonic around. The whole team at Orion are wonderful, but my editor Kate Mills always pulls the best out of me even when I don't think it will happen.

My daily chats with my father keep the world in perspective and my mother keeps me grounded with her prayers. My poor family puts up with me dragging them off to concerts, trailing them through churches and graveyards, and subjecting them to strange playlists. I am forever asking them random questions when my thoughts clearly haven't been with them, but with my characters. I am the frequent cause of great embarrassment when I mention my books or quiz some stranger about their lives. I would be lost without their love and support, especially that of my husband, Chris.

Author's Note

Bosworgy, the cabin in *A Cornish Stranger*, is based on a cabin that exists and is owned by the National Trust. It is called Powders and was built by the marine artist Percy Cecil Thurnburn, called "Powder" by his friends. He built the cabin in 1930 after he had bought the land from the Tremayne Estate in 1920. It is his boat, the *Iron Duke*, that can be seen rusting in the cove near the cabin.

I had tremendous fun discovering new music as well as revisiting old favourites for this book. I have compiled a Spotify list which you can find on my website, www.lizfenwick.com.

The Third Wife

Lisa Jewell

In the early hours of an April morning, Maya stumbles into the path of an oncoming bus.

A tragic accident? Or suicide? Her grief-stricken husband, Adrian, is determined to find out. Maya had a job she enjoyed; she had friends. They'd been in love.

She even got on with his two previous wives and their children. In fact, they'd all been one big happy family. But before long Adrian starts to identify the dark cracks in his perfect life.

Because everyone has secrets. And secrets have consequences. Some of which can be devastating . . .

A Cornish Affair

Liz Fenwick

Running out on your wedding day never goes down well. When the pressure of her forthcoming marriage becomes too much, Jude bolts from the church, leaving a good man at the altar, her mother in a fury, and the guests with enough gossip to last a year.

Guilty and ashamed, Jude flees to Pengarrock, a crumbling cliff-top mansion in Cornwall, where she takes a job cataloguing the Trevillion family's extensive library. The house is a welcome escape for Jude, but when its new owner arrives, it's clear that Pengarrock is not beloved by everyone.

As Jude falls under the spell of the house, she learns of a family riddle stemming from a terrible tragedy centuries before, hinting at a lost treasure. And when Pengarrock is put up for sale, it seems that time is running out for the house and for Jude.

A Seaside Affair

Fern Britton

The warm and witty new novel from a treasured TV personality

When the residents of Cornish seaside town, Trevay, discover that their much-loved theatre is about to be taken over by a coffee chain, they are up in arms. It is up to hotshot producer and Cornish resident Penny Leighton to come up with a rescue plan. Armed with her contacts book, she starts to pull in some serious favours.

Actors soon descend on the town, all keen to take part in a charity season at the theatre. One of the arrivals is Jess Tate, girlfriend to TV heartthrob Ryan Hearst. His career is on the rise while hers remains resolutely in the doldrums. But when opportunity comes, it isn't just her career prospects that are about to change. Trevay is about to put on the show of its life — but can the villagers, and Jess, hold on to the thing they love the most?

The Lie

Helen Dunmore

Cornwall, 1920, early spring.

A young man stands on a headland, looking out to sea. He is back from the war, homeless and without family.

Behind him lie the mud, barbed-wire entanglements and terror of the trenches. Behind him is also the most intense relationship of his life.

Daniel has survived, but the horror and passion of the past seem more real than the quiet fields around him.

He is about to step into the unknown. But will he ever be able to escape the terrible, unforeseen consequences of a lie?